RED SKY WARNING

RANDALL SAXTON

—

RED SKY WARNING

Saxton Law, PLLC
www.saxton.law

Madison, MS

Copyright © 2016 by Saxton Law, PLLC

All rights reserved. Published in the United States by Saxton Law, PLLC.

www.saxton.law

Saxton Law, PLLC and the portrayal of the capital letter S inside a diamond are registered trademarks of Saxton Law, PLLC.

Library of Congress Control Number: 2016911186

ISBN 978-0-692-75317-0

Manufactured in the UNITED STATES OF AMERICA

1 3 5 7 9 10 8 6 4 2

First Edition

Er·i·tre·a a country of northeast Africa bordering on the Red Sea named after the Roman term for red, *erythraeum.*

1

Hudson Jones was pacing, and he didn't like it. Departure time had passed almost an hour earlier and he still hadn't been told to board. No one could give him an answer as to whether the jet was prepared or if it was a technical hold up. There were only so many times he could flick through the reconnaissance notes without going crazy. He knew the details. There was nothing else to review, not after reading them in Mississippi, again in the aircraft and then going over them thoroughly during briefing on the base.

Almost everyone else had called, except Fitzpatrick, the one call he was waiting for.

At this point, the president himself could call and Hudson still wouldn't be any more impressed. It was just the wait that was excruciating. Sixty-four minutes late.

The room was small and tucked away. He couldn't leave because it was the only room with the right line. Greene had called an hour and a half ago to wish him luck. Lauren was at his house with him and Hudson had spoken with her briefly. She understood this time, though he could hear the reservation in her voice. She was trying to hide it. Hudson reassured her that he would be fine, that he would be home next week. He then spoke to Greene again who reminded him to pick up a newspaper in the morning before the meeting. And to not even worry about the second part of the mission until the legal proceedings were out of the way. It wasn't that he needed reminding; he couldn't really forget that.

It had been over three years since he'd been in this position. The last international trip he'd been on was just before he'd proposed to Lauren. It was a trip to northern Iraq to investigate reports of black market weapons dealers targeting U.S. envoys.

Although Hudson had told her not to, Lauren had stayed glued to the television and newspapers, becoming more and more stressed and anxious with each report of a roadside bombing or car explosion in Baghdad or Fallujah. Even though she knew he was in the north, the news of the explosions rattled her. After he'd returned, at the end of the four weeks, Lauren threatened to call off the wedding unless he transferred to a different position, one that required less travel.

If she ever found out what had happened while he was in Iraq, she would have probably called off the wedding immediately. Greene had said as much when Hudson had told him one evening when they were fishing on the Coast a week before the wedding. Hudson's investigation had opened a few doors too many for some officers who were involved with the smugglers. They were getting kickbacks for allowing the crates of firearms to go missing.

When Hudson tracked the weapons back to the company, one Colonel sent several officers to Hudson's room at the barracks to take care of the investigation in other ways. At that point Hudson had been expecting intimidation. He'd been waiting for it, almost baiting it, once he'd figured out it must have been an inside job. Without some action from the guilty party, Hudson was at a dead end in his investigation.

The other officers hadn't covered their tracks, and after Hudson had cornered them with the evidence in an unused warehouse between Kirkuk and Dokan, they were more desperate than ever. It was only the second case of live fire Hudson had been involved with, but he'd gotten some good shots in. He'd been lucky. Hudson knew it. And he swore that he wouldn't go into an investigation, no matter how simple it seemed, without an aide again. When Lauren had made her demands, he was more than happy to take domestic issues only…until now.

It had been a little over thirteen hours since he'd landed at Joint Base Andrews in Maryland. He had caught a ride on a C-17 from the 172nd Airlift Wing out of Mississippi.

From the plane he had seen that the last of the red sun streaking over the horizon was fading. Hudson gave it a moment's glance, glad to see the sky again after being in the darkness of the back of a cargo jet.

Seventy-eight minutes late. Impatience had waned, dripped off to the side and dissolved.

Now he just waited.

The job was easy, but the risk was high. Following procedure would get him and Mervyn, a specialized member of the U.S. Army's 1st SFOD-D, into the country. If everything went to plan, Mervyn, playing the role of the "tourist," would then be released to the U.S. Ambassador. Once they were there, under the guise of some other official business waiting to be airlifted out of the country, the team would trek through the desert for the unofficial and undocumented part of the mission, using Mervyn's unique skill set. After the international attention, the outcry of an American tourist being captured, the Eritrean officials would stay clear of any vehicle that might have a passing resemblance to a U.S. official vehicle.

And that was Hudson's job in the courtroom, to make sure the intensity of international scrutiny was enough to sway the Eritrean President and his advisors into turning the captured tourist over to the embassy. By now, the information of the capture of an American tourist, the fact that he's being held by another nation, would have been wired through to the international news desks at the Washington Post, Wall Street Journal and New York Times. Fox News would run with the story in the morning. The media pressure would bring the international political pressure. That was how these things worked, Hudson thought, as he spun a pen on his finger. Then it would be up to him to present the easy way for the Eritrean government to save face and return the tourist.

The newspaper in his briefcase would remind the government of the international pressure. It was subtle, like most of Greene's techniques. It was through Greene that Hudson had learned to present the legal solution in a way to make the defense think of it themselves.

That reminder of international pressure should be enough to make Hudson's first task go quite smoothly. The Eritrean president didn't need heat from either Israel or Iran, particularly with both having unofficial military bases in his borders. If either Israel or Iran had the slightest reason to be irritated with him, or each other, then Eritrea would be nothing but a pawn in any military fall out. It was in his best interest to find a quick resolution to the Tourist-gate, as Hudson imagined Fox would call it.

Hudson started counting. It was an old habit. He decided he would count days. Days since he'd met Daniel. Days since he'd introduced him to Lauren. Days since the first briefing and Greene had outlined the procedure to Fitzpatrick and his assistant. Hudson counted fifty-six. Things had moved fast. It was an old habit.

There was more at stake here than he'd been told. Hudson knew that. There was another motive for Fitzpatrick, some other pressure he was facing or some other operation whose success Fitzpatrick wanted partial credit for. That was fine for Hudson. He didn't mind what games the higher ranking officers wanted to be part of. Hudson had his own reasons for being there, in that windowless room in Israel, that the Admiral wouldn't have understood either. Hudson tapped the photo on the table then slipped it into the back of his military identification. He'd been carrying it around for fifty-six days.

The rest of the base was quiet. In a few hours the officers would come back but now, at this hour, it was strictly a skeleton crew. Hudson stood up and straightened his uniform. He left his cap on the table and walked to the door, pushing it open and looking out into the base. He heard turbines far off, somewhere near the airfield. The blades of a helicopter sat motionless outside the window. It was the only window he could see, obscured by a stationary helicopter. He had no idea where the Department of Defense Learjet was that was supposed to ferry him into Eritrea. A golf cart was at the bottom of the stars. He assumed someone would collect him when the call came but if not, he resolved to take the cart to the runway. Even from the top of the stairs he could see the keys in it.

That's when the phone rang. The shrill digital tone cut through the heavy silence. Hudson picked it up after the second ring.

"Something unexpected has come up." Fitzpatrick's tone was heavy and serious. "There's been a change of plan. Lieutenant Miggs is waiting for you on runway seven."

The line clicked. Silence.

2

The parking lot outside the restaurant was mostly empty when Hudson Jones pulled off the street and pulled into the first spot farthest from the restaurant door. He pulled his coat over his broad shoulders and closed the car door. The evening Mississippi air had a romantic charm to it that he'd almost forgotten. There was a sense of optimism and freedom that wove between the humid breaths of wind. It had been a while since he'd been able to breathe in that mixture of scents and when he tried to think of the last time, he couldn't. It certainly wasn't in the last two weeks. He felt a little guilty about leaving Lauren at home like that. Telling her he was meeting Daniel at seven, when he wasn't due there until nine, but some space would do them good. The air was too thick to talk any more at this point.

Hudson stood with his eyes closed, hands stuck in his pockets and face turned to the slight breeze. He stood there for a moment then turned to the restaurant. The Prince Of East Africa was a small shop front at the left of the complex. The other three stores were all closed at this hour; a small accountant, a deli, and a realtor. Hudson must have driven past it a dozen times in the last few months but had never given it too much thought. When Daniel had given him the address over the phone, Hudson said he knew the street and the intersection but he couldn't picture what was there.

There were ten tables in the restaurant but only three were occupied. A group of four sat at the back past the small bar and two couples sat on either side of the front door. A waiter dressed in a black silk shirt and black chinos walked towards Hudson, all smiles.

"Good evening, a table for one tonight?"

"I'm here to see Daniel, actually."

"I'll let him know you're here. Would you like to wait at a table? Or the bar? Wherever you like."

Hudson nodded and walked towards the bar and sat on the stool. It was a few minutes before Daniel had a chance to come out of the kitchen.

"Hudson," he said, extending his hand warmly. Daniel wore an apron tied around his waist and his black shirt sleeves rolled up.

"We just had a late order come in," he nodded to the larger table at the back. "Can you wait a few minutes?"

"Not a problem."

"So sorry. Can I get you something to drink? Ask Ali here, that's my brother. He'll get you anything you want and I'll be right back."

Hudson ordered a Jack and water and nursed it against the napkin while he looked around at the wood carvings over the bar and the landscape mural on the opposite wall. It was a detailed painting overlooking a city with the mountains in the background, contrasting with the buildings.

Hudson had met Daniel a week ago at the gym. There was no point in just sitting on a stationary bike and pedaling next to someone. Hudson always talked to whoever was on the bike next to him. Sometimes, he'd be lucky enough to stumble upon another gym rat who was more than just the casual fitness junky and once they'd sized each other up, they'd set some race between them. It was good for Hudson's competitive spirit.

Daniel wasn't one of those gym rats. There wasn't a race when Hudson started talking to him two weeks earlier while on the bike. Instead Hudson had just asked where he was from. Eritrea, Daniel had said. Africa. He'd only arrived in Mississippi four months ago and was working in his brother's restaurant.

"Why did you move to Madison?"

Daniel smiled. "My brother moved here last year. He'd read in a magazine that Madison was one of the best cities for families in America."

"So you moved here because of a magazine article?"

Daniel laughed. "Yes."

Hudson shook his head, laughing. He'd never considered a magazine article to be reason to choose a city to live in, but why not? There were probably worse ways to make that decision. Hudson hadn't been a part of his parents' decision to move to Madison but he figured they must have had a reason. Maybe it had been for him, for the same quality of family life that Daniel's brother had read about.

"How many kids does your brother have?"

"None yet."

Hudson laughed again. "Forward planning. Fair enough. Is Madison everything the article said it would be?"

"It was a short article," Daniel said. "All we ever knew about America was from magazines and TV and movies. It's different."

Hudson nodded. There were places he only knew about through media and the movies too, and he wondered how different it would be from the impression he had on screen. When he'd first moved to France he'd experienced the same culture shock. Now he wasn't as naïve or wet behind the ears. Time does wonders for perspective.

He'd seen Daniel two more times that week at the gym but only in passing. They gave each other a wave across the room until they'd crossed in the parking lot and Daniel said he needed to talk to Hudson about something and they'd swapped numbers. Hudson figured it was something to do with that cultural difference or some other advice someone new to America might need. There was something about Daniel he liked, and he was happy to meet Daniel at the restaurant when he finished work.

The glass of Jack was half finished by the time the two couples near the door finished and paid. Ali was clearing the table and serving the table at the back when Daniel came back from the kitchen. He apologized again for making Hudson wait and took a tonic water from behind the bar.

"It's not a problem. You've got to serve the customers."

Daniel nodded and pulled up the stool next to Hudson. "You asked me before if my brother has children," Daniel said. "I have three children. When I left Eritrea I had to leave them there with my uncle. There was a very small chance for me to escape. The government doesn't want anyone leaving, and I had planned my escape with the children and then that window closed. Another one opened, but it was very small and I had to leave right away without them. It was the only option. So I escaped to Yemen and then came to see my brother here, and began working in this restaurant to save enough money to bring my children to Mississippi." He pulled a photo from his wallet, a small picture of three children. "Sarah, Helen and Robel," Daniel said pointing at them. He handed it to Hudson.

"Aren't they sweet?" Hudson smiled, nodding, and put the photo down on the bar.

"It broke my heart to have to leave them there but now I work here every day to bring them here, to one of the best cities for families in the United States." Daniel paused, swallowing hard. He pulled another piece of paper from his pocket and pushed it in front of Hudson. It was a magazine clipping. Hudson unfolded it and read through it. Another Eritrean refugee living in Seattle was contacted by a group of kidnappers in Africa demanding a ransom for his daughter. The group had imprisoned her with dozens of others and kept them hostage until the families paid the ransom.

"I'm a little familiar with the regime there," Hudson said, pushing the article back.

"Since President Mustafa cancelled elections and ignores the constitution, things have been getting worse and worse," Daniel explained. "There's no one to keep him in check and the country is a mess. That's obvious to anyone. But people are getting desperate. So many people are starving and they have to do what they can. There is a lot of violence. Now there are gangs of men who patrol the border and they kidnap people who are trying to escape. Some of them they convince to get into their cars, because of the climate, but most of them are taken by force. Last week they called me." Daniel's voice was almost a whisper now. He drank another sip of the water.

"They have my children."

Hudson nodded, taking this in. It was not the kind of discussion he had been prepared for. "They called you?"

"The morning I called you," Daniel nodded. "I had this impression that you were the kind of man that could help me. I know you work with the government in some way."

"How much are they asking?"

"Half a million total. I don't have that kind of money. Can you help me?"

Hudson stared at his drink. He didn't want to make any promises he couldn't keep. Daniel was a wreck, and there was a way. He just didn't know how yet. Hudson put his arm on Daniel's shoulder. "There must be some way," he said. "I'm not sure what it is. I'm not sure to what extent I can help."

"Will you find out?"

Hudson nodded. "I will speak to some people, but I can't promise anything. Not at this point. You understand that?"

"Yes. But you'll try?"

"I will make some calls."

Daniel put his head in his hands on the bar, taking deep breaths. "Maybe I shouldn't have left them there at all."

"You did what you had to." Hudson pushed the photo back to Daniel.

"No, you keep it. Just keep it until you've made the phone calls, then you can bring it back to me."

"I can't do that."

"Please."

Daniel was a stoic man who had kept his emotions in check even while talking about his children being kidnapped. But there was something in his eyes that told Hudson that there was no argument; he had to take the photo.

"I'll bring it back to you in a few days."

He slipped the photo into his wallet. "You let me know if the kidnappers get in touch again. In the mean time, write down what they said and any other details you remember about them. Any special words they used, their accent, any background noises you hear. That will be important. And then keep yourself busy or you'll go crazy worrying about it."

"Yes, yes. Of course." Daniel nodded.

Lauren was already asleep when he got home. The light over the dining room table was on but the rest of the house was dark. He poked his head through the bedroom door and saw her lying on her stomach, sleeping peacefully, her dark hair pulled back into a ponytail. The blanket had fallen down to her waist and Hudson smiled when he saw that she was wearing his university shirt from Montpellier. It sagged and hung on her even as she lay there, falling off and showing her slender shoulder.

Hudson walked back to the kitchen and pulled a glass from the top shelf of the cabinet and poured another glass of Jack over ice. He walked out to the porch and sat in the wooden seat with the lights off. The moon was high in the sky, illuminating the trees a block over. They swayed in the breeze.

Hudson took the photo out of his wallet and looked at the three kids. Sarah had her arms around the other two. They were all smiling and looking up at the camera though the youngest was laughing at something to the side of the photographer. In the far distance behind the kids who looked like they were on some sort of balcony, was the same outline of the mountains Hudson had seen on the wall in the restaurant. Hudson pushed the thought away of where the kids might be now. What the kidnappers would be doing to the kids now shouldn't be pondered by anyone, least of all Hudson as he sat there waiting for midnight to come around and make him tired enough to ignore the other voices bugging him about more pressing personal issues. He took a big breath and let it out slowly. Daniel would have nothing else to think about these nights.

Hudson wondered for a moment what it was that gave Daniel the impression he could help. He was always attentive to not wear anything in the gym, or generally in public, that gave away his positions. It had been something carried over from his days in Montpellier. There was something about the anonymity that Hudson found attractive. He couldn't remember mentioning anything to Daniel about work while they spoke on the bikes, but he couldn't be sure – there was a calming and relaxing air that hung around Daniel. There was a sense that you could tell him almost anything. Hudson couldn't place it exactly. Perhaps it was Daniel's empathetic ear and the way he listened to conversation. Hudson had been similarly accused in the past. And it certainly wasn't the first time that someone had been quick to spot authority in Hudson's demeanor. His broad shoulders and confidence carried a weight that brought with it a level of instant respect and reverence when he entered a room. It had once or twice brought about some conflict when a newly appointed superior had mistaken Hudson's assured manner as some kind of affront to their own authority.

He slipped the picture back into his wallet and drained the rest of his drink from the glass, turned off the living room lamp as he walked through and made his way to bed.

Hudson had planned on coming in early to the office to look into Eritrea, but the intelligence reports Hudson had been expecting to arrive over the weekend hadn't come in yet, so he could spend the entire morning reading about Eritrea. Lauren was still asleep when he left for work. He kissed her lightly on the forehead and left a note on her bedside table with a refilled glass of water.

The office was empty.

He made a cup of coffee, settled into his desk, and then began reading the government briefs on Eritrea. The general information was easy to find, that since the end of the war with Ethiopia, Eritrea had been ruled by one party and by one man. President Mustafa had risen to power while much of the rest of the world had their attention focused on the Persian Gulf. The constitution had been written then promptly filed to collect dust by Mustafa who had cancelled three elections in the first ten years of his rule, and had made no attempt at any democratic process since. Their human rights and media freedom ratings were some of the worst in the world. Despite that, relations with the US and the EU were still strong. Relations with the neighboring countries weren't as friendly.

Hudson flicked through the reports and memos about the small African country. Eritrea had become the first country to turn its entire coastline into an environmentally protected area, but other than that, there was nothing that stuck out as strange to Hudson. The stories of border wars and unofficial body counts in short wars were too common in that area.

Gerald Greene sat behind his desk with case notes in front of him. He absently chewed his lip as he flicked through the folder. The greying flecks in his short trimmed hair caught in the light from where Hudson stood in the doorway.

"Sir?"

"Yes, Hudson?"

"How much do you know about Eritrea?"

"It's a dictatorship with unofficial ties to militant groups. Though still on good terms with the State Department, at this point. You knew that already?"

"Yes, sir."

"Why do you ask?"

"There is a case of kidnapped children of an Eritrean national, now a resident of Mississippi that I'm looking into."

Greene considered it. "A friend of yours?"

Hudson nodded. "Do we have any people there who can aid us?"

"Where were they kidnapped?"

"Over there," Hudson confirmed. "It does not appear to be a diplomatic issue at this point, sir."

"Our only contacts are diplomatic. So it's unlikely."

They swapped a glance. They both knew Hudson was going to continue to delve into the case whether he had a direct order to or not.

"Continue to look into it," Greene said, making the choice easy for Hudson. "Though it's unlikely this can go higher at this point."

"Understood, sir."

Hudson walked back to his desk, and sat there with another coffee. He pulled the photo of the children from his wallet again and looked at it. A knot was forming in his stomach, a tiny fist tight with anxiety. These children would be reunited with their father, Hudson told himself. He couldn't go back to Daniel and say it was hopeless. There were other avenues; it was just a matter of figuring out which ones. There was no military aid Hudson could tap into.

Hudson considered his next step. It was clear it had to be a personal crusade.

The restaurant was closed when Hudson pulled into the parking lot and glided into the same spot as the previous night. He knocked on the door and when Ali recognized him, he opened the door. Daniel was in the kitchen preparing food for the evening and cleaning up after the lunch crowd.

"Hard at work?" Hudson asked when he walked into the kitchen.

"You've got to keep busy," Daniel replied, and Hudson nodded. "I haven't been sleeping. But if I keep busy then maybe I can tire myself out."

"Can you take a break?"

"Of course."

They sat outside the back door of the restaurant on milk crates. Daniel pulled out a pack of cigarettes and lit one. "I haven't smoked in ten years," Daniel shrugged, offering the pack to Hudson who declined politely.

"I made some calls and spoke to some people," Hudson explained. "There are processes we can go through, but it will take time. Possibly quite a bit of time. I'm sorry I can't bring you better news."

Daniel rubbed his hands together absently, nodding as he took it in. He wasn't sure if it was good news or not, but then decided it was better than an outright negative answer. The fatigue showed. His eyes darted around the street, distracted by anyone who walked past. He stubbed the cigarette out against the wall and threw it in an old tomato can. Hudson thought his face looked longer than the previous night, but it could have been the light in that back corner. Daniel picked at a Band-Aid over his left index finger then was just as quickly taken with another thought.

"I wrote this out last night," Daniel said, pulling some folded notes out of his coat pocket. "At about three o'clock. It's all I can remember from the call, and all that they said. And anything else that I could think of that might help."

Hudson looked over the scrawl on the sheets of paper. The handwriting slid down the page, spread out more the further Hudson flicked through the nine sheets. "It's very thorough."

"I knew that everything might help, somehow. So I wrote down everything I could think of."

Hudson folded the sheet up and pocketed it.

"When did you escape?"

"About six months ago." Daniel stared across the street. "Almost a year ago I had everything lined up to escape. There was a trip I had to take for work and I'd pulled some strings to get the kids to be able to come with me. I had stolen a taser and dismantled it so I could reassemble it in the hotel room. The plan was to take out the guards in the hotel room and get down to the street. I had things worked out with some people I knew in Cairo. Then we'd be able to cross into Israel."

"That must have been hard to organize," Hudson said. "I was under the impression that it was near impossible to get out of there."

Daniel pulled another cigarette from the pack. "I worked in the government."

"You're ex-government?"
Daniel nodded.

Hudson leaned against the wall. This opened up a whole lot of other possible options. "Why didn't you tell me last night?"

"I'm not sure." Daniel shrugged. "I'm not entirely proud of my work."

"What happened in Egypt?"

"Nothing. It didn't happen. Less than a week before everything was meant to happen, someone else working in the defense department did almost the same thing with his wife when they crossed to Yemen. Security was increased and the travel permits for the children were revoked."

"What part of government?"

"Foreign Ministry."

This information could speed a lot of things up.

"About three months later, I was on a trip to Cairo and the opportunity presented itself," Daniel said. "It was a wide open door. And I had no idea of knowing when it would be open again, even just a little bit. I had to take it." His voice hung with regret and he said those words again, repeating it like he was still trying to convince himself. "I had to take it.

There was a split second where the guards had their back turned as we were heading back to the airport. Abdel's car was open. I climbed into the boot and he closed it, then his driver took off. I stayed in different abandoned flats for weeks. Someone would come and take me to another one, leave me with some bread and a bag of apples. then leave for another few days. I had no idea how long it would be until I was out of there or when someone else would come. I found out later it was three and a half weeks when I was taken to Israel and was able to get out. I was lucky. I had some contacts and enough cash from Abdel and some on me so I could get on a plane coming to America. I was lucky."

"Then you came to Mississippi?"

Daniel nodded. "Then I came to Mississippi. Eventually. And I've been cooking since."

He threw the cigarette in the can where the smoke spiraled up. "Abdel told me the kids had been taken away from Asmara and were hiding out where they couldn't be found. I hadn't spoken to them since I left but Abdel assured me they were safe and that he had connections to get them out. He sent me a short message saying they were heading to Egypt. Next thing I heard from him was the phone call the kidnappers forced him to make."

"They have him too?"

Daniel nodded. "He rescued me and I must rescue him."

"In your work with the foreign office, did you have access to any sensitive information? Something that we could use? My superiors are more likely to pull the right strings if they see that there's something in it for them."

"I know what you mean," Daniel nodded. "There is some information I have that they might be interested in."

The drive to Jackson was not a long one but each stop at a traffic light seemed like an hour to Hudson. At every moment his mind raced. Now Daniel had opened up this whole other possibility, another opportunity to get more people behind it and make quicker and deeper inroads than he could have by himself. The knot in his gut was dissolving. He hit the steering wheel with excitement while his mind raced through different approaches to getting into Eritrea.

The trick, Hudson realized, was presenting it to the superiors in a way that showed them the benefit of rescuing Daniel's children, and making them feel that in someway it had been their own idea. That was particularly true with Fitzpatrick, and no one knew how to get what they wanted out of Fitzpatrick quite like Gerald Greene.

The Greene household was on top of a hill with a longer driveway than most. The drive passed the neighboring properties and circled around the lawn at the front of the two-story house. Cynthia Greene opened the door dressed in a simple white shirt and pastel blue pants. It set off the white accents to her hair tucked behind her ears with the purple-framed glasses. She held some jigsaw pieces in her right hand.

"Hudson," she exclaimed. "Come in, come in. Is it just you?" She looked to the car but saw it was locked.

"Just me, this time. Work never stops."

"Of course." Cynthia put a hand on Hudson's shoulder. "How's Lauren? I was going to give her a call, but I just haven't gotten around to it yet."

"She'd appreciate that," Hudson said. "She really would. She's ok, but, well, it's not easy."

"Of course not," Cynthia nodded, leading Hudson through the house, past the wall with pictures of their two sons in uniform and the photos of Gerald with each of the previous three Presidents. "He's down at the bottom of the garden, fixing the pond. One day he'll finish that darn thing. Tell him to give me a wave if you want me to bring you anything."

Gerald Greene was on his knees bent over the pond when Hudson got to the bottom of the garden. The pump was in pieces, spread out over the rocks and lawn. Gerald's arm was deep in the water, pulling at something in the pipe. He sat back on the rocks when he saw Hudson walking down the garden steps. Hudson had helped Gerald install the pump last summer but it had almost immediately had problems.

"Damn thing shut off again." He threw his arms in the air. Hudson handed him the towel hanging over the chair. "I'm glad I hadn't moved the koi back yet."

Although Hudson had initially been forced on Greene by the CIA as they needed someone in an undercover JAG role for certain operations, Greene was one of the first to recognize the talent in Hudson Jones when he moved back from his time in Montpellier. He'd taken Hudson under his wing in the first few months after he had been assigned to the JAG office at Mississippi's Joint Force Headquarters and threw him work that others in his position might have deemed too demanding, or needing more experience. For Greene, that didn't matter. He knew Hudson could handle those cases. Plus, as Hudson was actually a local Jacksonian and had graduated from the Mississippi College School of Law, he was able to easily maintain his cover as a JAG attorney and fulfil both roles. And his faith had been repaid with interest.

Hudson was resourceful and reliable and at times offered a particular insight that Greene had come to appreciate and rely on.

A year after Greene had first put his faith in him, Hudson had come into Greene's office, anxiously asking if he could talk openly. Greene sat back, surrounded by smaller prints of the same pictures of the same visiting Commander in Chiefs that hung in the entry to the house, and asked if it was a personal or professional matter. Hudson confirmed it was personal. Greene told him to grab his coat.

Greene took him out for a drink at a bar on the other side of town, in a hotel where the staff seemed to recognize him. There had been celebratory drinks after certain cases but Hudson recognized this as something different. Greene sat him down, ordered them each a beer and leaned back in the booth to listen to the younger man.

Hudson had been hesitant when he first went into Greene's office, but he had no one else to ask for advice. "I think I want to marry this girl," Hudson had said.

"It's a natural thing to want to do," Greene replied in his commanding growl. "And I wholeheartedly endorse marriage. It's a wonderful thing to do, depending on the girl."

It was a side of Greene that Hudson had first been surprised to see, but had come to appreciate and rely on.

"Hudson," Gerald said, looking at the younger man's work attire, while he had his sleeves rolled up to avoid the pond muck. "I thought you'd gone home early today."

"I left the office early but I was still working."

"Your new pet project?"

Hudson smiled. "I guess you could call it that."

"Any ideas how you're going to do it?"

"The department will help me."

"And just how are you going to convince Fitzpatrick to do that? You do remember that I'm the only person in the Department of the Army that knows of your side relationship with the CIA? "

"The contact is ex-government."

"And he's…?"

"And he's willing to give us intel that Fitzpatrick would be interested in."

"You're a smart lad, Hudson."

"Thank you, sir."

"Have you told Fitzpatrick?"

"Not yet. I came to see you first."

Gerald nodded. "I could do with a drink, how about you?"

Cynthia brought out a tray of beer and snacks then disappeared back inside to her jigsaw puzzle. Hudson recounted Daniel's story and escape to Gerald as they sat on the porch.

"Three kids, you said?"

"Yeah, three."

"That's a hell of a choice to be forced to make," Gerald said, chewing on some peanuts. "Did he tell you what the intel is?"

Hudson shook his head. "No. Just that it was sensitive, classified and related to military."

The light was fading fast and Hudson decided he should get home before it was too dark.

"Hudson," Gerald said, stepping between Hudson and the path. He looked over his shoulder to make sure Cynthia was still in the house. "I'll make the call to Fitzpatrick and get the ball rolling." He dropped his tone from his usual commanding baritone. "This is not the right time to lose your self in work. There's more at stake than you might realize. A miscarriage is hard on both of you, but she needs you now. You have duties as a husband, and they're possibly more important right now than your duties to your country. You're a dedicated lawyer, no doubt. But there is a time for balance." Greene let his military face slide just a little, showing a more tender side that few men he worked with had ever seen. "Take it from someone who came far too close to making that same mistake."

Hudson nodded, understanding.

"Take tomorrow off," Gerald said in his natural authoritative tone. "I'll make the call and we can have a meeting with Fitzpatrick on Thursday."

"Yes, sir."

Lauren was washing the dishes when Hudson walked through the door. He dropped his briefcase at the door and walked through the living room to the kitchen. His wife had her back to him, and stood barefoot in track pants and his Montpellier shirt under a thin black cardigan. Her hair was tucked behind her ears. He walked up behind her and put his arms around her waist.

"I was just going to heat up some left overs for dinner. Is that ok?"

Hudson kissed the back of her neck. "No. I'm taking you out."

She bent her head back and rested it on his shoulder, taking a deep breath. Her eyes were red. He kissed her forehead. "Let me dry these for you," he said. "Then we can go.

3

At that time of the morning it wasn't particularly hot but it was uncomfortable inside the shed. The dirt floor didn't make the best place to sleep but there was no choice. There hadn't been any choice for longer than Sarah could remember at this point. She'd given up counting the days. No one else seemed interested to know how long they'd been tied up, shackled to the floor, inside the tin shed.

Whenever she announced the day count, the other hostages would look at her with some silent hate, a burning gaze that cut through her and told her to be quiet. Then yesterday she realized she didn't know at all. When she thought about it, she wasn't even sure it was yesterday any more. Maybe it was a week ago. She couldn't even be sure of that.

Helen was still curled against the tin wall and sleeping but Robel was awake. She smiled at him, trying to make her brother smile. If she could make him feel better to start the day then it made things easier. Robel crawled over to Sarah, the large chain almost comical on his ankle, and she ran her hand through his hair before holding him.

"I had a dream about papa," Robel said. His voice was quiet, dried out and parched.

"What happened?"

"He was driving in a car looking for us. We could see him through a window," Robel looked up at Sarah, a smile hanging on his lips. "He couldn't find us but we could see him."

Sarah pressed her brother's head into her shoulder and looked around. There were no windows in the tin shed. Light cut through holes in the tin, gaps in between the roof and the walls, and small different sized holes in the walls. If there had been any movement, if the dust had been kicked up at all, then the light would catch it. Sarah would sit watching the dust move through the light, the beams lit up and slicing through the humid and hot air in the shed.

The weight of the shackles pulled on Sarah's leg. She tried to slide a finger down to scratch it but was no use. She turned the cuff around, shaking it back and forth, until the itch went away. With Robel resting on her chest, they both fell asleep for another short while. There was more movement around the shed when she woke again. The other prisoners were awake. She had no idea how long she'd been asleep. Helen was awake now and throwing pebbles across the small room, bouncing them off the dirt floor on to the far wall where they hit the side with a dull metallic sound and bounced back onto the dirt.

Abdel sat in the far corner of the tin shed. "Good morning," he said to Sarah. He always tried to stay in an upbeat mood for the kids, like everyone else shackled to the floor in the tin shed, but Sarah could see the strain on his face. Behind the smile, past the dirt and beard, was a deep concern. It burrowed into his brow and though he tried to hide it, tried to push it aside and remain strong for the three children, Sarah could see it burrowing deeper each day. He stayed in the corner and barely moved out from there. When they were shackled to the floor that first night, Sarah wasn't sure how many nights ago but she knew she'd seen three full moons through the holes in the shed, Abdel was pushed into the far corner.

Everyone was spaced around the shed with little room to move. Metal rings were drilled into the base of the wall and the chains ran around their ankles. To save space the three children had been shackled in the same amount of space as the other people had to themselves.

Abdel sat in the corner by the door, opposite Sarah. He could move enough to come and comfort the children when needed but stayed in the corner as much as possible.

When their car had been pulled over, a tire shot out as they reached the border into Ethiopia, he had remained calm. He'd kept his voice steady and kept explaining things to the children about how they were getting into the other car and they were going for a ride with these other people.

Sarah exchanged glances with him and he smiled and winked at her. She knew things weren't right but she went with it. She trusted him and kept reassuring her siblings about the drive to the shed that would be all they saw for the next few months. It was only when they'd been pushed into the humid shed in complete darkness, dragged in and shackled to the ground, that Robel and Helen had started to realize that Abdel wasn't in control.

The lock on the door clicked and the door opened, the light pouring through blinding the prisoners. A waft of fresh air came through the hut. Sarah closed her eyes and turned away. Despite the hunger it was difficult to get excited for food. It was the same meal twice a day. Kitcha fit-fit. The thought of the spices and yogurt made Sarah's stomach turn. The door slammed against the tin wall and the smaller guard kept his gun pointed into the darkness of the shed. Helen and

Robel blinked against the light, trying to see past the guards but the tray with the plates were put down quickly and the guards stepped back, closing the door and leaving the half dozen prisoners in darkness again.

Sarah watched Abdel smile at Robel, showing some excitement about the food, and copied him. She wiped the spoon on her dirt-stained top and handed it to Robel and did the same for Helen before she took one for herself. She ate a few spoonfuls and swallowed it down then passed the rest of her bowl to her younger siblings. She put her head back on the tin, but the wall was already too hot and she turned to lay on the ground, flat on her side while Robel leaned against her, eating the ration. She closed her eyes. The light through the holes in the wall would travel across the floor and be shining on the other side of the shed before the door opened again and any more food came through. She didn't mind. She resigned herself to the empty stomach, preferring that over the nausea that the constant bland meal of wheat kitcha gave her.

Sarah felt a tapping on her head and opened her eyes. Abdel was sliding his half eaten bowl across to her, pushing it with his foot. She sat up and smiled at him, whispered a thanks and picked at it. She left most of the kitcha in the bowl, and ate what she could of the yoghurt and other liquids. Her mouth was already dry. Her head ached from the dehydration already and she didn't want to eat more spiced bread to dry herself out any more.

Across from Abdel, sitting at the back of the shed, was an Eritrean man in his early twenties, who had been shackled in the tin shed for two months before Abdel and the children had been captured. His clothes were dirty and torn and stained with sweat marks. His beard made his face look even more tired. He'd been crossing the same part of the border Abdel had marked out and had been captured while he hid in the flat landscape from the military vehicles. The choice was between following the armed men in the balaclavas or running into view of the military truck crossing the top of the hill. They led him to their small vehicle, slamming him against the door and pounding his ribs for good measure, before driving him back to their camp and making him call his sister in south London. He lay huddled and beaten on the floor of the shed during that first night and he didn't move for the longest time. Addis just lay there as the moonlight shifted through the holes in the tin walls.

Two brothers in their early thirties sat on the other side of the tin shed. They'd been separated by the kidnappers and shackled on either side of Addis. They would speak quickly and in low hushed tones between each other. The younger one, between Addis and the children, had taken to playing magic tricks for the children once or twice a day whenever he was in good spirits. He would use slight of hand tricks to make the small pebbles disappear from in front of Helen and appear behind her ear.

The children had learned to be quiet. Every time Helen or Robel had let out a cry in the first few days a pounding came on the wall of the tin shed. In the middle of the third night, Robel woke up crying. The thumping on the tin wall came. Three hits then it stopped. The rattling died out in the still night air, like the world's thinnest church bell. That still night air was sliced again by Robel's screams. It didn't scare him into silence now.

With the hot air hanging in the dark moonless tin shed, the hard dirt all that was underneath them save for a threadbare blanket, his crying had set in for the evening. Sarah moved over to her brother but her comfort didn't bring him any peace. The screaming echoed around the metal walls and scared Robel even more, adding more and more to the wailing. Addis and the brothers stirred but they didn't do anything. There was nothing they could do. They kept their head down though Sarah could see Addis staring at her, staring past her to the holes in the wall above her head.

Abdel moved over to Robel and ran his hand through the child's hair, trying to sooth him. The door swung open and the silhouette of a guard yelled at them, screaming at Robel to be quiet. The sight of a gun pointed directly at him and his sister didn't help.

"Shut him up!" the guard snarled. "Make him quiet."

Robel howled louder, the light from outside the shed shining off the tears on his cheeks.

"Quiet or I will shoot him!"

"He's four and he's scared," Sarah said. "What do you think he should do?"

The guard stood stunned. The white of his eyes glared back at Sarah who was too tired and not entirely awake to be as scared as she later realized she should have been. The guard hesitated, unsure if he should slam the butt of the gun into the ten-year old's face or let her stay.

"Do you think this is a good way to make him calm?" Sarah looked around at the metal cage. The sound of Sarah's voice, the tone alone, settled Robel. He looked at his sister then back at Abdel.

"He's quiet now," Abdel reassured the guard. "He's quiet. You can leave him."

The guard glared at Sarah, forgetting where his gun was pointing, then lowered it and shut the door and twisted the lock into place. Sarah moved her and Robel around to a slightly more comfortable position and fatigue overtook them both. That was the last time Robel had cried.

The plates of food had been placed back in the middle of the room on the tray and left there until a guard would come and collect them in an hour or so.

There was never enough to fill anyone up and so they were always eaten completely and scraped clean. Even then there was enough to attract the flies, and heaven only knows how they got through the small holes in the metal. If any amount of food was left there then other things would be brought out into the heavy and sticky air with the promise of a meal of fit-fit.

The older brother and Addis were both lying on the ground with their eyes shut. At this point of the day the metal on that wall got far too hot to lean against and lying was the easier option. Robel and Helen were playing a game of tic-tac-toe with the pebbles in the dirt.

"Sarah," Robel said. "Tell us another story about papa."

"Yeah," Helen said, putting the rocks down.

Sarah lifted her head from the sandy floor and rolled onto her back. In the beginning Sarah had told the stories to remind Robel and Helen of their father and his promise of moving them to America. Then after they'd been caught and locked in the tin shed, the stories had turned into reassuring tales that they would get out of here and that their father was working on a way to get them away. After she'd run out of all the stories about their father she could remember, Sarah had begun telling stories, some of them myths that she remembered small parts of and others were based on the detective stories he used to read her at night, and putting their father in the center as the hero.

"Did I tell you about the time papa was swimming in the sea and he swam down and found a mermaid trapped in an old pirate ship?"

"No!" Robel said. His eyes were open wide and he leaned forward. "When?"

"It was about two years before Helen was born," Sarah said. "Papa was swimming one day and he decided to go swimming down very deep. He swam past all the fish and down to the bottom of the sea. And what do you think he found?"

"A pirate ship?"

Sarah nodded. "A pirate ship. The masts and the sides were all rotten and just laying there. So papa climbed on the ship and thought he would walk around and see what he could find. There were old cannons and there was a big hole in the bottom of the hull that made the ship sink. That's when he found the mermaid."

"What did he do?"

Abdel was listening to Sarah. Everyone was. The tales of their father's exploits and his ability to save them were a light of hope, brighter than the pinprick stream of sunshine moving through the dust. When Robel or Helen had that tone, when they were about to ask for another story, everyone's eyes opened and turned to Sarah. It had slowly become a stand out point of the day in captivity.

Although he would have denied it, even Addis had been captivated by the heroic stories. It might have been the only part of each day where he paid attention to what was going on around him instead of retreating inside himself. The adults knew they were mostly fictitious, they knew that Sarah's stories were parts of an Osiris myth and they knew that their father was not currently walking across the desert with an eagle on his shoulder, nor was he on the other side of the Red Sea with a small but dedicated army of followers preparing to march across to the hut and lead them to freedom. They didn't believe in the stories. But deep in some part of each of them, they wanted to, and they let themselves go with Sarah's storytelling.

Abdel sat in the corner like he always did. His hands were behind him, bent around the corrugations in the tin and pressing against it. On that first day he leaned against the wall and felt it give slightly under his weight. The metal was thin. There was no doubt. He looked at the joint in the wall and there were only a few points where the metal had been welded. While he listened to Sarah's stories, or watched the kids play with the pebbles in the sand, he was continually rocking back and forth, pressing against the metal and feeling it bend. One small joint had given with a popping snap sound four days earlier but it was only a small victory. In the corner he was safe. Whenever the door swung open, the guards were too concerned about intimidating the rest of the prisoners to check on Abdel on the corner.

Abdel first met Daniel years earlier when he was living in Asmara and working as a concierge at the Hotel Intercontinental. With an Eritrean mother, Abdel was the ideal candidate to be recruited by the foreign office and work undercover at the hotel where most foreign dignitaries stayed when visiting the Eritrean capital. He worked with a modest efficiency and collectedness that quickly made him a popular favorite for the clientele. Any request made would be fulfilled and that kind of service opened many doors for Abdel. There were many meetings where Abdel was drifting through in the background, the trusted concierge, ensuring all was well with the service as national leaders and high-ranking officials absently discussed classified state business. To most people it wouldn't have made much sense but the daily cables from the Egyptian office ensured that Abdel was informed on the matters. Small details that most assumed would go over his head were the actual reason for his employment. No one suspected a thing until Abdel met Daniel.

Daniel and his superior in the foreign office were meeting with representatives of the Arab League and Israel within the same week. It wasn't the first time Abdel had served Daniel. They were familiar with each other and Abdel would immediately order the double espresso Daniel would always order. For Daniel, like other frequent visitors, Abdel was a welcome face at the hotel.

After the meeting with the Israelis, the other officials left for the government offices and left Daniel behind. He had the afternoon to visit his wife in the hospital where she was with their first-born. Daniel went to the bathroom and came back to Abdel at the concierge desk and asked for a taxi to be called for him. "Not a problem, sir," Abdel said. "And congratulations."

"Sorry?"

"I heard the you had a daughter."

"Thank you," Daniel smiled. "What else did you overhear?"

"That was all, sir."

Daniel nodded slowly. "When do you get a break?" Abdel hesitated then checked his watch. "Let me buy you lunch."

The two of them bought a sandwich and walked through the park. Daniel showed Abdel a picture of Sarah. "She was born yesterday afternoon."

"She's wonderful."

"She is. Do you have any children?"

"No," Abdel said. "Not yet."

"So," Daniel said in a low tone. "What else have you heard in that conference room?"

"I don't know what you're talking about," Abdel said. "I'm just there to make sure everyone gets their espressos."

"No one else suspects anything," Daniel persisted. "But I saw you react when the ambassador mentioned Mustafa. A concierge wouldn't know who he was."

Abdel looked back at Daniel with a frown. He was careful to hide the panic he felt swelling inside him, the heart racing and the urge he had to get the hell out of there. "I didn't hear that," he insisted. "Was that when I dropped the spoon? I may have reacted from that."

Daniel shrugged. "You're good. But you're lucky it was only me who saw it. I'm not going to say anything but I need you to tell me who you're working for."

Abdel looked at Daniel and knew he could trust him. "Egypt."

Daniel nodded. "My allegiances don't necessarily lie with the President." He waited for Abdel to acknowledge it. "But I need you to tell me if the Israelis say anything about the Dahlak archipelago when they're here."

Abdel nodded. "I can do that."

The two shook hands. By even just saying these things, both of them ran a high risk of being locked up in the Adersesr prison with the other thousands of dissidents and political prisoners. Neither of them could say why they felt at ease with the other and admitted to these things in public.

The relationship between the two developed into a friendly communication. Because of their positions it was not possible to spend much time together but there was a brotherly connection growing. It was the next May when Daniel walked through the front door of the hotel at half past eight. He pulled Abdel aside.

"Someone else spotted you."

Abdel felt that panic grow again. It started in his gut, wrenched at his heart and gripped his throat.

"Not you, exactly, but they know there's an informant in the hotel," Daniel said in a hushed tone, looking straight at Abdel to make sure he focused and understood every word. "I intercepted the memo from the foreign office to the state police and ran some interference. In an hour they're going to come here and arrest one of your co-workers. Do not leave before then. I changed the details in the memo to point to one of the room service staff. He's on our informant list. The state police have no record of it. Nothing will happen to him once they get him to the office and he reveals he's one of ours and the minister confirms it. But that only gives you an hour maximum after they leave until they come back and clean out this place."

Abdel nodded, his mind racing a hundred miles an hour.

"I'll give you an address. Wait half an hour after they leave, then go. It's a dry cleaner. There will probably still be police here then. Can you make it look like you've gone out to get something for a guest at the hotel?"

Abdel nodded.

"Good. I'll meet you there."

Daniel paid for a coffee he didn't order with a hundred nakfa note. The address of a dry cleaner was written at the bottom.

For the next hour Abdel was a wreck. He calmed himself, and pulled himself together. He had trained for intense circumstances like this. One slip up here and he would be caught. Just one false move, one small error to give anyone an idea that he had anything to fear or knew that they were coming, and the suspicion would be all over him. He served a regular guest and sent his customary wine to his room. He waited for an hour and still there were no police. Had Daniel been wrong? Were they being watched? Had he been caught?

There was no way for Abdel to contact him. He wondered about going to the address but wondered if that would be a trap now. Just as the nerves were clawing at his gut and he was about to have a cigarette for the first time in two years, the police came into the foyer. They were exact and precise. The three agents moved through the hotel with intimidating efficiency and dragged the assistant room service manager out in handcuffs.

Just as quickly as they'd appeared, they were gone. While everyone else looked around in stunned silence, Abdel was steadying himself. He drank some water and checked the time. With a list of phone calls he had to make he was able to focus on business and work. That took twenty-two minutes. He walked to the front door and looked around, feigning interest in the taxis. There was one armed police agent sitting in the foyer. Abdel checked his watch. He walked upstairs and took account of everything. He would have to leave personal items behind so it didn't seem he was running away. He took what he could of identification without seeming suspicious.

He walked back down to the foyer and spoke to the front desk manager.

"Is there a bellboy free?" Abdel asked.

"Not at the moment. What do you need, sir?"

"I need some dry cleaning picked up for the guest in room 214."

The manager checked the computer but found no listing for dry cleaning. It wasn't unusual since regular customers just dealt with Abdel. "Don't they usually drop it off?"

"It's a different one," Abdel shrugged, rolling his eyes. "They're fussy about it."

"I can have someone do it in an hour."

Abdel frowned. "Look, I'll do it. It's on the way for some other things. I'll be back in an hour or so. You'll be fine until then?"

"No problem, boss."

Abdel walked across the foyer to the door. He started doing math puzzles in his head to keep his mind occupied and to not make his walking look deliberate.

"Excuse me. Stop one second."

Abdel froze then turned to see the agent in the foyer walking towards him. "Yes?"

The agent reached out and put his arm on Abdel's shoulder. "You wouldn't have a cigarette, would you?"

"I do." He pulled the freshly opened packet of cigarettes from his pocket and handed them to the agent. "Keep them. I'm trying to quit anyway."

And with that Abdel walked out the front door without suspicion, having just bought himself an hour before the hotel started looking for him.

Daniel was pacing in the drycleaners. He was getting impatient. His absence from the foreign office would be noticed soon. Getting a flight for Abdel out of the country through the foreign office wasn't difficult. Getting one without any police agents on it, just for the off chance they recognized the hotel concierge, on such short notice was more difficult. By the time Abdel came through the drycleaner's door there was no time to explain. The car was out the back and they took off, driving through the traffic and trying not to draw attention.

"Put this on," Daniel said, handing him a uniform. "Your cover is as a co-pilot. It was the best I could do."

"What type of plane?"

"I believe it's a Douglas C-47."

"I've never flown one that big before."

"You fly?"

"I have. Only small ones.

"The pilot is aware of your situation, to some degree. He'll cover for you. Once you're through the terminal, you'll be fine."

"You saved my life," he told Daniel when they stopped by the military airfield. "One day I might be able to do the same for you."

It was almost two years later when they met again, this time with Abdel working directly for the Egyptian ambassador. Six years after that he was able to hide Daniel in the back of his car as they left an airfield, then smuggle him out of Africa, promising to bring his children to safety.

A shadow passed along the wall of the tin shed as a guard walked by.

"They're quiet today," Addis said. Abdel nodded. There was definitely something different about today. The shadows on the wall, cutting through the beads of light falling through the holes, were usually much more frequent. There was much more yelling and discussion between the guards. Not today.

The younger brother had been leaning against the wall with his ear near the hole. He'd been listening to the guards talking. Today there was so little talk that he heard every word whenever they passed. When the radio crackled as the guard walked past and he spoke back into the radio static the brother's eyes lit up.

"American convoy," he whispered. "They said there was an American convoy coming."

"That explains it," said the older brother. Addis nodded, his eyes still shut. "It happened once before. They all go and hide."

"What's happening?" Sarah asked.

"There's an American convoy coming through," Abdel said. "The guards don't want to be caught so they're going to go and hide."

"Is it papa?" Robel asked.

"Maybe," Addis smiled.

Abdel leaned against the tin and started rocking against it with a new focus. It was important to not attract any attention. Who knew how on edge the guards were at the moment as they prepared to go underground and avoid any detection by the passing U.S. forces. He pushed his hands into the tin and rocked it, bending it. The next spot weld popped and gave way. Addis looked up. It was the most life Abdel had ever seen in the young man's face. Addis started to move across to the same part of the tin wall but the lock clicked and swung open. Light flooded into the room. Abdel froze and dropped his head to his shoulder as if he was half asleep. The guard looked around, his eyes narrow.

"We have extra food so you can eat more." He put another tray down and picked up the bowls from the morning. The second guard pointed his gun at the two brothers then stepped back to close the door, the strongest part of the shed, closing with a click. Robel and Helen leaned forward, reaching for the food.

"No," Addis said. "Don't eat it."

Robel looked up, his eyes pleading. There was food, enough there to actually feel satisfied for the first time in months, but he was being told not to eat it.

"They drugged it last time there was a convoy," Addis said. "An anesthetic so you sleep and don't make any noise when it comes past."

Robel looked up at Abdel and then to Sarah. She nodded and he lay back on the dirt floor. Helen looked just as upset and Sarah reached for them and put her arms around them while they watched Abdel and Assid work against the metal on the wall.

It was sometime in the mid-afternoon with the sun coming in from the other side of the shed when the younger brother heard the radio crackle and then shut off. Any sound of guards walking around outside the tin shed was gone. The silence of the desert town spread out like the heat. The convoy had passed the last town, or wherever their contact was, and was on their way.

The two brothers began working on the shackles with a broken off bit of tin. They worked it into the lock and twisted it off. The locks were heavy but not well made and the first one snapped open after five minutes. The older brother's hands were raw from twisting and bending the metal. The next shackles fell off quicker.

Abdel was still careful about attracting attention. He was working on the weak points of the shed with new focus but still unable to slam against the metal wall as much as he wanted to. Another spot weld gave way. Abdel pushed harder against the metal, bending it up and out. The tin was hot and as he pushed hard against, bending it back to make a hole, the heat burnt through his shirt. He kept pushing until the metal gave way enough that they could crawl out. Addis went first and blinked back against the bright light. He pulled Helen and Robel through and held them close, keeping them quiet as they huddled in the small amount of shade in the hut.

The sun beat down hard but the movement of air was a relief. The sweat and humidity and dust hung heavier in the air than any of them had realized. It stuck to the skin. It filled the lungs. For months now the only fresh air had come from the few times the lock clicked before the door swung open and a guard brought in food. Sarah blinked back hard against the light. A few other weathered tin sheds stood in the hard afternoon light. The other building where the guards were always going in and out of was on the other side. They were fine here as long as there was no noise made.

Once everyone was out of the shed and huddled in the corner, Abdel looked around.

"I think the road is that way," Addis whispered.

"I thought it was that way," said the younger brother. "That's north there."

"Stay here." Abdel said. "I'll find it."

He snuck through the shacks, bent over, looking for any sign of a road. It wouldn't be near the shed. That was certain. Abdel's legs ached. He could only move crouched over a few feet at a time. The muscles hadn't been used for weeks and now it was showing. If there was any need to run far and fast, then it would take a lot of effort, particularly for Addis.

When they had been brought to the small shack, blindfolded and shackled, Abdel had kept a track of the direction. He pictured a compass in his mind as they moved around after the turn from the main road. Navigation training had paid off in someway. He saw the minor road in the dirt past the guard's shack, with three vehicles parked there. It traced a line through the dirt and Abdel squinted into the harsh light to make it out. The major road was on the opposite side from where the vehicles were parked. That made perfect sense. A small dust cloud was at a distance along the horizon. As he squinted, he realized that it was the convoy moving quickly towards them. The intersection was at least half a mile away.

Abdel crouched down and rushed back to the group. A direct route would have been easier, but it would have drawn attention from anyone near a window in the guard's shack. The rest seemed to be mostly deserted.

"We have to sneak around these buildings," he whispered. "Then the main road is about half a mile away." He looked around at six anxious faces, covered with dirt and all blinking against the piercing sunlight. "The convoy is already on the horizon. We only have a few minutes."

"We can't run," said the older brother. "Addis can barely walk."

"We have to," Addis said.

Abdel nodded. "Come on." He led the way around the buildings, going further away from the guard's shack than he originally had, just as an extra precaution. When they reached the end of the houses he picked up Helen and the older brother carried Robel. "Wait until the convoy is in sight," Abdel said, looking around the corner to the guard's shack. "If we go too early the guards might see us."

They all watched the road, waiting for the dirt cloud to get closer. Abdel peered around the corner again. A guard was walking to one of the vehicles.

When he turned he saw Abdel's face and called out to the other guards.

"Shit," Abdel said. "Run. Go, run!"

The younger brother put an arm around Addis and helped him run to the road as it lay there in the sun, twisting and slicing through the landscape like some path to a promised land. They waved maniacally and called out to the approaching convoy, crying and screaming for them to stop. The dirt was hot and Sarah made good ground. She was waving her arms and yelling at the approaching military truck, running as fast as her tired and weakened legs would go.

A crack of a gunshot rang out in the dead hot air. Then another. Helen cried out and Sarah turned to see Abdel falling to the ground, clutching at his thigh. Another shot and Abdel grabbed his lower back. "Run," he hissed at Helen. She stood there, and grabbed his hand, trying to pull him to his feet. "Run," he yelled again.

Robel called out for Abdel, screaming and twisting, and the older brother dropped him on the desert ground, unable to hold the child while he struggled to keep his own legs pumping. Another shot rang out, landing in his right shoulder and sending him sliding across the dirt. He cried out in pain, pulled himself to his feet and kept going.

The military convoy slowed and pulled to a stop. U.S. soldiers jumped off with the guns drawn.

Two grabbed the fleeing prisoners and threw them to the ground, covering them from any more gunfire. Sarah turned and looked back at the camp of disheveled huts and sheds. One of the guards had run out from the shack and grabbed Helen, screaming and kicking, and was dragging her back. A shot was fired from the military and it hit the shoulder of the guard who kept pulling her back into the shack.

Another hit the nearest shack as another guard pulled Robel behind the wall. A few shots were fired back and hit nothing but the dirt. Sarah cried out, screaming for her brother and sister, and as the soldier ran out to reach her she turned and ran back to the shack. She saw the guards climbing into one of the vehicles with her siblings and then piling into the other trucks, yelling at each other with weapons drawn and firing randomly at the soldiers.

A guard grabbed Sarah and threw her to the ground, hitting her in the back of the ribs then hauling her up and throwing her into the back seat with her siblings. Helen and Robel were both crying, a weapon from the front seat pointed at them as the vehicle took off over the dirt track, weaving through the shacks and away to the next town. Sarah looked back as the brothers and Addis were pulled into the military convoy and Abdel's dead body lie there on the hot dirt, the blood already drying out in the sand.

She felt a hand grab her shoulder and turn her around to face the front, then a hand hit her face. The guards yelled at her, screaming, but the blood was racing through her ears, her chest heaving and pounding from running and the screams of her siblings filled the cab. She clenched her jaw and pushed aside the screaming and yelling that was swelling inside her. She took her siblings hands and held them, mustering all the strength she could to stay calm for them and watched the U.S. convoy grow smaller in the reflection of the guard's mirrors.

4

It had happened quickly. Only two weeks earlier Hudson had been being tested at Camp Peary, a place most people outside of the CIA referred to as The Farm. Now he was on a military aircraft on the way into southern France. He flicked through the notes and then put them away. He'd read over them countless times at this point.

The idea of studying a semester abroad had been in the back of his mind for some time before he'd been approached and asked to apply. To say he was a stand out in his class was an understatement. There were high expectations for his future already. After the interview process with the Dean of the School of Humanities and Social Sciences at Mississippi College, he was accepted for the exchange program, full scholarship. Little did anyone from Mississippi College know that he was just in the exchange program as a cover and his flight from Mississippi to Montpellier would include a stop in Langley for a briefing on his assignment.

Montpellier sits on the southern coast of France, along the coast from Cannes, Nice and Monaco. Apart from the reputation of the University of Montpellier, and being the oldest operating medical school in the world, it was the school's location that made it so attractive to those rich and powerful. It was in Montpellier where the sons and daughters of important and powerful people, the future leaders of the world's nations, the future major players on a global scale, were educated. That's why Hudson had been pulled aside from his training class at Peary and shuffled off to play the role of a simple college student from Mississippi College, getting to experience studying abroad at the University of Montpellier.

Hudson climbed the three flights of stairs to the apartment that had been rented for him. It was a small studio apartment with a balcony. He could see the cathedral in one direction and the Mediterranean in the other. He opened the windows and let the sea air blow through the room. He sat on the couch and closed his eyes for a while. The jetlag caught up with him and he woke up when a car alarm sounded on the street below. It was quarter past ten. He closed the windows and climbed into the bed.

The next morning Hudson rose and made a pot of coffee. He drank it in the sunshine on the balcony and watched his new neighbors on the street below. He watched the bus pass by every ten minutes and a handful of people racing to catch it. Every time he silently cheered them on, even those who seemed to be too far away to have any chance, then gave a cry when they climbed on to the bus before it took off from the edge of the road. There was only one who didn't make it, and Hudson watched as the man checked his watch and looked at the bus schedule, then after a minute of looking down the street, decided to walk.

Hudson showered and walked into the town square. The appointment at the tobacconist wasn't for another hour but he felt like looking around. Relaxing on the balcony and watching the French go by was enjoyable for some amount of time but he felt like exploring.

He walked down the Rue Francois Franque and past the statue of Louis XIV mounted on his horse. He had an appointment at the tobacconist at one in the afternoon and that meant there was plenty of time left to explore the new town.

He walked past the citizens speaking French and smiled to himself. Just to hear another language as he passed everyone in the streets brought a smile to his face. He sat in a café and ordered a coffee and listened to the conversations. He could pick out the main parts of the conversations around him but following it was more difficult. The speed with which they spoke would take some time to get used to. This wasn't Mississippi anymore, or even Virginia.

The tobacconist was on a small side street opposite a hat store. The store was small with shelves lining the walls and extending to the high ceiling. A glass cabinet was in the middle of the room with the expensive cigars. Along the walls were different, less expensive cigars and tobacco, cutters, cases, pipes and rolling papers.

In the front window were a few other examples and a rotating Zippo lighter case. The wooden cases smelled of fine tobacco. It was ingrained in the wooden finish and hung in the store, not in a dense restrictive way like the smoke that hangs in a college bar, but in a refined and appealing way. Hudson hung around in the store, looking over the racks of cigars and cigarillos. A humidor hummed in the corner keeping the cabinets at the right humidity. When the other customers had been served, bought their boxes of Corojos and Madruos, Hudson approached the counter.

"Hudson," the man behind the counter said. He was a slim man in his early forties with hair cropped short beneath his brown felt cap. A few days of light grey stubble hung on his jaw line.

"Julien," Hudson said, stepping forward and reaching out to shake Julien's hand.

"Nice to meet you," Julian said. He lifted the middle part of the counter. "Come on through."

Behind the storefront was a small sitting room with a kitchenette. A window opened out to the courtyard of the building and the breeze wove through the curtains into the room. Julien brewed some coffee and Hudson looked through the bookcase. Most of the titles were in French.

"When did you arrive?"

"Yesterday afternoon."

Julien nodded. "Usually the students take a while before coming to see me."

Hudson shrugged. "I didn't have anything else to do."

Julien put two espresso cups on the table and set the coffee maker on the stove top. "You've been given the brief?"

"About the surveillance, yes, I have."

"The important thing to remember is that you're here as a student," Julien said. He leaned forward in his seat when he spoke. "Officially as well as practically, you're a student. You're here to enjoy a semester in France, to continue your studies and perfect your French. If you start to struggle academically then it will affect other things. It's that whole experience of studying abroad that is key. The surveillance is secondary."

Hudson nodded and watched Julien pour the coffee.

"Just between you and me," Julien said, "when you look back on this, it's the semester in another country that will be most valuable to you. But of course if there's any information you pick up that you think might be valuable then that's beneficial too."

"The class list has a few foreign names on it that I thought were interesting, but there's just one I've been told to keep an eye on."

"That's often the case. It's a very attractive university to send any one who's able."

"You studied there?"

Julien nodded. "I did a similar program that you're doing, but decided to stay here in France instead of returning to Langley." He raised the espresso. "To your stay in Montpellier."

Julien had found himself living in the south of France in an apartment similar to Hudson's. Julien had grown up in New Jersey with a French mother and for him the change to the French lifestyle wasn't as difficult as some other Americans had found it. He'd met Paulette while he was studying at the university and she'd come back to Virginia with him.

When he'd finished his studies they'd moved back to Montpellier and Julien took over her family's tobacco store. He continued his role in Montpellier doing surveillance for the CIA. Although he lived a civilian life, he was the contact for Hudson. For over a decade, Julien had been a supportive figure for the various students who were on exchange at the university, as well as the point of contact for the CIA.

"In my fifteen years of doing something like this, there have been a few interesting pieces of information but there's not been any need for the student to do anything else."

"If there is, then let me know. I'll be willing to do what I can."

Julien frowned. "I'm getting that impression. But remember – you're here as a student. Enjoy that while you can."

Hudson nodded, taking it in, and putting the empty espresso cup back on the table.

"If you need anything, then just stop by the shop and I'll make sure it's taken care of or delivered to you. If you need more tutoring too, then I have some friends who can help out. Or you need information on Montpellier, then just stop by."

Hudson nodded. "Everything seems pretty taken care of in the apartment so far."

"Do you smoke?"

"No."

Julien chewed his lip. "Maybe you should start." He pulled out a pouch of tobacco and some rolling papers from the drawer and slid them across the counter. "Take these. It might come in handy."

Hudson still had another week before classes started and he spent most of it wandering around the city. The town square became a favorite place to loiter. The French lifestyle was different than what Hudson was accustomed to and he soon developed an interest in sitting with a coffee and people watching. He'd take a book but usually didn't even pick it up, preferring instead to just sit and watch the citizens pass him by. There was a man in his seventies that Hudson saw at the same café several days in a row.

Hudson approached him and started talking to him in his improving French and listened to stories of how he'd come to the same café for the last thirty years. Before that he had driven around the coast selling suits to distinguished customers and, after meeting a Montpellier girl, working as a tailor across the road between drinking espressos. Hudson was getting the impression that the women in Montpellier were possible of ensnaring you if you weren't careful.

"I sold suits to Cary Grant one time," Charles said. "I was selling them in a hotel and I saw him in the foyer. I thought, why not? The man knows his suits. He bought three off of me."

Hudson nodded, smiling, letting the old man tell him the stories.

"He wore one in that Hitchcock film. Did you see it?"

"Which one?"

Charles shook his head. "With Grace Kelly."

"Rear Window?"

"No."

Hudson shrugged.

"La Main Au Collet. It was about a thief."

"I don't know it."

"Do you smoke?" Charles asked Hudson while he stuffed his pipe.

"No," Hudson said.

"Good, good. You look like an athlete. Are you an athlete?"

"I work out a lot and I used to play football and compete in powerlifting competitions."

"Football? You're too big for football."

"American football." Hudson mimed a quarter back pass.

"Yes, yes. That football. I understand." He rubbed his beard. "I must go. My daughter finishes work and we have lunch on Tuesdays."

"It's nice talking to you."

"Yes. Maybe I'll see you here next week. And you can tell me if you want a suit."

"I'll think about it," Hudson said.

"Just let me know. My son will make you one. A very good suit."

When classes did start, Hudson's command of
French was more complete and more fluent than he'd
anticipated, although he was still appreciative that his
classes were held in English. Speaking was becoming
less of a difficulty. There were two other students from
the US in his lectures and they gravitated to each other.
Keith Manning was from Seattle and Joey Lorca came
from San Diego. This was Joey's second semester in
Montpellier. After class, they went out drinking at a
few smaller bars Joey knew.

Hudson's urge to get home and get rest before
morning lectures was strong but he remembered
Julien's words and relaxed. He ordered another Jack
and water and relaxed in the bar. Joey lit another
cigarette and started telling a story about heading up to
a party in an ancient building near Marseilles at the start
of last spring.

In the second week he found himself in the
same study group as Nyan Kham and getting close to
the object of his surveillance was suddenly easier.
There was a joint research assignment due at the end of
the semester and in the five person group was Nyan
Kham, who promptly invited the group to his apartment
for a party that Friday.

Hudson already knew some things about Nyan,
the son of a high-ranking Burmese general. Nyan was
the same age as Hudson, twenty-three, and was the
eldest son of Khin Kham, had studied at the military

academy and was working his way through a law degree. Hudson had tried to guess why Nyan might be of interest to the CIA but had put the thought away; it wasn't his place to know why. He remembered Julien's words again – he's there as a student first and to observe the movements of Nyan secondary. Any information would be part of a large picture, Hudson figured, and he wasn't privy to that larger information.

Nyan's apartment was further up the hill and looked over the rest of the city and out over the sea. It was a penthouse apartment and already pretty full of people when Hudson arrived with Joey. Nyan was in the kitchen making another drink for himself and he greeted everyone with energetic backslapping.

The doors to the balcony were open wide and most people were out there where a DJ was spinning the decks. Nyan called out and pushed through the crowd, saying something in Burmese to the DJ who quickly changed the song.

Melody was standing at the bar and ordering a vodka tonic when Hudson first saw her. She wore a short strapless black and white dress and red kitten heels. Her hair was tied back in a loose bun. Hudson ordered a Jack and water and introduced himself.

The three campuses of the university were all connected somehow and Melody was in her second year of studying pharmacy at the campus across town. She'd grown up in a small town outside Bordeaux and moved to Montpellier for college. Her English was fluent from a semester she'd spent studying in Vancouver but they continued to speak in French.

"Whose place is this anyway?" Melody asked.

"It's Nyan's. You don't know him?"

"I came with other friends." She pointed at two other girls outside on the balcony. "I guess they know him.

"Nyan," Hudson grabbed the host's shoulder as he walked past. "This is Melody."

"Hello."

"Hi. This is a great place."

"Yeah," he nodded, looking around as though it was the first time he realized that it had a spectacular view. "It's pretty great. You're all set with drinks? Yes? Great."

Nyan disappeared back through the crowd with as much confusion and bluster as his appearance. There was a particular charisma that followed him around. Despite his smaller frame, he commanded attention no matter which corner of the room he was in.
Melody was telling a story about the fountain in the middle of the square, about the history of the merchant who built it, and how it related to other fables from Montpellier. Hudson nodded along and drank his drink until Melody suggested they leave the party at some time around 1:00 AM. They walked through the square back to her apartment.

They left the window open all night, making love and breathing the warm summer air that rustled the loosely hanging curtains. Hudson woke in the morning, blinded by the harsh sunlight and the church bells a block away ringing loudly. They dressed and walked back across the square, stopping for coffee then going their separate ways.

Hudson walked slowly back through the town. His head was aching still and he pushed the hangover back as far as he could. The structure of the city and the architecture was still amazing him with all the older apartments and small doors, mismatched windows and colors to the buildings. He stopped in each square and looked at the statues. He read the brief sign under each street name explaining who it was named for. When he got back to the apartment, he opened the windows, poured a glass of iced water and napped on the couch.

The next week went smoother for Hudson as he became more accustomed to the French way of life and the university schedule. Between classes on Tuesday he had a coffee with Nyan and realized that just keeping up with him was hard work. Nyan had an exuberance and energy that was difficult to match. His charisma and popularity made everyone who came in contact with him seem to seek his approval in some way. He never asked for anything, but when he even suggested an idea, it was taken upon immediately. Hudson wondered if Nyan's father had a similar energy and charisma, if that's what kept him in power. The group project wasn't due yet and neither of them were that keen to start yet – there were other assignments and projects that demanded more immediate attention. They decided to go out for a drink later that week with Joey.

Hudson met Melody for dinner on Thursday night and she cooked what she had in the kitchen, putting together a meal of some kind of risotto and wine from her uncle's vineyard outside Bordeaux. Hudson stayed the night again and went to class from her place. Over the next few weeks they grew closer. They started spending nights at Hudson's apartment to have some space from Melody's roommate.

One weekend they took a train to Aix-en-Provence to visit the grave of Paul Cézanne. Hudson knew the name but to Melody he was a cultural touchstone. Prints of his work hung around her apartment and as they walked through the city to the cemetery, her chatter became nearly obsessive about the late painter. She smoked her way through a pack of cigarettes at a café, recounting stories of Cézanne's life and his work, and the way he painted. It didn't take long until Hudson had a full appreciation for what Cézanne meant to her, even if he didn't have as much of an appreciation of the man's work as Melody did.

It was on Sunday a few weeks later when Melody and Hudson were sitting in a bar with Joey, Nyan and some of his friends whose names Hudson didn't remember, when Nyan suggested getting away from the city. There was a week free of classes coming up.

"Marseille," Joey said.

"Really?"

"Totally. There's this old chateau outside the city. We went there a while ago. It was amazing."

"We can all stay there?" asked one of Nyan's friends.

"There are plenty of rooms. We could book the whole thing. No problem."

It was decided – they would bring in a few other friends and the twelve of them would book the chateau for four days to get out of the city. Nyan said he knew a friend who could come and DJ the nights away. Joey said he knew a friend in the city already who could hook them up with alcohol and other possible things they might have a need for. Hudson sat back and rested his head on Melody's shoulder. Getting out of the city, as much as he loved the city, was going to give him a break he needed after the papers waiting to be completed next week.

Hudson walked Melody to the university in the morning and spent the next few hours in the library going over his notes and other references. The library environment encouraged study. Every time he stepped through the doors, Hudson felt inspired to pick up a book and drain it of information, to fill his mind with the words and knowledge and learn everything he could. To remain focused on the assignment at hand and the research that the day required was a challenge in itself.

In the afternoon Hudson walked through the streets of the old town and found his way to the William The First tobacconist. Julien was working through the inventory when Hudson opened the door.

"Ah, dear boy. I wondered when you'd come through these doors again."

Hudson laughed. "You've missed me?"

"Ha!" Julien could see Hudson was more relaxed than the last visit. He walked more relaxed and sure of himself, and it was a good sign that he was settling in. "How has the month treated you?"

"Classes are fine, Montpellier is fantastic. And on top of that, I met a rather captivating girl."

"Ha! So you're going to be trapped by these Montpellier women too?"

"Not quite. She's from Bordeaux."

Julien nodded. "You might be safe then." He handed a cigar to Hudson.

"How is everything with you?"

Julien rubbed his short beard. "Can't complain. I've just found out I'm going to be a father."

"Congratulations."

"Thank you." Julien lifted the bench. "Come on through." Hudson made himself comfortable in the chair while Julien made a pot of espresso. "What's to report?"

"I'm regularly seeing Nyan and have become close to him. We're doing a report together later in the semester and I see him every few days. The only things I've picked up are things he says about classes and about bars. He just socializes a lot."

Julien nodded. "I read that in the brief."

"He's quite charismatic."

"Leadership breeds that kind of trait."

"There are a group of us, including him, who are going to Marseilles for a few days in two weeks. An end of summer party since we don't have classes."

Julien put the cups down. A frown crossed his brow. "Was that his suggestion?"

"Going away was, but not Marseilles. Why?"

"Has he mentioned anything about Majorca?"

"No. Why?"

"Just curious. There's some information coming out that, well, if he'd mentioned that then it might be interesting."

"It would be easy for him to have suggested that. The parties at his apartment always have a club vibe with DJs and things like that."

Julien rubbed his chin. "Keep an ear out for that."

"Anything else?" Hudson raised his eyebrow. If he knew what he was looking for instead of just vaguely listening then he would be more helpful.

Julien looked back at him, knowing exactly what the young student wanted, but knowing the less he knew was also helpful. He weighed it up as he poured the coffee. "You have to remember, Hudson, that he's not your friend. You have to keep him at a distance. There is a chance he's involved with gun runners. Intelligence suggests he might be playing some part and it would be helpful to stop the arms smuggling before it becomes a problem."

"Smuggling them through Majorca?"

Julien ignored Hudson's question. "Who suggested Marseilles?"

"Joey, another American."

Julien nodded.

"Surely he wouldn't be doing something with all of us around. There would be a better chance for him to do whatever he wanted to do by himself. Right?"

"Not always."

"So what do you want me to do?" Hudson was a little deflated, feeling more like a pawn than he appreciated.

"Just stay vigilant. Stay attuned to what's going on. Then we'll take the next step if, and it's a big if, if anything happens."

Hudson understood. "Do you need the address of where we're staying?"

Julien nodded. "It's probably a good idea to always let us know where you are going, especially with the target."

Melody stayed at Hudson's house the night before they caught the train to Marseilles. She lay in bed in the morning with the sheet pulled up loosely around her hips.

The morning light trickled through the room and caught the perfect curve of her body. Hudson stood in the doorway to the bathroom watching her chest rise and fall.

"Can you pass me my cigarettes?" she asked.

Hudson pulled the pack from her bag but it was empty. "Hang on," he said. He opened the drawer of the dresser and pulled out the pouch of tobacco and rolling papers. "Here you go."

"You always said you didn't smoke."

Hudson shrugged. "It was a gift. I'll have a shower, then we can go."

"Ok," she said, focusing on rolling the cigarette. She sat up in bed and reached through in her bag for her lighter. She exhaled the smoke and smiled at him, posing like a sixties French film star. Hudson lingered in the doorway, looking over her body, then turned and ran the shower. They made love again in the shower before getting dressed and heading to the train station.

Melody rested her head on Hudson's shoulder and dozed most of the ride along the coast. She couldn't even remember how many times she'd taken that train along the coast. For Hudson, the views were more breathtaking. The water rolled out from the shore, the rising cliffs and smaller coastal towns. He wanted to nap and rest, but every time he opened his eyes and looked around, there was another view he couldn't take his eyes off.

By the time Melody and Hudson arrived at the chateau, everyone else was there and unpacked. They found their room at the west end of the second story and then went back down to the balcony where everyone else was sitting with a drink, looking out over the coast, while Nyan was telling the DJ what to play for the rest of the afternoon. Melody slipped her shoes off and put her feet on the railing while Hudson looked through the kitchen to find what else there was to make a drink.

"Whose is this?" Nyan held up the pouch of tobacco with the William The First logo on the side.

"Hudson's," Melody said as she rolled a cigarette. She ran her tongue along the paper and sealed it. "Does anyone have a lighter?"

Nyan looked at Hudson and tapped the tobacco pouch against the table. "You don't smoke," Nyan reminded him. "One hundred percent finest Virginian tobacco."

"No," Hudson said, remaining calm as he sat next to Melody. "Not now. But that was a gift."

"A gift?" Nyan's eyes were lit up like a cat that had the mouse pinned in the corner, considering how to pounce.

Hudson nodded.

"I'm sure it was." Nyan dropped the pouch on the table and went back inside to make himself a drink. For the rest of the afternoon, as the sun set over the coast and everyone took in what they could of the last of the late summer sun, Nyan sat scowling at Hudson. When someone made a request to change the music Nyan insisted the DJ be allowed to do what he wanted. When Bethany suggested they start cooking and that the cookout should probably be tomorrow night, Nyan demanded it be done tonight. Hudson ignored him as much as he could and played cards with the others. Or talked to anyone else. Or walked around the chateau with Melody.

Nyan had been making odd remarks for the last few hours. As the sky darkened, so did Nyan's mood. Almost everything he said for the last hour had been some attack against the western world and, more specifically, the US. Hudson dismissed it with a shrug. But now Nyan had set into a rant, leaning forward with his arms on the table, his knuckles white as he gripped the table to make his point. His most faithful followers nodded along. Others shrugged it off, agreeing

passively with Nyan's claims of imperial meddling in a
vain hope that Nyan would be satisfied and he would
drop it. There was no stopping him. Hudson didn't act,
and that just urged Nyan into a fuller diatribe.

Nyan was trying to provoke him now. Hudson
took another sip from his Jack and water. It calmed the
nerves but he made sure it didn't fill him with any false
bravado. All it would take is one slip now, just one
misspent phrase, that let on that Hudson knew more
than Nyan had said, anything about Burma or his
father's position in the military rule there, just one slip
up and it would be a whole new game. At this point
Nyan had no concrete evidence. On some level he
knew, but he couldn't do anything about it as long as
Hudson stayed mute and played dumb when
questioned. Nyan's anti-American rant continued. It
was directed directly at Hudson sitting at the other end
of the table. He realized he was squeezing Melody's
hand tight and let it drop. He had half a mind to leave
the room, but realized that too would be a false move.

Then Joey stepped up. "You're a hypocrite,
Nyan." That simple sentence broke the stream of words.
Joey might have been unaware of the tension, certainly
unaware that it was all directed towards Hudson, but he
had some nerve to interrupt Nyan, ranting and gripping
the table hard with his slender hands.

The silence didn't last long. "How? How am I
the hypocrite? You're the hypocrite." There was venom

and hate in Nyan's voice. Arrows pointed directly at Joey sitting there with a head full of alcohol.

Joey shrugged. "Maybe you're right. Let me get you another drink. What are you drinking?"

And Nyan realized at the same time as everyone else around the table that Joey had set him up. It was the empty glass of Jack and water that did it. Everyone looked at it at the same time. Keith laughed. Melody hid her smile behind a hand then lifted her vodka to her lips. The glass sat there like a smoking gun. The drink had been drunk and Nyan's fingerprints lingered on the cool glass, suddenly showing Nyan's complete argument being built on hypocrisy. All of a sudden the Calvin Klein jacket hung heavier on Nyan's shoulders. His Nikes now seemed glued to the ground. The argument he had earlier about sour mash bourbon being a better drink than the Jameson's whisky that Pierre preferred came back like an echo. Everyone at the table became aware of the remixed Michael Jackson tracks playing in the background and every other part of American culture that Nyan had dragged with him to Marseilles.

It was mid-morning when Hudson and Melody climbed out of bed and went downstairs. Pierre had cooked a breakfast and it soothed the aches of the night before. Nyan was noticeably absent but no one made any particular mention of the fact, assuming he would come down when he was ready. Everyone had their separate plans for the day and after the frittata and bacon and crepes had been eaten, they went their separate ways. Pierre and most of the others were heading to the water and were trying to talk Keith into coming with them. Joey had decided to go for a short hike. Hudson had talked Melody into going into the city for a few hours to look around. The architecture and other historical elements of these towns still fascinated him. Melody had agreed to come with him on the condition that they visit another artist's grave.

They walked around the Marseilles cathedral before heading down to the waterfront. The previous night's scene played over and over in Hudson's mind. He was sure he did the right thing in not doing anything, and the more he went over it, the more he was convinced of it. What would come next is what had him worried. Nyan knew for sure now that Hudson was not just another American student on campus. How would it affect their relationship? What would the fall out be? He needed to talk to Julien, to tell him the circumstances had changed, but how? These questions swam around his mind and he kept pushing them away.

"What are you thinking?" Melody asked him.

"The architecture," Hudson lied.

"It's the same as in Montpellier."

"But it's not the same as at home."

"You're such a tourist," she laughed.

Hudson shrugged. He looked at the buildings again. "Doesn't it make you wonder about how they built it? All these perfect arches and domes were made with an amazing workmanship. It's amazing."

Melody shrugged. "Sure. But they're everywhere."

They walked along the waterfront until Melody said she needed another coffee and they sat outside a hotel overlooking the waterfront. The need to speak with Julien was growing and when Melody said she needed to go to the bathroom, he walked to the concierge and said he needed to make a phone call. As it rang, Hudson decided he would be vague, only disclosing what Julien asked. That was the best way.

"William The First Tobacconists," a female voice said on the phone.

"Is Julien available?"

"I'm sorry, he's gone to Marseilles for the week."

"Marseilles?" Hudson repeated.

"Yes. He'll be back in a few days. Is there anything I can help you with?"

"It's more of a personal matter, actually. Could you tell me where he's staying?"

There was a pause, and the sound of movement. Then in a lowered whisper, "Mister Jones?"

"Yes."

"He left a message in case you called. There's an address. Can you write it down?"

It was a place in the third arrondissement not far from the hotel Hudson was standing in. After visiting the grave site with Melody and talking about more sightseeing, she decided she would go back to the chateau and meet the others at the beach. Hudson walked towards the other cathedral as she disappeared on the bus then headed towards the address in the third arrondissement. It was a small hotel off the square.

"Hudson," Julien said, closing the hotel room door. He led Hudson into the hotel suite where another American operative was sitting. Rick was in his late thirties with short-cropped hair. His muscular frame was hidden beneath a dress shirt and chinos.

"Any fresh news?"

Hudson told the two of them about the previous night's episode, stressing his passive role and the humiliation.

"What did he say this morning?"

"I haven't seen him today."

Julien and Rick exchanged glances. "We believe there will be movement tonight," Rick said. "There's a small unregistered ship off Isle Gaby. It's a replica of the ferry that goes across the Mediterranean and we believe the weapons shipment will be leaving from there tonight."

"And you're trying to stop it?"

"Intercept it at the best, or else observe the transaction. At this point the information of who is involved is a major part of future operations."

"It was your information about Marseilles that made us look in this direction instead of the Spanish islands," Julien said.

Rick was chewing his lip as he ran something over in his mind. "It would be beneficial to have you on site in some capacity," he said eventually. "To observe, if nothing else."
Julien nodded.

"Can you tail the target tonight?"

"You think he'll leave the chateau and head out to the island?"

"Exactly."

"I can follow him, somehow disappear from the party and tail him to the harbor."

"We'll be watching the harbor from another safe house and we'll be able to contact you once you get there."

Rick pulled out some radio equipment and a small device that looked like a hearing aid. "Put this on after you leave the chateau. It's convenient but a little obvious in broad daylight. We'll be able to contact you through that radio when you're in range."

The chateau was quiet when Hudson returned. It seemed everyone was still down at the beach. Hudson poured himself a juice and picked at what was left of the frittata. He was looking in the cupboard for something else to snack on when Nyan walked down the stairs.

"Morning, Nyan."

Nyan walked past him to make a pot of coffee. "Morning, Hudson."

"How's the head today?"

"It's fine. Nothing some sleep and caffeine can't fix. Do you want some coffee?"

"Sure, thanks."

Nyan leaned against the counter and looked piercingly at Hudson, still trying to figure out how to get him to slip up or betray himself.

"Is the cookout happening tonight?"

Nyan nodded. "I think I have to go and pick up some other things in the city."

Hudson nodded. "You don't have to do this. There's still time to change your mind."

"Not really," Nyan said, staring coldly. "I've already ordered the extra meat from the butchery."

Hudson scanned his friend's face for a clue, for a break, but there was none. There was just the façade, only the cold expression and the calculating eyes. Where even yesterday there had been compassion and empathy, now there was not. "So we'll start cooking at sundown?"

"I guess that will be best. I'll have to go in just before then since we have no where to store it all."

"Do you want a hand?"

A bemused smile crossed Nyan's face. He almost let out a laugh but shook his head, amused, instead. "I think everything will be taken care of by then. I'll just give them the directions to get back up here."

The heavy weighted silence was broken by Keith's laugh as he led the rest of the bathers back into the chateau. "Mojitos for everyone!"

Nyan took the boiling coffee pot off the stove and poured it into two cups, handing one to Hudson. "Salut!"

"Coffee?" Keith asked. "What's with the coffee? It's cocktail hour, boys!"

Melody slipped her hand around Hudson's waist and kissed him. Her lips were cool from the water.

Hudson sat on the balcony for the rest of the afternoon with his sunglasses on. At every point he kept track of Nyan, watching his movements and making sure that at every second he knew where he was. As soon as Nyan made any motion to leave Hudson would have to take off after him.

The western sky was turning red when Nyan slipped off from the balcony and headed to the door. The last hour he'd been toying with Hudson by getting up every five minutes for a different reason. Hudson admired the collected demeanor Nyan carried with him.

He was smooth and as charismatic as ever, still making jokes and talking to everyone on the balcony, but with some focus on the continuing mind game he played with Hudson. It was like an eagle with eyes on its prey, even as he volunteered Hudson to make the fire in the yard before he returned with the extra meat.

Hudson realized he was snookered and that he had to accept, and that it meant everyone would hold him accountable, not letting him leave. The pure gall and brazen behavior was amusing. Nyan watched Hudson in a mirror while he pulled on his shoes. Hudson stayed still, ignoring Nyan moving towards the door. Hudson kept his feet up on the balcony railing as Nyan walked down the road and into the shadows.

There was no time to make up an excuse or figure his way out of the chateau. Hudson slipped out the back and took off down the back road so the rest of the party couldn't see him leave. On the main road he saw Nyan in the distance climb into a white Audi and take off down the hill towards the city and the harbor.

The rattling of the bus coming around the corner stopped Hudson panicking and he ran to the bus stop and raised his hand. The Audi was speeding away and there was no way to catch them in a bus, but Hudson knew where he was going.

The city was dark and the sky was grey when Hudson made his way to the port. He'd gotten off the bus a few stops early to make sure Nyan wasn't waiting for him at the bus stop. The main streets were as busy as always in the late summer as people were out enjoying the humid night. The side streets were less busy and as he neared the port he saw the white Audi parked near the water.

Hudson stopped behind the wall, put the earpiece in place then walked casually in the shadows of the building. By the time Hudson caught up to him, Nyan was halfway across the square. Hudson took off down the parallel street and wove his way back to the other side of the square in time to see Nyan and his associates moving out onto the boat.

"We can see you there, Hudson," Rick's voice said through the earpiece. "And the target appears to be moving towards the smaller yacht. Continue to follow the target but at a distance."

Hudson turned to make sure no one else was following them, that there were none of Nyan's associates following him at a distance to catch him. He did a double take – Melody was following him. As she rounded the corner he reached out and grabbed her wrist, slid his hand over her mouth, and pulled her against his chest.

"What are you doing?"

"I was meeting Nyan to help him with the barbecue meat."

Hudson looked at her in disbelief. "What?"

"He told me to meet him at the store at the next square. It's near the dock. Are you going to help too?"

Hudson released his grip. "Sure. Lead the way."

The radio crackled. "Hudson, where are you going? You're going out of our sight here."

"I have a visual," Julien's voice came through the radio.

"Is it this way?" Hudson asked Melody. He turned to look at her over his shoulder. One hand held his hand, and in the other was a small pistol pointed directly in his back. "Melody?"

"I have a visual," Rick's voice crackled.

Nyan appeared on the other side of the square with two bodyguards. They walked slowly across the square. Nyan took the pistol from Melody and smiled at Hudson, caught in the trap perfectly.

"Hudson, stay calm," the radio crackled. "We haven't got a clear shot but it's coming."

"You couldn't just stay put, could you?"

"Nyan, it doesn't have to go this way."

"That was your choice, that you should have made a long time ago, Hudson. I have business to take care of and you got in the way."

"Come on, Nyan. You can stop what you're doing. I'm your friend."

"No, you're not. You never were, Hudson. You're a liar and a hypocrite. You only came to my parties to drink my wine and eat my food because it was your assignment. You had nothing personal invested in it. Until now."

Nyan turned the gun away from Hudson and pointed it at Melody and fired a shot into her abdomen. She screamed and Hudson cried out, looking at Nyan. Melody collapsed into Hudson's arms in the middle of the square. She reached out to him as the blood flowed out over her quickly, stopping him from lunging at Nyan. Hudson bent over Melody and looked up at Nyan who looked back with cold calculating eyes and a slight hint of a smirk. Nyan pocketed the pistol again then turned and ran out of the square. Melody gasped for air, her eyes pleading for Hudson to do something to save her. Her hands were covered with her own blood, reaching for Hudson. Her fingers gripped his shirt then fell loose again. Hudson shook, shocked and enraged. He let her body fall and stood up. A crowd had gathered in the small square.

"Do not pursue the target," Rick's voice came firm through the radio. "Repeat, do not pursue. Return to safe house."

Hudson stood in the square watching Nyan disappear into the shadows, into the grey night that hung over Marseilles and felt more than Melody's red blood pouring out amongst the stones of the square. He looked down at Melody's lifeless body then at the crowd starting to form. Sirens were wailing a few blocks away and getting louder. Hudson took off down the street, Melody's blood still on his hands and shirt.

5

Daniel was almost half an hour early, and he was anxious. He'd tried to take his time. He tried to stretch out getting dressed, or leaving his brother's house later to miss the bus, but he was still early. Anxiety gnawed at the bottom of his stomach. Hudson had reassured him that it was almost a formality but still he couldn't help but feel some trepidation. His heart raced. His palms were sweaty.

The coat of his new suit was draped over the arm of the couch and he sat there with his mind wandering completely. He absently brushed a stray thread off the thigh of his trousers. Then, when the barista started frothing milk, he turned as if suddenly realizing for the first time that he was in a café. He ordered a coffee and returned to the couch. His mind raced and he picked up a newspaper to keep himself occupied. It didn't work. As he flicked through the paper, the print smudging slightly on his thumb, his focus was somewhere else. None of the pictures or headlines registered with him at all.

There had been another phone call demanding the money. The line was distorted but still he could make out Sarah's voice. He was working every night at the restaurant but still barely even had a tenth of what he needed to bring his children back. He'd looked into other work and started office temping but the work was not as frequent as he'd hoped. One office had given him two days work the week before, but there had been nothing since.

Nine hours in an office followed by seven more in the restaurant had driven him into the ground. He managed to keep his voice calm and steady, reassuring his daughter that he would bring them away soon. It was when she told him that Abdel was dead that he started shaking. The kidnappers had taken the phone from Sarah and yelled at him. The message was clear even through the static and distortion. He hadn't been able to sleep after that. He checked his watch and counted the hours until he was supposed to be back at the restaurant.

Hudson entered the café and stepped up to the coffee table and couch where Daniel was sitting. Whether he was unaware of the shroud of respect that engulfed the café or was simply ignoring it, Daniel couldn't tell. Hudson commanded some air of respect as it was, simply in how he carried himself and the way he walked, but now with his formal attire, Daniel saw it compounded.

"You look tired," Hudson said.

"It was a rough night."

Hudson ordered a coffee for himself and took a seat. "How are you feeling?"

"Other than tired? Nervous and anxious."

Hudson put a hand on Daniel's shoulder. "There's nothing to worry about," he said in a comforting and direct tone. "These people want to help you. They see you as a person of importance and will do what is in their power to bring this to a close."

Daniel took a breath and nodded. He wasn't sure if it was the message or just Hudson's presence that made him realize that more fully. He was put at ease simply by being near the direct and clear thinking Hudson. He certainly needed some peace of mind after the last twenty-four hours.

"How's business?"

Daniel smiled. "Good, good. There was a profile in The Clarion-Ledger about the new trend of Eritrean restaurants. It sparked some interest."

"There are other Eritrean restaurants in Madison?"

"I don't think there are," Daniel laughed. "I don't know what the paper was trying to say."

"That was last week, right?"

Daniel nodded. "Tuesday, I think."

"Lauren said something about that."

"The word is out on the street."

"We should get going," Hudson said. He motioned for Daniel to put his wallet away. "Let me pay for these. They're on the government."

Sarah had sounded calm, Daniel realized. There had been some strange serenity around her when she spoke. While he was picturing her tied and gagged with weapons, probably one of the Soviet supplied AKM rifles, pointed at her head, her voice was steady. It sounded almost like she was in control even when the voices in the background were barking commands at her, telling her what to say, there was a steadiness. She told him about Abdel being shot and while the voices in the background told her to say the others were dead too she ignored them and said she and Helen and Robel were fine.

For Daniel, hearing that they were kept in a small tin shed was almost a relief. His mind had been racing to alternatives every night during the last few weeks. Human trafficking in Eritrea was far too common and with his daughters captive, with Abdel and Robel there too, he had no idea what would happen. His work at the foreign office only made things worse.

He'd read files of other cases of kidnapping and trafficking. He'd heard from his colleagues about forced labor and worse. It was poorly policed and almost unofficially tolerated by the state. Even those who avoided the kidnappers as they fled Eritrea weren't safe. The illegal status of Eritrean refugees in the neighboring countries made them susceptible to those willing to exploit them.

There were four people already in the small conference room when Hudson and Daniel entered. Hudson took a seat at the same end of the table as Daniel and introduced him. At the head of the table sat Colonel Fitzpatrick and his assistant. Fitzpatrick sat his heavy frame far back in the chair and in a position to watch over proceedings. To his right was Major Greene who, despite not being the highest-ranking man in the room, certainly commanded a certain level of respect. He rubbed his hands in front of himself and picked up the metal pen from the table. He tapped it absently on the pad as his eyes flicked through the notes he'd jotted down.

Fitzpatrick leaned back in his chair with his eyes fixed on Daniel. The muscle in his jaw pulsed. Sergeant Donald Mervyn sat to the side near Hudson. He was a solidly built man with short black hair. His hands were on the table with fingertips touching, and he extended a hand to Hudson and Daniel, then resumed the same position with a straight back and careful gaze taking in the proceedings.

"Thank you for coming in today on short notice," Greene began. "We're told you have some information that might help us, and that we might be in a position to help you."

Daniel swallowed hard. His mind had been wandering, back to the phone call. Back to the strained tones in his daughter's voice.

"This is a preliminary meeting to gauge the situation," Greene said. "It's rather informal but we'll be taking notes and what not, if that's ok with you."

"Sure."

"We understand that your children are currently being held hostage for a ransom. And that you've been contacted by the abductors."

"That's right," Daniel said softly. "Yes."

"When did they first contact you?"

"A little over two months ago. My friend from Egypt called. He had been hiding the children in his truck and driving towards the northern border. There was an ambush, he said, and they were taken hostage. They demanded a large amount of money. I've been recording any conversation since." He pulled out a USB stick and put it on the table. "The conversations are there in mp3 format."

"It was always by phone?"

"Yes."

"Are they aware of your previous role there in Eritrea?"

"No. No, I don't think so."

Fitzpatrick's assistant leaned across and muttered something in the Colonel's ear. Fitzpatrick nodded.

"Can you tell us the position you held in Eritrea?"

"I was in the foreign office and had contacts in the military from my time as an officer there. I served in the war with Ethiopia." He paused. The expressions around the table all held a certain weight of expectation. "I have some knowledge from there particularly about the military base north of Keren, that might be helpful to you."

"Can you tell us about your training?" Daniel looked down at the table, anxious now with uniformed eyes on him. He took a sip from the cup of water on the table in front of him and then began. "I was enlisted in the mid-90s. I served in the war with Ethiopia and then transferred to the foreign office two years after that. My wife was also employed by the military. For the last three years, she worked as an assistant to a general. She was collecting information, in case it proved to be of some use. I always told her not to," Daniel said with some appreciation of the situation. "But she did."

"Why did you decide to leave?"

"Conditions were getting worse. Particularly for people like us," Daniel hesitated. It had been so long since he'd been able to talk about it openly and he'd still not adjusted to that aspect of living in America.

"Since 2002 it's been illegal to be a member of the Protestant church. There are only four recognized religious institutions in Eritrea. If you're not a member of those, then you're forbidden to worship and are persecuted. Even other denominations of Islam are persecuted. For the last few years we've had small weekly congregations in different homes. We even had to have Robel baptized in a friend's living room. Some friends were caught and they just disappeared. We had to stop the congregation for a few months after that, just as a precaution."

"How did you escape?" Greene asked.

"My wife died last year. We'd talked about leaving before, but after she got sick it wasn't really an option. I promised her that I would get the children out of Eritrea. There was a conference soon after her death where I was serving as assistant to the ambassador. I managed to get a few strings pulled and organize some passes and travelling visas for the children. They were to be taken from the hotel while I was at the conference and the meetings with other ambassadors. Then at a point between the conference and the hotel I was to join them. It had been planned for months.

Two weeks before the conference, a colleague of mine went missing in Israel and it looked like he'd done the same thing we'd planned. The official line was that he had been abducted, but no one thought that this was what had happened. He'd fled, just left and gone. Then the president cracked down on visas and any travel permits that came through. The children's permits were revoked. There were extra police with each envoy to embassies and conferences.

I was in Cairo two weeks later. I have a contact there, a friend, Abdel. He works in the state department and was overseeing security for a meeting of the Arab states." Daniel sipped the water again. These were things he didn't particularly want to talk about but knew he had to get out. He'd told people some details, some level of what happened, but now as he went through those actions he'd taken not even six months ago, Daniel was feeling that rise of guilt and anxiety that he'd had to learn to deal with. After all, what kind of father was he to leave his children there?

"It was a split second decision," Daniel said. "Just one that we made, no discussion. And once it was done, there was no going back. It couldn't be undone. We've known each other for years but of course we could never make it seem that way at those meetings. So he pulled me up for a breach of security. There was something 'wrong' with my identification. I was pulled into another office and left there for an hour, missing the final meeting. Then I was taken to another location, under suspicion of breaching security and being some sort of security risk. I was quietly taken across town before the meeting ended. The rest of the Eritrean envoy went directly to the airport. They were told of my arrest and there were some meetings about it. Or so I was told. I was a low priority for the state – Abdel made sure the charges were enough to keep me in isolation so no one could track me, but not enough to cause a stir between diplomats."

"Then what happened?"

"I stayed in a few abandoned flats around the city for a few weeks until I was able to be smuggled out of the country."

"I mean as far as your arrest."

"On paper, I'm still in an Egyptian prison in isolation."

Fitzpatrick and Greene exchanged glances, impressed. Hudson let a smile escape before pouring some water from the pitcher on the side of the table and drinking half of the glass.

"The children were already staying outside Asmara. They were not using my surname, as a precaution in case there was trouble with my position." He stopped and pulled out his wallet. "This is a photo of them." He slid a photo across the table to Greene who passed it around. Hudson looked at it, the same photo he'd seen before, and put it back in the middle of the table. Mervyn's gaze lingered on it then he flicked his eyes back to Daniel as he continued. "Abdel smuggled me out of the country and then relayed information to me about a plan to bring them to Egypt then out of Africa in the same way. He told me he was driving a freight truck across Sudan and would be able to stow them away. That was the last I heard from him before the abduction."

"And the most recent?"

"They called again last night." Daniel didn't even look up. "They called last night. They killed Abdel but the children are still alive."

Donald shifted uncomfortably in his seat.

"The friend who was bringing them to Egypt?"

"Yes. He's dead. I guess they shot him."

A heavy silence rolled through the room. "What else did they say?"

"Sarah was talking. They always make her talk. She said the other children were fine. She was calm," Daniel was a mixture of concern and pride. She told the kidnappers to be quiet while she was talking, and they listened. A shot of fear had run through him when he heard her say it, a sharp jolt, but the noise in the background stopped. "She said they were fine. Then one of the kidnappers cut her off and demanded the first payment in a week."

"How much is that?"

"About twice what I've got together."

Greene looked sideways at Fitzgerald who was chewing his lip. He sighed, a breath full of importance. The chair creaked as he shifted his weight and leaned forward on the table.

"We have another operation under way in Eritrea that could better succeed with your information," Fitzgerald said in a low commanding tone. "If that's the case, then we will be able to expand that operation with Mervyn here and a team of Deltas to encompass the recovery of your family."

Mervyn nodded slowly. He tapped his fingertips on the desktop, the first time he'd unclasped his hands for the whole meeting. "We have information on the base north of Keren and the bases around Asmara."

"OK," Daniel said hesitantly.

"For the operation to succeed, we need classified information on Eiraeiro and Adersesr."

A chill shot down Daniel's spine. Just the mention of those names were enough to do that to most Eritreans. Especially one who had worked in the government and, for years, had prayed daily that there was nothing that betrayed his views on particular issues. People went into those prisons and didn't come back. They disappeared. There had been colleagues of Daniel's, people he knew casually, who vanished. There were rumors they were in Adersesr, but there was no way to know.

After the break up of Daniel's church congregation, there were whispers that the reverend had been taken into the murky depths of Adersesr. There had been times Daniel had a document or file come past his desk, often unintentionally, that detailed treatment of prisoners in that disparaging hell. Unless he needed to, he would barely get past the first page. The light description was enough to give him nightmares. The details on the prisons, the inmates, the guards, conditions, treatment and architecture were all hard to find. It was a black hole of information.

Finding himself on the other side of those bars, having a file about him and being locked up in one of those dark pits of suffering was always at the back of his mind. There didn't even have to be a reason, just the slight suspicion of betraying the state from someone close to the president. He walked a fine line most days. And now he looked up, pushing away the fear and distress that those two names brought, and looked at these uniformed men. They sat forward in their chairs, leaning slightly. Mervyn tapped his index finger absently on the tabletop near the photo. Daniel looked up at Greene and Fitzpatrick. "Yes, I can help you."

"Captain Jones," Fitzpatrick said. "Some of the details to follow are highly confidential, and should only be heard by those involved in the mission."

Hudson looked around, a little taken aback. "Of course." He began to stand.

"I'd prefer if he stayed," Greene said. His tone was authoritative, even when talking to his superior. The issue was not up for discussion. "If JAG is going to be involved with this operation then I insist Jones is the contact and operative."

Hudson was disorientated. Until now he hadn't been entirely sure of his role in the operation.

"I'd prefer if he stayed too," said Daniel, with a little less conviction than Greene.

"If that's how you feel," Fitzpatrick said to Greene, "then he should be properly informed of all the details as soon as possible." With that issue out of the way the mood in the room settled.

Greene turned back to Daniel. "When you're ready, please proceed. Let's begin with Adersesr."

*

Mervyn climbed into the vehicle. He was still tired from the flight. After the flight back from Africa, he'd had three days in California, at home in Santa Clarita, before the flight this morning to Mississippi. He'd surprised his fiancé at the school where she worked. He'd arrived as they were packing up for the day and told her he was home for just a few days and they were going away for the weekend.

Melissa threw an overnight bag together while he filled the car up at the gas station on the corner and then they drove up the coast to his father's condo near Half Moon Bay. They walked along the beach and ate crabs at the restaurant on the pier. They walked through the craft markets the next morning before driving back and seeing his family.

They'd become accustomed to his brief and sudden visits. Mervyn had come to recognize the looks on their face too, no matter how much they tried to hide it. The happiness they had of seeing him was a thin veil over the constant reminder they had that he would leave again just as quickly. It was the nature of his work.

It was a veil Melissa had grown too accustomed to. During the last visit, almost four months earlier, he had promised the coming and going would stop soon. He would transfer to another division in twelve months when they got married. He would be around more. But now his duty was to his country and Melissa accepted that more than she understood. She knew it was something he had to do. There was no changing that. She'd learned to enjoy the time he was home, when that happened, and continue with planning the wedding. The first few times it had been harder. Now she was able to deal with it better. Even in the quiet moments she had to be a steady voice of reason when Donnie's mother called her.

Donnie shrugged off the fatigue and stayed up talking with his parents and brother. He was up at five and with the words of his mother still ringing in his ear, always the same, "Remember to call, Donnie," as he boarded the flight to Mississippi. Hours of meetings in closed offices didn't help keep him awake.

Mervyn hadn't been paying much attention to the streets as Hudson drove. He snapped out of it when Hudson pointed out the Eritrean restaurant.

"That's his restaurant?"

"He works there. It's his brother's restaurant."

"I can't imagine getting a call like that."

Hudson had run the scene through his head a bunch of times too. "And our position has to remain clinical and unemotional."

"Exactly," Mervyn said. "What are you meant to say? Your kids look fine, just thinner, but we don't know where they are?"

Now Hudson understood. "You were on that team of Deltas that picked up the escapees?"

Mervyn nodded. "I saw the children," Mervyn said. His voice was heavy, dragged down with the emotion of remembering. "The eldest almost made it to us."

"Sarah."

"Yeah, Sarah. She was near the road. I could almost reach her and pull her behind the vehicle. But she turned and ran back for her brother. I didn't believe it was them until he showed us that photo."

"What happened?"

"The patrol was on route to the Sudan border when we just saw the escapees running at us and waving frantically. We stopped and then realized we were under fire. We helped two of the escapees into the patrol and took cover. Some of them got shot and the kids were screaming. After the girl, Sarah, turned back to the building we ran after her, and pursued the other vehicle but they were able to take off too quickly."

Hudson stared straight ahead. He replayed that conversation in the conference room, trying to remember Mervyn's reaction.

"That was when they killed his friend, I think. During the escape."

"Not because of the ransom?"

"Not from what the other escapees said. He'd made a hole in the shed and they'd crawled out of it."

Hudson tried to take it in. He didn't notice the light change to green until a horn blared from the car behind them.

"Have you seen action?"

"Not that kind."

"Some things you can deal with. You can deal with it and forget it. Maybe it's not so healthy that we can, but it's doable. Some fights, some hits. Some sniper kills. Then there are things like that. Seeing that girl running across the sand, barefoot and screaming, then turning around to go back for her siblings." Donnie got quiet. "That's something I wish I could forget."

"It's something we'll set right," Hudson said. "Something we'll be proud to remember."

Hudson parked by the hotel and waited in the lounge bar while Donnie checked in and went up to his room. Donnie washed his face and changed into more casual attire before coming back down. Hudson ordered a Jack and water and Donnie had a light beer. They sat at a table near the window overlooking the river. When the light across the river began to fade Hudson drained the last of his glass and headed home.

Lauren was in the shower when Hudson walked through the front door. Her green dress was laid out on the bed. He undressed and slipped into the shower after her. When he'd dressed in chinos and a buttoned black shirt, Lauren was just finishing her make up. Over the years Hudson had learned just how much time he had to kill while she got ready. She looked stunning; it was undeniable. Hudson held the door open for her and set the alarm as she walked out to the car.

He asked her about her day and listened attentively as they drove across town. The first week back at work had its ups and downs but she was settling back into the routine.

She ordered a wine and he ordered a Jack and water as they looked over the menu. He ordered the filet steak, and Lauren had the chicken risotto. It was after Hudson paid the bill, as Lauren was sipping the last of her white wine when he told her.

"I have to go away for work next week."

She nodded, then stopped. She knew he wouldn't have waited this long to tell her if it was another trip to Washington. "Where?"

"It's just for a week."

"Where?"

"Africa."

"Africa?"

"It's just one week."

"A week in Africa?"

"It's a special operation. They need my expertise."

She frowned at him for a moment then stood up. She picked up her bag and then her coat without looking at him. "They need your expertise?" She turned and walked out of the restaurant before he could say anything else.

Hudson smiled at the waiter as his card was returned then quickly picked up his coat.

"Lauren."

"Can you open the car please?"

He hit the button and she opened the door and closed it just as quick, not slamming it – that would be too obvious. That would give away too much of the shape and color of her emotions. Hudson slid into the driver's seat beside her. "Don't close up. You start talking to me again and now you close up again."

"Because you're telling me you're going to Africa."

"For a week."

"It's still Africa."

"I'll be back in a week."

She crossed her arms.

"It's work, Lauren. Would you have this same reaction if they were sending me to Washington for a week?"

She didn't look up. She stared straight ahead and chewed her lip. "That's different."

"How's it different?"

"You would have told me before the end of the night if it was Washington."

"It's really not that different."

"You're choosing to do this."

"It's work. They asked me to do it."

"You're still choosing to do it. You could say no. What would be different?"

"You're right. I'm choosing to do it. But what's that got to do with anything? I'm choosing to go and do my job. It's my duty."

"You don't get it."

"What don't I get?"

"You just don't get it."

Hudson started the car. Lauren stared out the window as they drove across town. At the first red traffic light Hudson offered her something – "What is it that you're worried about?" But she didn't take it. She kept her arms folded tight and, although Hudson couldn't see, he was sure her lips were pressed into that tight thin line. It was that sign of stubborn indignation he'd learned years earlier, a gesture she'd inherited from her mother. That first time they'd both done it at the same time, years ago at one Thanksgiving, both mother and daughter disappearing into Lauren's parents' house and giving each of their husbands the silent treatment, Lauren's father shrugged and uncorked a bottle of pinot and handed Hudson a glass. It was that same shrug that Hudson had learned to mimic whenever Lauren got her back up.

When they pulled off the route home she turned. "Where are we going?" It was Hudson's turn to give her the silent treatment – another lesson he'd learned over a glass of pinot. Lauren, like her mother, would come back to talking sooner or later. It was too much in their make up.

"There's too much you don't know," Lauren said. Her voice was quiet now and that direct slicing tone had softened. "There's so much that you have to keep classified even from me, and I get that. I do. But there's so much you don't know and you can't or won't tell me."

Hudson pulled off the main road into the car park outside The Prince Of East Africa.

"I need you, Hudson."

"Just trust me."

Lauren hesitated, looking at her husband, the darkened street, and then gave in. She unclipped her seatbelt and climbed out of the car. She walked quickly behind Hudson, reaching for his hand as they crossed the car park.

Although the parking lot was almost empty outside, the restaurant looked like it had served an entire infantry. Daniel and his brother were busy clearing tables with the other staff. A waiter came over to Hudson. "I'm sorry, sir. We actually close in fifteen minutes and the kitchen is already packing up."

"It's ok," Hudson said. "I'm a friend of Daniel's. We're just here for a drink."

Lauren shot him a suspicious look then followed him to the bar.

"Mister Jones," Daniel exclaimed from across the room. He ran to the bar. "It was so busy tonight."

"It looks like it." Hudson turned to Lauren. "Daniel, I'd like you to meet my wife, Lauren. Lauren, this is Daniel."

She cooly shook his hand then crossed her fingers in her lap.

"I'll get you a drink. What would you like?"

"A house white wine and a Jack and water, thank you Daniel. But there's no rush. It looks like you're busy."

"Very."

"I'll have a soda water instead, thank you," said Lauren.

"Jack, soda water. I'll come back."

Hudson waited until Daniel had returned to the kitchen.

"Daniel is from Eritrea. He came here six months ago after his wife died." Hudson knew he was messing some chronology up, but that wasn't too important right now. "He left three children back in Eritrea." Hudson pulled out the photo from his wallet. "Helen, Robel and Sarah."

Lauren looked at the children's faces for a moment then put the photo back on the counter.

"And they need JAG legal advice?"

"They were kidnapped several months ago while escaping Eritrea with one of his friends. They're being held for ransom. His friend was killed two weeks ago."

Lauren's face changed and she picked the photo up a second time.

"I'm not part of the operation to get the children, or whatever else the Deltas are doing there. But I am needed for the preliminary part of the operation. Since I'm the one closest to Daniel and can do the part of the operation that JAG is required, Gerald has requested me to be part of it."

Hudson let the words hang in the air while Lauren looked through the picture. He wouldn't have to tell her the whole story, that as a trained CIA field operative, he was the only person who was qualified to accompany a Delta team on a small scale extraction.

"One soda water," Daniel said. "And one Jack." He smiled at Hudson, his face freer of anxiety and worry than Hudson had ever seen him. "Your husband is a great man," he said.

"These are your children?"

"Yes," Daniel said. "Helen, Robel and Sarah. It's Helen's birthday tomorrow."

Lauren nodded and put the photo back on the counter. She slipped her hand in Hudson's and sipped her soda water while she listened to Daniel talk about the three children.

Hudson kept an eye on the clock above the counter and after half an hour he bid Daniel a good night and took his wife home. She kept her hand on his thigh the entire drive home then led him into the bedroom and, for the first time in months, they made love while the Mississippi breeze blew through the night.

6

Donnie Mervyn had only seen the islands of the Dahlak archipelago from the helicopter to Yemen. The submarine trip into the Red Sea had been uneventful. Anytime he was on a submarine for any length of time, Donnie was immediately disorientated. He had to rely on his watch showing Zulu time since his body clock was completely unreliable.

Located at the southern end of the Red Sea, some 60 miles offshore from Eritrea's port of Massawa, was Dahlak. It was common knowledge that Dahlak was used as a covert submarine base for the Israeli navy in their war against the Iranian networks smuggling weapons into Hamas and Hezbollah. Common but not confirmed. The U.S. looked the other way while the conflict was subdued and not between the two nations. And now, the U.S. used the base to sneak Donnie into Yemen, the closest country to Eritrea from which Donnie could put Hudson's plan into action.

From the small hotel he was staying in, he walked the streets taking countless photos of mosques. His knowledge of mosques was quite small before he arrived. But now, after seeing more than he'd thought possible, he was able to tell the difference between designs and periods. He was, with some reliability, able to outline the features that made a mosque from the fifteenth century different to that of one from the nineteenth century or even a more modern one.

He didn't want to walk that far. His guise might have been as an American tourist traveling through the Islamic nations but he didn't want to wear himself out entirely. Donnie sat at the table outside near the window, far enough back from the footpath that the pedestrian traffic didn't bother him. He ordered a strong coffee and a soda water. The glass was already dripping with water when the waiter, an older man who looked like he'd been working in the café for the last forty years, placed it on the small crooked table. Donnie nodded thanks to the man and watched as he turned, put his hands on his hips and squinted into the passing traffic then turned back into the cool dark sanctuary of the bar.

Donnie undid another button on his shirt, letting the slight breeze roll through over his chest. The heat was oppressive. Through the crowd Donnie saw a man order a drink and sit in the bar opposite him. He faced up the street a little, trying to not appear to be watching

Donnie through his sunglasses. Donnie drained half the water and smiled to himself. He'd first noticed he was being followed yesterday when he was taking photos of the mosque near the water. He'd walked around the entire mosque, taking photos and stopping to admire each side of its understated Islamic architecture. Every time he stopped, he noticed the same man in chinos and a blue shirt standing not far away. There was no reason to walk around the entire building without looking at it, and so Donnie knew he was being followed. He ducked inside and joined the tour group just as they began.

While the plan was to get "caught," he certainly couldn't get entangled while still in Yemen. Without the capture by Eritrean forces, he would never be brought into Eritrea, thus preventing the necessity to bring in Hudson to defend him and cause the international attention that would keep the Eritreans at a distance as they travelled to rescue the children.

There hadn't been anything Donnie had done that any other tourist wouldn't do. There'd been no contact with anyone yet. It was all still to come. He didn't mind being followed. Joining that tour group actually added to the façade even more. But the fact they knew he was here amused Donnie. He'd nicknamed his shadow Scar, since the dark and determined eyebrows of his tracker made him look like a comical human version of the Lion King character.

Donnie knocked the coffee back, leaving a thick muddy residue of coffee in the cup and drained the water. He slipped into the crowd easily and watched as Scar tried to pick him out. He'd walked around the block and was standing at the other end of the square before Scar left the bar and figured out where he'd gone, completely unaware that Donnie had travelled around the block. It was partly a move to keep himself occupied, to amuse himself, and partly a way to reassure himself he could escape Scar's tail if required.

Donnie walked toward the markets. The sound of the cries of the vendors cut above the noise of the shoppers. The vendors' cries of fruit prices and discounted fabric hung in the air. It was a thick crowd and Donnie pushed past the sweaty and hot bodies.

The fish stalls carved out a thick stench down one alley. Donnie turned around, walking past Scar directly to avoid the stench of the seafood going bad in the heat. The water from the ice dripped beneath the market stalls and ran into small puddles on the dusty street. Donnie ensured he didn't react when he saw Scar. He turned, brushed shoulders with him and pushed his way through the throngs of people toward the fruit stalls. The polarized glasses allowed him to watch Scar without looking like it, and Donnie hid his amusement as his tail was forced to go down the fish alley further than you could stand. Scar pulled a handkerchief from his pocket and breathed through it while he pushed out of the crowd.

Donnie walked along the docks. The breeze rolled in more refreshingly now. The smell of the morning's catch hung in the air but it mixed with the scent of spices and the salt from the sea. It was much easier to digest.

"American?" A man asked.

"Yes," Donnie nodded.

"Why you so far from home?"

"I'm travelling to Mecca then Jerusalem." Donnie started the first part of his spiel. He'd given it to the guy at the hotel and the man sitting next to him on the plane. It was well rehearsed and Donnie knew part of the believability was in keeping some of the information to himself, only divulging it when it was asked for.

"Searching for all the Gods. That's a good thing to do," the man said, nodding to himself and brushing his collar. "How long are you here for?"

"Two more days." Donnie leaned against the pier looking out across the Red Sea. "Is this your boat?"

"No," the man shook his head. "Not my boat. My friend's boat. We sail tomorrow morning. You want to come?"

Donnie smiled to himself, considering it. Somewhere in the background he knew Scar was watching. "Come fishing? It looks like I'd get in the way."

"No, no." The man shook his head. He grabbed Donnie's shoulder. "It will be a good trip. Maybe you'll be good luck. You can see the fishing, then maybe we go along the coast. There's no tour that will show you that. The real Yemen experience."

Donnie laughed. "That's true. What time do we leave?"

Scar was still shadowing him when Donnie walked back across the square and into the town. He went upstairs to the hotel and showered. From the second story window he could see Scar smoking in the park across the street. He flicked the newspaper, briefly looking up at the hotel then back down. Donnie was careful not to go too close to the window. He was pretty certain Scar had no idea which room he was in and he planned to keep it that way.

As Donnie walked down the stairs to the street again he checked the other exits. There was an exit through the staff kitchen to what he could only assume was the back street. He wouldn't be able to check it with Scar following him. There was another one through the laundry room and it looked like it went the same way.

Donnie lingered at the front desk, picking up a few travel brochures, then headed into the heavy warmth of the Yemen evening. He bought cigarettes at the newsstand and slid them in his shirt pocket, leaving the brochures on the counter. Donnie used a shop window to glance behind him and saw Scar pocketing the forgotten travel brochures. Donnie smiled to himself and decided to look for a decent seafood restaurant.

Donnie woke early and showered without turning the lights on. Enough light fell through the curtains to have some idea of what he was doing. He took only what he needed and slipped down the stairs, skipping the fourth one that creaked, and waited for a moment before slipping out the exit through the laundry. Donnie waited at a bus stop for five minutes to see if Scar had followed him out the back of the hotel but the street remained empty.

The last of the crimson dawn was fading over the sea as he walked through the streets to the dock. Donnie smiled to himself. He'd known he'd be approached by the Yemeni agent at the docks but hadn't expected the agent to sell the act so convincingly. Donnie hadn't even been sure it was the agent or just a fisherman at first, but the code words checked out. Donnie arrived at the dock and kept up the American tourist act.

"Are you sure I won't be in the way?" he asked agent Al-Hadi.

"Please, please. It's a big fishing boat." Al-Hadi smiled, shaking his hand. He showed Donnie to the top of the boat where he could look out over the Red Sea and the rest of the crew untied the ties from the dock. It was only when they were well out of the harbor when Al-Hadi climbed to the top of the boat and shook Donnie's hand.

"Ali."

"Donnie."

"It doesn't look like you were followed."

Donnie shook his head. "No. There was one guy following me around for the last few days but I think I left him back at the hotel."

"I saw him yesterday."

"Any idea who he was?"

"No, not at all."

The motor hummed as they left the shore and headed along the coast then further into the middle of the sea. Donnie didn't realize how loud the motor was until after it had been shut off. The three crew members dropped the nets and went about their business. Ali and Donnie sat on the roof of the boat. Donnie snapped a few pictures out of habit of the tourist guise.

"It was a weird light this morning. Is that normal?"

"Not uncommon but it was a bit strange. I think it had to do with a mixture of a front coming in and the dust storm late last night."

Ali pulled out a small pair of binoculars and looked along the western horizon.

"Anything?"

"Not yet."

It was nearly an hour later with the sun still cutting flat along the east and the trawler edging further away from the coast when Ali let out a cry. He pointed along the horizon. It was a small dot but it grew quickly. As the Eritrean navy vessel approached, Donnie swapped glances with Ali.

"They'll pull up beside us," Ali said, keeping his eyes on the navy ship. "And let us know we've travelled inside their territorial waters. It's possible they'll take us back to Yemeni waters but they'll probably escort us into the port at Massawa and book us. Then we'll be in the country under a legal pretense."

Donnie nodded. He'd been over the plan before. There was not a detail that he didn't know, but with the naval ship pulling closer and dwarfing the smaller fishing ship, it was good to be reassured. Donnie turned and kept taking a few photos of the Eritrean coast while Ali went into the bridge to wait for the radio call. The three crew members hauled up a net full of fish. The light flashed off their shiny scaly bodies as they struggled in the net, while the waves peeling off the naval ship rocked the fishing boat.

Donnie turned to look at the ship approaching. The size of these ships seemed completely different when you're on a small vessel near the hull, Donnie thought. He could hear Ali talking on the radio.

Donnie couldn't make out any words over the engines now, not that it would matter – it wasn't a language he was fluent in. Donnie saw a small boat being lowered to the water and some officers climbing into it.

"We've got trouble," Ali said. His head was poking over the roof. "They didn't go for the foolish fisherman act."

"What?"

Donnie saw Ali slide a pistol to him across the metal roof then disappeared below again. Donnie moved between the boat and the pistol, using his body to block the view of anyone on the Eritrean navy ship from seeing him pocket the pistol. He rolled over the side of the bridge to the opposite side. Ali was loading another pistol. "They're boarding us."

"And then?"

Ali shot him a look – complete uncertainty.

The boat shook as the other boat connected with it. Ali turned the corner, hands raised, calling out to the Eritrean officers. The other fishermen called out something. Donnie saw one being forced to his knees, hands behind his head. There was shouting that Donnie could make out. All his training told him to turn, to cover himself with the metal railing and to fire at the officers boarding the fishing boat. But he caught himself.

He fought the urge to wait on this corner and ready his elbow for an Eritrean face, to break the nose to stun, then grab the automatic weapon slung over the shoulder. Instead Donnie threw the pistol into the water and turned, hands raised, and let himself be caught.

A shot was fired and he saw Ali go down. Blood mixed with the water on the deck quickly. Before he could orientate himself, before he figured out what was happening, the butt of a rifle hit his head. The blow forced him to his knees, and a hand on the back of his neck held him down on the cold water, seeing Ali's blood float across the deck. Donnie's hands were cuffed hard behind him and he was pulled up, then pushed over the side of the boat to the small raft below. The other fishermen sat there, handcuffed, silent and shocked. Donnie looked around, trying to see what he could. A soldier stood over Ali's body as the small raft pushed off the fishing vessel, leaving it floating in the middle of the Red Sea. Donnie strained to see what happened to Ali as hands grabbed him and forced him up to the deck of the navy ship. Another blow to the head threw him around again. And then there was darkness.

Donnie was kept in a dark and wet room in the bowels of the navy ship. He felt the sides of the ship shake as the engines turned and the vessel steered back to an Eritrean port. The smell of salt and metal mixed with oil in the air. It was cold, and Donnie figured it was beneath the water line. It was the coldest he'd been since the morning he woke in Mississippi. The blows to the head had disorientated him and with the bag pulled over his head he'd lost most sense of direction, but he was sure he'd been pushed down stairs. He heard some other movement.

"Ali?"

A hand hit the metal wall above Donnie's head and a gruff voice barked some order in Arabic. Donnie couldn't understand it exactly but the message to stay quiet was clear. A fist smashed into his stomach for extra effect.

Donnie doubled over, breathing in the harsh oily, salty fumes until he felt the ship dock. Minutes later a hand pulled him up by the collar and threw him back through the door then up the stairs. He walked where he was led, through some sunlight then back into some dank musty area. The bag was pulled off his head and he gasped at the stale air, free of the fumes of petrol and salt. When his eyes adjusted to the light he saw that he was in a small cell with the three fishermen and two other prisoners.

No one said anything. Two guards stood outside the bolted bars of the cell and kept half an eye on the six prisoners. Donnie looked around. There was sunlight through the bottom of the far door, but not the window. The cell was too far inside to make a break for it despite the unattended firearm sitting on the desk.

Getting through the gate would be the first step. Donnie looked back to the cell. The fishermen were all looking down at the floor. Two of them had blood on their shirt or cheek.

The other, the youngest, had no signs of violence but looked shaken into silence. He had been athletically running around the boat and making sure the fishing nets were pulled up properly, but now he sat like a shell of a person. The other two prisoners, who looked like they'd been locked in there for some time, were either asleep or trying to be.

The sound of a key in the aged padlock woke Donnie. He was groggy, his head ached and he was suddenly aware of a sharp pain in his right shoulder when he was pulled to his feet by the guards and pushed down the corridor on the right. The youngest of the three fishermen was led to the left. Donnie tried to look around, to see where the fisherman was being led, but another blow to the ribs with the butt of a rifle brought his attention back to the hall and the room he was thrown into.

Donnie was pulled up and put in the chair. The handcuffs were tight around his wrists. He tried to lean back against the chair but it offered no support. He had no idea how long he'd been in there when he heard the lock turn on the metal door. It closed with a thud and from the shadows stepped his interrogator. Scar. The trashy tourist attire was gone and replaced with some high-ranking military uniform. Donnie suppressed any sign of recognition. He pretended he didn't recognize the heavy eyebrows and the harsh gaze that spilled from beneath them.

"You thought you could get away?" Scar was teasing him now, trying to bait him gently.

"I've never seen you before."

Scar's fist slammed into the table, echoing around the room. Donnie couldn't even see the walls clearly but he had the impression it was small. Cold and small. Scar pulled out a file and spread out the photos of Donnie meeting Ali, climbing on the fishing boat, and looking around with the binoculars.

"What were you doing on that fishing boat?" Scar's voice wasn't rushed or hard, almost calming, but still full of sinister intent.

"I thought it would be a good way to see the Red Sea."

Scar chewed his lip. "On a fishing boat with strangers? That doesn't sound like a safe type of tourism."

Donnie didn't say anything. There was nothing Scar could prove and Donnie knew it. Scar knew it too. There were too many missing connections. The only way to get past this stalemate was for Scar to force something from Donnie to connect the dots. The muffled screams came from down the hall. Scar looked at Donnie, as the scream of the younger fisherman echoed through the concrete corridors.

"I know you weren't out there for the fishing." Scar motioned towards a thick folder left unopened on the table. "What were you doing?"

Donnie knew it was a fake, a folder just there for show and intimidation. "Enjoying the sea. I'd never seen the Red Sea before."

"That's not true. And I know it. And you know it." Scar walked around the table. "This will be easier on you, and on him–" another cry, a whimper, echoed down the hall "–if you tell me now."

Donnie sat in silence. He had been detained illegally and any other abuse would make the case worse for Eritrea. He wasn't able to point this out; he couldn't argue his case for legal protection without conceding some point that would let Scar know he wasn't simply an unfortunate tourist.

Scar walked to the door and pulled it open. An Eritrean soldier in infantry uniform entered the room and stood by the door.

"It seems you need some time to think things over. You're in a very vulnerable position, mister Mervyn. I suggest you take some time to think about that."

The handcuffs were not as strong as Scar had hoped. They were old standard issue and with the sweat now dripping down his forearms and wrists, they were easy to maneuver. It would be easy for Donnie to manipulate the lock. He'd done it before. But breaking out, overpowering the guard – it just wasn't an option. Donnie would escape; he'd be able to get out of the concrete tomb of a prison but not without betraying his position and bringing more attention to any other operation that was about to take place. Again, Donnie repressed the urge to fight out of there.

Scar walked out of the room and clicked the lock on the door back in place. He walked down the hall as he heard the first blow knock Donnie to the floor.

When Scar returned Donnie was sitting on the chair. The blood above his eye had started to harden. The air was thick and heavy. Donnie's shirt was heavy with sweat and had more than a few drops of bloodstains.

"Did you fall?" Scar sat down opposite him. "That's unfortunate. You should be more careful."

Donnie looked up at Scar. The interrogator's shirt was clean and crisp, completely unlike anyone else in this sweltering hellhole. "This can't be legal, what you're doing to me. I'm just a tourist out for a sail."

"That's not what your fishermen friends say."

It was a ruse. Donnie knew it simply because only Ali was an agent on that boat and he'd been shot. There was no way for the fishermen to know anything. "They probably say anything you beat into them."

"You don't have much faith in your friends."

"I don't know them. I only met them on the boat today."

"When you went for a sail? To see the Red Sea?"

Donnie swallowed hard. The dehydration was setting in.

"I'll admit you had a good cover," Scar said. "But you're not as smart as you like to think you are, mister Mervyn."

Donnie just looked back. He tried to match the stare but the dehydration and fatigue were taking their toll. His right eye had started to swell. A door slammed in the hall, echoing through the whole building.

Scar chewed his lip then stood up. "You've had enough time." He motioned to the guard in the corner who picked Donnie up and pulled him to his feet. Donnie was led down the hall then thrown in a small concrete room. There was no furniture and no light. The door clicked shut with a metallic thud. The air was still musty and stale but it was cooler. Donnie gasped, leaning against the cooler concrete walls. The floor was wet. The only light came from a slim glimmer beneath the door where Donnie saw the guard's feet standing still.

Donnie moved into the corner and leaned against the wall. There was nothing he could do but rest. He put his head against the wall. The concrete was hard and brutal. This place wasn't built for comfort. He closed his eyes but he couldn't sleep. Every few minutes a thud would rock the door and startle him into being awake. Sleep deprivation. He should have expected it. He tried to fight it, controlling his breath, calming his mind and fighting the delusions that came with being woken every fifteen minutes. It was going to be a long night, but it would end. There would be an end. He just had to keep reminding himself of that and stay calm. It would pass.

*

Lieutenant Miggs was a strikingly handsome man with his blonde hair cut short. His tall frame stood just in the light near the end of the runway. He stood at an angle with his hand on his hip and turned half way to the plane. He turned to face Hudson Jones as Hudson parked the golf cart at the end of the runway.

"Lieutenant Miggs."

"Jones." Miggs motioned towards the aircraft. "I'll brief you on the developments on board."

It was a a C-130, with just the crew and some other cargo. Miggs took a seat near the front of the cargo area and nodded to the crew for take off. Hudson clipped his belt in and waited for Miggs to get to the details. He didn't have to wait long; Miggs started into the developments before they'd even reached the end of the runway.

"Sergeant Mervyn was captured at approximately fourteen hundred this afternoon. The small fishing boat he was onboard was approached by the Eritrean naval ship Keren. He was taken into port by force."

"How much of the details on this mission are you aware of, Lieutenant?"

"Just those that I've told you, Captain."

Hudson nodded. There wasn't much difference from the original plan. The use of force was unanticipated, and if he could prove it then it might work to Hudson's advantage in the courtroom. He wondered for a moment if this briefing was part of the façade, but to do it on a secure US aircraft was strange. The mention of Mervyn's rank was also strange for someone not involved with the mission since he had been under cover. And then there was the wait, that ninety-four minute delay. Something wasn't right, but Hudson couldn't tell what it was just yet.

Miggs rifled through his folder and pulled out a piece of paper. "This communication came through half an hour ago."

And it was that communication that made the difference. Sixty-five minutes earlier the Eritrean office had contacted the US ambassador and the foreign office. They had denied all knowledge and reiterated the claim of the US tourist, as per orders from Fitzpatrick. Al-Jazeera had picked up the thread of the story already. Other news organizations weren't going to be far behind.

Hudson took a breath and rested his head in his hands. The plan hinged on Mervyn being taken in as a civilian. Being able to argue that the Eritrean navy, and by extension the government, had over reached its jurisdiction and taken a US civilian into custody was key to the whole operation. If there was any hint of it being a military operation on the part of the US then it would be a lot harder for Hudson in the court room. International pressure would also be in favor of the Eritreans.

"Is this all that has come through?"

"So far. Though I'm sure the ambassador has more information when we land."

Hudson chewed his lip.

"Prepare for a tactical landing," the captain said.

Hudson tightened the seat buckles around his chest while Miggs did the same. Then it came. The descent. It was quick, spiraling and dropping ten thousand feet in the quickest amount of time possible. Hudson hadn't had time to process what Mervyn's capture meant and now he was caught in a g-force that sent his blood rushing to his head and his ears popping. Hudson was out of practice with tactical landings. It takes a certain amount of energy out of you, some level of concentration to get through it. A descent at that speed, the demand it has on the body, can leave you ruined if you're unprepared. Hudson gripped the arms of the empty chairs beside him, holding on tight and with his knuckles turning white.

The Hercules flattened out then hit the tarmac. The land came in under the wheels smoothly. The aircraft came to a stop on the runway and with the engines still whirring and the blood still pumping around his brain, Hudson was led off the aircraft to the waiting ambassador's empty car. He reread the communication from Fitzpatrick's office on the way then filed it in his briefcase and chewed his lip as they drove through the Eritrean capital. Hudson thought the first part of the mission was merely a formality. Now it was turning into something else. This was not going to be as easy as any of them had anticipated.

Inside the US consulate the atmosphere was tense. Hudson left the vehicle and walked through the gates. He could feel the tension outside, hanging on the dry heat of the Eritrean night. He saluted the guards on duty and was led through to the ambassador's office.

The ambassador was pacing. His suit was disheveled with his tie askew, and his hair was brushed back clumsily. His face was red. Ben Archer had served as ambassador for almost six years. The pride of Archer's term as ambassador in Eritrea was the complete level of diplomacy. He'd been brought in to mediate other tensions with Eritrea and Ethiopia and liked to think that he was the reason their tensions hadn't blown into an armed conflict on at least three occasions.

His time at the embassy at Yerevan had been marked with strong diplomacy and no major conflicts between Armenia and either of its neighbors. Tensions were high, and that was to be expected, but the four years when he was there were noted for their peace and lack of armed conflict. It was that record he wanted to maintain in Asmara. It was not entirely about international politics for him at this point but also personal pride.

Lucas Dabwee sat in the leather lounge, his left leg crossed over his right and his foot tapping slightly. His jaw was clenched and he looked unamused as he listened to the ambassador's rant. As far as Hudson could tell, Dabwee had been listening to the same speech for most of the evening.

"Hudson Jones, JAG," he said, shaking hands with Archer and Dabwee.

"I cannot believe this," Archer said. "You have no idea what trouble this is for me. And what good do you think JAG can do now?"

Hudson took a seat opposite Dabwee and pulled the communications out of his brief case. "This is all I've heard so far. Can you tell me what else has happened in the last two hours?"

"What hasn't happened?" the ambassador mumbled. "You have no idea what work you've undone."

"You're assuming he is a spy? Just because of what the administration here is claiming"

"Ambassador, if you don't mind," Dabwee said. "I'll just get Captain Jones up to date."

The ambassador sat down, still raging, and drank from the water on the desk.

"Early this afternoon," Dabwee began, "at around sixteen hundred, Yemen announced that one of its fishing boats, a private vessel, had been captured by the Eritrean navy."

Hudson nodded.

"This happens more than you'd expect because of disputed water territories and an over anxious Eritrean navy. Usually they either escort the ship back to Yemeni waters or to an Eritrean port to fine them, intimidate them, then turn them around. That sort of thing. This one was different. Instead of just Yemeni fishermen they discovered a US national, a tourist named Donald Mervyn. The Eritrean government has not released any of the fishermen, the ship, or Mervyn."

"But this isn't so straight forward as asking for the return of a civilian?"

"Unfortunately it isn't. Or else you'd have an easy job," Dabwee said. "At eighteen hundred the Eritrean president issued a statement claiming Mervyn was a spy working with Israel and the US on an operation based in the Dahlek archipelago."

"Based on?"

"Wild speculation, it seems. And a case of wanting international attention."

"Attention?"

Dabwee nodded. "Within the hour, Iran, Egypt and Libya had issued statements calling for UN investigation into the espionage claims, and a monitor on US involvement in the region."

"It's a play for power."

"Exactly. In the larger scheme of things, if Eritrea can make enough noise and get the backing of these larger Arab states then it puts them in a better situation with any possible conflict with Ethiopia."

"And there's always a conflict with Ethiopia," Archer said. "Now you know why this is bigger than just your court case to get a US national out of an African prison," Archer said.

"But they can't prove he was a spy," Hudson said. "So we just make the case he's not and have him returned. With that proven false, they'll return to their shell."

"It's not so straight forward," Archer said. His face had turned a deeper shade of red. Dabwee shook his head. "For the immediate case it is. But now that the allegations have been made, that the issue has been raised, it brings a whole lot more into question. Any US presence, even the current presence in the country, will be called into question."

"It could be used as a pretense to send the US packing."

"Ambassador," Hudson said. "You seem upset."

"Well, I'm certainly not happy about the situation."

"An American citizen has been unlawfully detained, with no evidence," Hudson explained. "It's our duty to see justice through and have him freed."

"That's not the problem," Archer said. "That part's fine. But you don't have to deal with the diplomatic fall out of a situation like this."

*

Hudson woke early and did some light exercise while the coffee brewed. Jet lag and little sleep wasn't a great cocktail to wake with but there wasn't anything else Hudson could do. He had to be as alert as possible before court. Three sets of fifty push-ups, then he showered and shaved and ate a small breakfast of eggs and toast with the pot of coffee while he read through the newspapers the embassy had provided.

He perused through the pages, scanning for anything that mentioned Eritrea, the UN, or US international policy. The New York Times and

Washington Post ran stories of a conflict between the two administrations over the capture of a Yemeni fishing boat with an American tourist on board. The Guardian reported the Eritrean claim that the captured American was working as a spy. He checked Al-Jazeera and saw that they were reporting similarly; raising more questions than they were answering.

There was no way that the Eritreans could prove their case and they had to know it. But the lack of an overwhelming international outrage wasn't going to play in Hudson's favor. After pulling on his uniform, he walked downstairs and met the ambassador. Archer's face was calmer than the night before, but he looked tired. The impeccable suit and a tie in a trinity knot didn't cover the fact he'd been up most of the night talking with Washington and any Eritrean representative who called. There were bags under his eyes and the same pile of newspapers next to him as the one Hudson had left in the room.

"Good morning, ambassador," Hudson said, pulling a seat up to the table. He was tired too. He'd spent the night going over other ways to pull up the Eritrean and UN counsel without giving much of his own hand away.

"Morning, Captain."

Hudson refilled the ambassador's coffee cup and poured a cup for himself. "Any developments?"

"Nothing positive."

"Anything disastrous?"

"No, I guess not."

Hudson nodded, stirring the cream into the coffee. "Then it will be fine."

"I'm sorry if I don't share your optimism."

"There's nothing they can prove here. He was on a fishing boat and from what I understand he was in Yemen for a few days before."

Archer folded The Guardian back in half and placed it on the table, conceding that Hudson had a point.

"What are you afraid of here?"

Although Archer would never admit it, his experience at keeping the peace had left him anxious of any conflict. Any claim of spy or espionage was out of his depth. But he would never let anyone know that. He was determined to get through this crisis too, and keep his legacy as a peace broker. He just hoped that it didn't blow up into a full blown crisis.

"I don't know what your role is in this," Archer said. "I don't believe you were in Israel for the reasons I was told, and just happened to finish your investigation yesterday. And what I'm afraid of, as you put it, is that you and your superiors are keeping me in the dark, leaving me unable to do my job."

Hudson sipped his coffee gently. "I see what you mean."

"So will you enlighten me?"

"After court this morning," Hudson assured him. "You will be briefed, don't doubt that. But at the moment it's better to see how things play out in court."

Archer glared at Hudson for a moment.

"Sugar?" Hudson offered the bowl of raw sugar cubes but the ambassador shook his head.

"This morning's hearing will be overseen by a UN mediator," Archer said as he slid a small folder of email transcripts in front of Hudson. "It's strictly a hearing to see whether it is a trial that will be sanctioned by the UN or if it is an Eritrean domestic issue."

Hudson nodded. "Do you know who the Eritrean counsel will be? Or anything about the mediator?"

"It's possibly going to be overseen by a Japanese official, Kaori Okayama, but that hasn't been entirely confirmed yet. A Norwegian official and Brazilian official were also seen on the same flight out of New York." Archer leaned closer. "The Eritrean state will not roll over on this, I hope you understand that."

Hudson looked up. "I'd figured they would hardly be a push over in their own court."

"President Mustafa issued a statement earlier this morning and, from what I've heard from the palace, he's taken a particular interest in this."

"Is that strange?"

"It's not unusual," Archer conceded. "It is an international affair. But the office that issued the statement is run by a particularly cunning and manipulative man. You shouldn't overlook that. Saeed Araya's ambition is no secret and if he wasn't so close to Mustafa, Mustafa would not have lasted this long in office."

"What does that ambition have to do with this?"

"If he's involved, then he sees an advantage that he wants to exploit. I'm not sure what it is yet, but he wouldn't be involved simply for the exercise of it."

Hudson read through the email transcripts between the embassy and Washington while he finished his coffee. He didn't have any particular plan other than to ensure Mervyn was released to the embassy and not kept imprisoned. Any other legal or political fall out from that, he would have to deal with as it arose. Once the hearing was over he would have a better idea of where he stood, what the Eritreans were arguing and how far they were from being able to pin any case on Mervyn.

After that he would be able to work with Mervyn on the second part of the mission. Without Mervyn's release, it was pointless. For the other matters, it was best to keep an open mind.

An hour later Hudson and the ambassador were sitting in the dignitary's car waiting to leave the embassy. A media circus had formed around the court and the embassy was waiting to learn from the Eritrean police as to when the hearing would take place.

"This is Araya's doing," Archer said. "He would ensure the media was there."

Hudson rubbed his chin and tried to keep the mood light. There had to be something to counterbalance Archer's strained and weary face.

"Are there any good traditional restaurants here in the city?" Hudson asked. "I ate some traditional Eritrean food once and it was quite good."

Archer looked at Hudson incredulously. He couldn't comprehend how the head legal on this issue could be talking about cuisine at this point. Hudson turned his attention back to the street outside without an answer. Twenty minutes behind schedule, the motorcade of US official vehicles took off from the gates and wove through the streets to the courthouse.

The media pool was thick and, as Archer had feared, there was a line of protesters wrapped around the block across the street. Protestors drew attention and that's what Archer had been hoping to avoid at least at the preliminary hearing.

Donald Mervyn was sitting at a table in a bare room to the rear of the courthouse. The cut above his right eyebrow had been stitched up quickly and he'd been allowed to shower and shave. He'd been beaten, and some of the bruises were visible. The treatment he'd been through wasn't entirely apparent as he sat in a basic suit handed to him by Scar that morning.

"Mr Mervyn," Hudson said as he walked through the doors into the small room. "I'm Captain Jones. This is Ambassador Archer." Mervyn shook hands with the two men and sat across the table from them.

Hudson began. "We have just a few moments to brief you on what is going on. Though usually this seems to be a case of simple bureaucracy, they are currently making a bigger case out of it." Hudson waited for Mervyn to understand what he said. He spoke to Mervyn in the most civilian way possible.

"They're trying to make a case to argue that you're a spy, for whatever reason. Today is just a brief hearing. The case will take place at a later date but right now we'll secure your release, move you to the embassy and then we will start process to have the charges dropped and have you sent home."

Mervyn nodded. "Today is just a formality?"

"Essentially," Archer said. "Because of the Eritrean claims, the UN has been called in and is overseeing the proceedings."

"It will be brief," Hudson said. "You won't be required to say anything or make any statement. Do you have any questions?"

"A lot," Mervyn forced a laugh. "But they can probably all wait until we get to the embassy."

"Shouldn't be too long at all, son," Archer said. The doors at the back of the room opened and two guards came through to escort Mervyn to the defendant's table. Hudson and Archer were directed through the door at the other end of the room, the same ones they'd entered through.

"See you in a moment," Hudson said. He picked up his briefcase and followed Archer.

"Captain?" Hudson turned to see a senior official calling him. The official motioned to the room.

"Go ahead," Hudson told Archer. "I'll be there in a minute." Archer hesitated and then went ahead as Hudson turned back to the room. "Yes?"

The official hesitated. For Hudson it all happened in slow motion. The door clicked behind him and then he saw the armed guard standing behind him to the left. The first blow of the rifle butt hit Hudson in between the shoulder blades. The second one pinned him to the desk.

"Captain, you are being held in suspicion of espionage."

"Are the UN officials aware that you're doing this?" A blow to his ribs winded Hudson and took any more questions out of his mouth. Two guards escorted him through the same door Mervyn had been led through, then through a small door at the back and into a police car. Mervyn was sitting handcuffed in the back and looked up as Hudson was pushed in with him.

"I thought you said it was a formality."

"Legally it would be." Another rifle hit him in the stomach and Hudson coughed hard as the door was slammed behind him. He was still catching his breath when the car took off down the street and drove away from the courthouse.

Archer was sitting on the defendant bench and looking back to the door nervously. The media was taking its place behind the two parties. The judge's seat was still empty. The loud rumble of the media talking and shouting over each other hushed quickly when the Eritrean counsel walked to the front of the courtroom. He reached for the microphone in the witness box and pulled it down towards him.

"The hearing has been delayed due to the arrest of another spy suspect. There will be no further statement at this time."

Archer was shocked. He looked around at the empty seats next to him. The roar of the media started again, louder and more intense. Questions were called out but the counsel ignored them as he exited the courthouse. Archer grabbed the arm of the Eritrean counsel.

"I want answers," Archer said.

"Our office will be in touch. I have nothing else to say at this point."

Archer looked around and took a breath. This was an outrage. That such a stunt would be pulled while the UN officials were in the same building was inconceivable. Archer collected himself and made his way back to the embassy, more confused than he'd been that morning. He walked directly to his office and told his secretary to get Washington on the phone and the Eritrean foreign office immediately. He closed the door to his office and took two valium as he looked out the window.

7

Hudson had no idea how long he'd been in the cell when the door finally opened. A guard pulled him to his feet and led him down the hall. There had been no sunlight and no regular food. Some water and bread had been slid into the room at different times but they didn't seem regular. Hudson had slipped in and out of sleep, light and disorientating, and that hadn't helped him keep track of time either.

Hudson was led down the halls and taken through another door. When he thought he'd be put in another room for even more questions, the door opened to the outside. It was night and the air, though it was still undeniably hot, was a relief. The skies were dark with little moonlight, but Hudson still had no way of knowing what hour it was. Before he could look around or get accustomed to the fresh air, he was thrown into a military truck with over a dozen other handcuffed prisoners. They were squashed in there uncomfortably.

It would have been surprising if they'd had enough room.

It was remarkable, Hudson had realized in his cell, how he'd adjusted quickly to these conditions. A breath of fresh air and some adequate drinking water was all he needed to be satisfied for the time being. It wasn't that he wanted these conditions to continue but since the conditions were what he had to put up with for now, half a cup of fresh water was almost a luxury. Two more men were tossed into the back of the truck behind Hudson then the armed guards closed the doors. A metallic sound of the lock sliding into place and clicking shut. The sweaty bodies pressed together beneath the truck's canopy pushing together and falling around as the truck accelerated out of the pen and rolled down the road into the night.

There was no light in the truck. There was no way to know how many men were in the back, or where they were. Hudson could feel other bodies pressing up against him. Their silence was unnatural. There were possibly dozens of handcuffed men in this small truck, all pushing against each other as the truck rocked its way down the highway, rolling towards wherever they were going, and not a single one of them spoke. They were probably all as disorientated as himself, Hudson thought. Woken from disrupted sleep and pulled out into the air then pushed into this truck.

"Mervyn?" Hudson asked the darkness. His throat was dry and it was difficult to raise his voice above the truck engine. "Mervyn?" he called out again into the silent black din of the truck. But there was no reply. The truck continued its rumbling journey away from the prison, shaking violently at the one time it had to idle at an intersection, and slamming the bodies of its prisoners together as it bounced along the unforgiving Eritrean roads.

There were small flood lights around the prison and it blinded the prisoners as they were pulled out of the truck. The soldiers were yelling in a language Hudson couldn't understand. The tone was enough – he just kept in line with the others. They were pushed into the door with their heads down. Anyone who looked up was hit in the back of the head, or the ribcage with a rifle butt.

Hudson was pulled aside by one guard and taken through a different door. Hudson looked up to see where the other men were being taken but a rifle butt reminded him to keep his head down. The air in the concrete prison was stale. A metal lock slid open and the guard yelled something at Hudson. He didn't know what it was. He looked up for a moment then the guard threw him into the small cell. The metal lock slid closed followed by the click of it locking, and the guard's footsteps going back down the concrete floor. The sounds of yelling guards could still be heard in the cell.

Hudson looked around. There was one other body in the cell. It was in the corner. By the faint light Hudson could make out a long tangled beard as he rolled over. Hudson leaned against the wall for a while, then lay down on his side against the cold concrete floor. His head hung down to the side. The concrete floor was uncomfortable but at least it was flat. Hudson rolled onto his back, feeling the side of his ribs where the rifle butt had landed. He spread out and tried to relax, shutting his eyes and wondering if he could ever sleep on this concrete floor.

It was early but already light when Hudson was awoken by the guards bringing food in to the prisoners. He squinted hard against the pale glow and looked around. There had been a full moon but he hadn't seen much from the truck to the cell. Even now he couldn't see much. From where he sat he could see crowded cells running down the length.

Small plates of food were pushed through to the waking inmates. The cell Hudson was in was much smaller. A plate of dry bread sat in the middle of the cell. In the opposite corner was an older man, a beard hanging down from his tired face, slowly putting the food in his mouth and chewing. It was more out of habit, a need to go through the plate, than the desire to eat. Hudson swallowed hard and took a sip from the small tin cup on the floor. It was warm. He didn't care. Hudson looked across at the other crowded cells. The wire cells ran as far as Hudson could see, bigger than his own but much more crowded. "Why are there only two of us in here?"

The older man looked up slowly. "We're special cases."

"Special cases?"

"The President wants to take care of us, for some reason. Despite being locked up in here for decades," the man said, "news of my death would be bad news for the President. It would cause him problems. As for you, I'm guessing it's because you're international. He doesn't want that kind of difficulty with your government. You don't even want to know what's beneath the ground."

"There's more beneath us?"

The old man nodded. "Shipping containers of prisoners beneath the ground."

Hudson wasn't expecting that answer. He'd read reports of the treatment of Eritrean people but hadn't been prepared for that sort of disregard for human life.

"Entire shipping containers?"

"Like sardines.

"How deep?"

The old man shrugged, sadly. "Hard to say."

Hudson looked around, taking it in and trying to fathom that he was a lucky one, encaged with access to sunlight and fresh air.

"Hamid Abraha."

"Hudson Jones." Hudson nodded. "So why does the president need to take care of you?"

"There are some factions in the government, within his own party, the People's Front for Democracy and Justice, that are dormant and agreeable. Being in here has as good as gotten rid of my influence, but they may not be dormant if they found out he'd had me executed."

Hudson took this in and started slowly eating the bread.

"I was a leader in the party at the start of the war of independence. I was with Awate when he fired the first shots. After Awate died the next year, there were few strong enough to maintain a strong ideological grip and a commanding focal point over the liberation front. Some strayed from the cause. Others didn't. We made do among a few of us, but it came to a head in the seventies and Mustafa began to work his way through the party, manipulating his way through the shattered ranks to seize power."

Hamid paused to sip from the rusted metal cup next to the worn and ripped mattress. "As he and his faction of the party gained more control, the ideology shifted. Mustafa's power was unquestionable. Once independence came to the country, he turned his focus towards us to get rid of any possible challenge for power."

"How long have you been in here?"

"On and off since the end of the war of independence. Permanently since '96."

"Are these men all political prisoners?"

"Primarily. Some are from protesting the regime, or being too involved with the other factions during the war of independence. Most are here after refusing to do their military service." Abraha didn't look up. "Mustafa conscripts the young men of the nation into his military with no end date. It's not easy to get out or be released from service. Since they're conscripted they aren't paid a living wage. If you're caught deserting your post you're either shot or, if you're lucky, you find yourself in a shipping container beneath the desert. So, many of the young men just refuse to serve, and end up in here or one of the other underground prisons. And that's not a fate that's much better."

Hudson had read about these places. But reading about them and the intelligence reports about secure prisons for the enemies of the states and being inside one are entirely different situations. For most people, getting out is not a formality. It is not a matter of letting justice run its course or to wait for your day in court. These are elements of freedom that Hudson had become accustomed to. It was his way of life. It was often he who made sure that day in court was just, balanced and fair. That was in the United States, a democracy whose integrity was unquestioned. A nation whose very existence was built on democracy and freedom, so much so that they exported it. Now Hudson sat in a prison in a country with one of the worst human rights records of the last half of the century and the worst ranking of freedom of press.

Hudson knew the international laws. He knew the finer points of the Geneva Conventions, the military protocols and the laws of war, and the other international agreements that were signed in Stockholm, Washington and London. He also knew that Eritrea was a blacked out region when it came to those agreements and that if he was in the prison for too long, the UN pressure might just wane and slip, and his time in an Eritrean prison would become much more permanent than he'd have liked.

Still, he had faith in the system. His faith in the United Nations and the international laws he had defended for his entire professional life held strong. He had faith in Archer and the other dignitaries and, if it came down to it, Greene and Fitzpatrick. For now, he had to be patient.

It was sometime in the afternoon, Hudson guessed, when he slid across the cell to where Abraha was sitting. "Tell me about the war."

Abraha leaned back and peered out the small gap in the cell door. The sounds of the prison were dull and distant. There were no guards around but Abraha spoke quietly anyway.

"We'd been trying to convince Awate to declare an armed element of the resistance. The political aspect was well represented but it just wasn't making any ground. There had to be a military aspect to Eritrea to fight for independence. Awate had led units against the other occupying forces before but he didn't feel ready for a full engagement with the Ethiopians. You have to understand," Abraha leaned towards Hudson and lowering his voice even further, "he was the only one who could unite all these scattered forces into a force that was capable of taking on the Ethiopian army."

Abraha sipped again from the small metal cup. It was clear that he was used to rationing his water. "He waited. He felt the time wasn't right. Then in August in sixty one he felt he had the support he needed, and that everything came together. He issued a decree to the Ethiopian leaders that declared the beginning of an armed resistance. They tried to change his mind, to urge him to reconsider and he just said that if they want to avoid the armed conflict then they have to lower the Ethiopian flag and raise the Eritrean."

Abraha smiled. "They sent a unit to capture him in the village where he was living. We were waiting for them. He knew the first strike would have to be a defiant and definitive victory. It had to be with full force and then it would inspire others to join us. We'd doubled in size by then, over a dozen soldiers, but we still didn't have the arms by then. They were still on their way from our political allies. So Awate snuck out of his house. He'd been expecting the military to come after him, trying to cut off the head before the snake had truly awoken.

He was too smart for that. When the military trucks came to his house, he was in my attic. His family was across the country near the southern coast. The Ethiopians couldn't find him so they burned down his house and terrorized his neighbors. He watched it with the rage growing. Three of us crossed the street to his house and pretended he'd run off through the darkness towards the riverbanks. The troops took chase and we started to put out the fire on his house and make sure it didn't spread to the neighboring houses. When I came back to my house he was sitting in the kitchen in the dark, watching the scene outside. He was defiant, a man determined to set things right." Abraha paused, then added wistfully, "That was the last place I could call a home for almost three decades."

"That was before the first shots had been fired?"

Abraha nodded but didn't speak. The sound of a guard shuffling past the door caught his attention. He leaned in closer to Hudson. "About a week later eleven of us rode into the west with the sun on our backs. We split and went different ways. The first strike was to take out some police posts. It was strategic. It was a symbolic attack against the ever-present authority we had to deal with and it would get the attention of our

countrymen and the Ethiopian leaders. They were sure
Awate would carry through with his promise of
violence but they weren't sure how or in what way.

"I followed Awate up Mount Adal. We waited,
then fired on the post on the northern side. We didn't
think it would be a quick attack. We were prepared for
a long battle but there were other issues. The three of us
waited until the agreed time then we fired on the post.
The police fired back immediately. The plan was for the
other divisions of the revolutionaries to take control of
the smaller posts and then join us on Mount Adal to
take out the larger post. But they took longer than we'd
anticipated. The police had back up closer than we'd
been led to believe.

I was really just a kid and more confident of
myself than I ought to have been. There's nothing like a
full gunfight to bring that out. Firing one or two shots
and disappearing is one thing but this was completely
different than anything I'd experienced before. It was
loud, dusty and intense. Oh, definitely intense. Awate
kept talking to me and saying things like keep my
position, to keep still when all I wanted to do was run,
and to keep my aim steady as I fired into the police
posts.

"Eventually the other men joined us. We had
three positions around the post and it confused the
police for a while. It lasted seven hours. It wasn't a
stand off. It was a full engagement. We hadn't prepared

for a seven-hour battle. Dohen made a dash for the store shed to the back. While we drew the fire to the right, he fought his way around the flank with a pistol and carried out cases of rounds for us. I have no idea how he survived. It was a miracle."

Hudson nodded, taking in the story. A seven-hour battle baffled his mind. He hadn't faced that kind of engagement and had no idea how he would react under that intense fire. He didn't even want to think about it.

"It wasn't the victory we'd been aiming for," Abraha said, "but it wasn't a defeat either. We took no casualties and we made a few blows to their numbers. We certainly made our cause known and made an impression on the Ethiopian leaders. Our numbers grew quickly over the next month and our next strikes were definite victories. We claimed a small town on the southern border and held that for a few months. Momentum changed a year later."

Abraha grew thoughtful. "There was a battle in May when we'd stretched out towards Haykota. We were ambushed. I was shot in the leg. Awate was injured in the shoulder, but not badly. A few others were injured far worse. His shoulder injury was bloody but really wasn't much more than a scrape. The bullet wasn't even lodged in him. There was something else at work and Awate died that night. That's when momentum changed for a few years. We were on the run and trying to get a firm footing anywhere, trying to stay in one place long enough just to steady ourselves. That was a difficult time."

There was a rush of voices outside and a banging on the wall. The clang of the metal door on the concrete wall echoed down the hall and reverberated through the cell. It came again and louder. The voices were yelling, then a gunshot and the voices fell silent. The sound of the metal door still reverberated through the prison. After a minute Hudson spoke up, his mouth was dry and felt like cotton. "What about Mustafa? When did he join you?"

"The first time I met Mahmoud Mustafa was about ten years after Awate died. He was an idealistic young man full of more energy than he knew what to do with. He'd spent some time travelling through the east but I never knew where. Much of his time had been spent studying philosophy and war. He was incredibly well read. He could talk for hours about Marx or Sun Tzu or Napoleon, and sometimes he did.

He joined us in Asmara when we were about to return to the southern villages. It wasn't always safe to be in the cities but it helped. Small groups of us would go back when we could. We'd talk about what we were doing, and the volunteers would help us gather supplies. Students always liked hearing what we were doing and often a few would return to the villages with us and take up arms with us. Mustafa wasn't a student. He had been but when we met him, he'd just returned from some sort of trek that had opened his eyes to a lot of things. He just wanted to talk about our philosophies and tactics. He wanted to hear about the battles too – a lot of students did – but he was even more eager to just talk about the tenants of Marxism and how they could apply to an independent Eritrean nation.

We spent about two weeks in Asmara that time and were enjoying ourselves, as much as living in hiding can be enjoyed, until we heard the news from Basik Dera in the north." Abraha closed his eyes for a moment and screwed his face up. His voice was shaking when he started speaking again, still with his eyes closed. "They'd put the whole village in a mosque then set it on fire." Abraha shook his head. "Can you imagine that? The Ethiopians were trying to gain an upper hand over us by setting fire to our countrymen, then shooting any of the villagers who made it out alive. Their lack of humanity was meant to inspire it in us, or something like that. As if proving they were more sinister and heartless could actually lead to some sort of peace offering.

It did the opposite, of course. More students joined, about fifty in one night, and we made plans to leave the next morning in small groups and make our way back to the other units. They were spread out over the countryside but we had certain meeting points. We were meant to meet them outside Asmara on the way to Tukul."

The sound of footsteps up the concrete floor startled Hudson and Abraha. They both realized there'd been almost no sound outside since the gunshot. They'd lost track of things and hoped their talking hadn't drawn any unwanted attention.

They exchanged a glance as the lock slid open. Two fresh cups of water in the same beaten and stained tin cups were slid into the room then the metal lock slid closed and the footsteps receded. Hudson drank thirstily but knew he had to ration this cup. He suppressed the urge to knock it back and sipped at it carefully, making sure not to spill any and checking for any leakages, then put it on the other side of the small room, just far enough out of his reach that he would be reminded to ration it.

"Did you have any idea of what he would become?"

Abraha took a breath and let it out slowly. "Maybe later, after he'd served with us for years and became part of the leadership group. But before that? Not a clue. Our focus was always on the enemy or staying alive every day. You think differently when that's the focus. And war changes people. Have you experienced that?"

"I've only had very small confrontations," Hudson said. "But I've seen what you mean."

"Three weeks after we came back to the unit there was some idea that part of the division should spread further south down the coast. Since we were already packed there were five of us who volunteered and we headed down the highways until we got to Ona. We stayed in one of the farmer's huts and talked to the elders about what was happening around the country. They'd heard from travellers about the massacre in Basik Dera.

It's difficult to look at an old man, a man about my age now, and tell him that all this suffering is for a better future when you know it was one of his cousins in that burning mosque. That's what the Ethiopians were trying for, you know, to turn the desire for revolution against us. Some would tell us the bloodshed wasn't worth it, especially if they'd lost family, innocent family, like that. Others would encourage us.

Two days later, word got out that we were there. The village supported us. The elders supported us. We had no idea who had let slip that the five of us were in the village. By the time it got back to us that the Ethiopians were on their way, it was too late to make a run for it. If we even tried to make a run for it, to make a break for the next village, then we'd be guessing on direction. It was not a smart move. We'd lost men before because they'd done that same thing.

The very moment you hear that the Ethiopians are coming, you make a decision in that same moment.

You stay, or you go. But you don't hesitate. And it was too late for us to leave. So we stayed. We hid under the floorboards of a hut, our faces pressed to the dirt. We were given small canteens of water and we stayed there. The rumbling of the Ethiopian trucks came hours later, from all directions. They surrounded the village as it was turning to night and demanded to know where we were. That same elder stepped forward and told the sergeant that we weren't there. The sergeant hit him and knocked him down to the ground. Mustafa was pressed up next to me under that floor and gasped when he saw the old man fall to the ground. The man's son stepped forward and told the sergeant that we'd left an hour earlier. The sergeant shot him.

For Mustafa, it was a total shock. He'd told me he'd seen men die when he was travelling, but maybe not in that same way. No one else would say a word. It was fortunate for us that the man they'd shot and the elder were the only two who knew exactly where we were. The others may have broken." Abraha stopped. "It was a horrific night. I can't go through the details again."

Hudson reached an arm out for Abraha's shoulders and consoled him.

"They killed over six hundred people from that village and started setting fire to the buildings. While their relatives were lying there dying on the ground, they made the other survivors watch the village burn to the ground. It was only a matter of time until they lit the hut we were in. There was one chance when a corporal left one side of the village out of view. We scrambled and crawled across the dirt and hid behind some other hut. We were trying to get out without any confrontation. We were badly outnumbered. My friend, Idris, was shot. He fell and kept firing into the crowd of advancing Ethiopian soldiers while we ran down the hill and further inland."

Hudson didn't want to say a word. The expression on Abraha's face said it all. There was no use for words, and there was no need to console him. These were old wounds that he rarely revisited. For now there was just a silence for his fallen friends.

"He was just a kid," Abraha shrugged. "Mustafa believed in the cause but he quickly learned that having read everything written on war philosophy or having studied Napoleon's battles is a lot different to hearing a military unit unload outside and knowing they're trying to hit you. Hearing the bullets fly over your head, tearing apart the building you're in and trying to press yourself so flat to the wooden boards that you become part of the dirt, trying to not cough or sneeze on the dust flying around the room.

Mustafa had studied everything on the topic and could debate you until you were worn out or come around to his point of view, but picking up a weapon and taking another man's life because it's you or him was something that didn't come as easy to him. He had to learn that."

Abraha sipped carefully from the cup, wetting just his lips that were hidden behind his white tangled beard. "He learned how to deal with it, or how to shut off the part that he needed to. Perhaps he learned it too well, I don't know. But that kid I knew then is not the man who rules today. He is changed."

Not much was said between the two men for the rest of the afternoon. Occasionally Abraha would ask Hudson a question about his service or why he came to Eritrea but mostly they slept. There wasn't much else to do in the heat. The cool concrete slab was almost a relief despite its unforgiving texture.

"Did you see much of the city?"

"Asmara?"

"Yes."

"I saw a little. The courthouse and piazza look pretty nice. It's mostly kept well."

Abraha nodded as he tried to picture it. "Do they still have the war monument?"

"The one with the tanks? That's there."

Abraha nodded again. "I'm sorry for asking so much. I don't get to ask people these questions much. The prison must be full if they're putting you in with me."

"Ask whatever you want."

Abraha drifted to sleep again. He woke with a start when the metal lock slid open. Another prisoner was thrown in the small cell. The guard threw him in then locked the door before the prisoner had even had time to pick himself up off the ground. He turned around and sat on the concrete, leaning against the wall facing the door. He gasped and looked around.

"Hudson?"

"I'm surprised they put you in here too." Hudson handed Mervyn his half full tin cup. "Drink it slow. They don't hand them out too often."

"You know each other?"

"This is the man I was sent to Eritrea to defend."

"They must be really short on cells," Abraha said.

Donald Mervyn sipped the water and leaned back against the wall. The cut on his cheek had begun to heal but hadn't been given any proper attention. It looked worse than it felt, making his right eye red and puffy. Hudson noticed a few other cuts on his face, and that Mervyn's wrists were raw from tight handcuffs. His ribs were bruised but Hudson couldn't see that. Mervyn kept one arm wrapped around his chest, subconsciously protecting himself.

"What went wrong?"

"I'm not sure," Mervyn said. "Everything was fine. I met the contact, got on his boat and we went out like it was planned. There had been a small man following me around Yemen and I hadn't thought much of him. I'd tried to lose him or see if he was following me but I thought I had. Then the fishing boat was boarded. The contact was shot and killed and I threw the gun overboard to keep up the tourist front. That was all to plan, except for Ali getting killed."

"That's what was meant to happen," Hudson said mostly to himself. He'd been going over it for hours in his cell trying to understand what had gone wrong.

"The man who followed me was waiting in the prison for me. It was he who gave me this," Mervyn motioned towards the swollen eye. "He doesn't know anything but he wanted to get me to confess to something."

"There's something else then," Hudson said. "Something that we overlooked or that was out of our control."

The rest of the night the men sat in silence, each in their own thoughts. Mervyn rested, drifting along in sleep for the first extended period since Yemen. Abraha continued his meditation and prayer. It was the only way he'd found to keep himself from going completely insane over the years of solitary confinement. He closed his eyes and worked back through situations. He lived them again, experiencing the smell and the taste of coffee or burnt bread from a fire. He focused on the

senses, letting them drive the memory. He went over
details. The seating positions of everyone in the room.
The way the light cut through the leaves. The light fog
over the river. The feeling of a hot day, the sweat
perspiring as they hiked through the highlands. Even
the ache of the muscles as he'd climbed mountains or
trekked, avoiding the Ethiopians during the war of
independence.

He was intent on experiencing the memory and
the feeling of everything, even if it was painful or
unpleasant. He remembered when he'd run all night to
escape the Ethiopians burning a village. The smell of
the burning wood, the cries of the people, the ache of
his legs as he willed them to keep going. He'd relived
the pleasant days with his family, or playing football
with his brother when they were children.

Over time he realized he couldn't pick only the
pleasant memories. He forced himself to confront these
memories emotions. There were times he'd spent nights
weeping as he relived his comrades deaths, or when he
remembered hearing of his parents' deaths. It was a
strategy that had helped. It kept him together and alert.
The solitary confinement, the small rations of food and
water, and the interrogations that had petered out after
the first few years – all of these he could keep balanced
by living in his memories.

The light bulb hanging in the cell was dim and
barely lit the corners of the cell. It hummed without

letting up. A moth had found some way into the cell and fluttered around the light. It banged against the globe, flying frantically around the dull light. Hudson looked up at the moth. Surely it had a better chance of bright light in the hallway, he thought. But somehow the moth had come into the pit in which Hudson had found himself. Even in the cell of a prison in the middle of Eritrea, a moth had found its way into the room, and insisted on butting its head against the glass for hours trying to get to the light.

The click of the metal lock woke them all up. The only opening to the outside world didn't open often. Its metallic click always brought the inmates attention whether they were conscious or not. It was usually to slide a tray of kitcha or a rusted cup of water into the room. Abraha hadn't heard the door open as many times a day as it had in the last two. That morning they stirred from their sleep, all three looking towards the door blurry eyed. The door swung open completely and two guards stood in the doorway.

"Hudson Jones?"

Hudson stood from the part of the cell he'd been sleeping in. He balanced himself against the wall and pulled himself together and stepped forward. Mervyn swapped a glance with him through the closing cell door. Hudson had been lying on the concrete with his face to the wall only a minute ago, and now he was collecting himself as the guards led him down the hall, trying to make sense of where they were directing him.

They led him to a smaller truck than the one he'd arrived in. At least, he thought it was smaller. It was the bright light of day and so much about that night was blurred under the haze of disorientation and fatigue, or just unseen in the dark. It was hard to say anything about the details of his trip to the prison.

Hudson was in the back of the truck by himself as it rattled along the highway. He sat on the wheel hub until the truck hit a hole in the road and Hudson's head slammed into the roof. He sat on the cold metal tray of the truck and waited for them to arrive at wherever he was being taken.

Archer was pacing the room when Hudson was led in between two guards. He was handcuffed and sat in a chair at the table.

"I demand these handcuffs be taken off Captain Jones," Archer said. "He is not being held as a criminal nor has he been charged with anything."

The guards didn't move. They stood at attention. Archer walked across and stood toe to toe with the most senior ranking officer. He looked up at the officer. "Corporal. Remove the handcuffs."

The corporal did not move. He looked straight forward, over Archer's head to the wall on the other side of the room. "I have been ordered to leave the prisoner handcuffed, sir. Those are my orders, sir."

Archer grunted in resignation and walked back to the table. He sat down opposite Hudson and pulled out a file of notes.

"You don't look so good," Hudson said.

Archer shot him a glance, incredulous. "I haven't been sleeping, thanks to this whole fiasco. And you're one to talk – you look like you've been sleeping on a concrete floor."

"I have."

Archer paused. "I'm sorry, I didn't mean to…"

"It's alright. It's not permanent." Hudson shrugged and shook his head. "When will I be released?"

"There have been a few meetings with the president, with the foreign minister and other representatives." Archer paused. "The matter hasn't been proceeding as we had hoped. The president is claiming that you and Donald Mervyn are spies. He's holding you on that pretense but without any charges. It's blown up to a much larger international issue than it should be."

Archer pulled out that morning's New York Times, Corriere Della Sera, and the Daily Telegraph. A picture of Hudson's face, an official DoD photograph, was on the front page next to photos of an Eritrean port, the US embassy or the Washington-based embassy of Eritrea. "President Mustafa seems intent on making this a major international issue. The Secretary of State is flying in this afternoon to handle the escalating negotiation for your release. So far we haven't made any ground."

"That's much more coverage than I thought this would get."

"Me too. The meetings last night were a two-hour long stalemate. The only thing we've been able to get ground on is this, here. They conceded that I can meet with you to brief you and see your state of health."

"I see."

"However, I haven't been able to get a location on Donald Mervyn. They refuse to say where he is or allow me to see him. They're hiding him well. And the president won't comment on his location or well being."

"He was put in the same cell as me last night."

Archer raised an eyebrow. "That's peculiar."

"We thought so too."

"How is he?"

"He's surviving, though the rations are low. He's been beaten. And he's also sleeping on concrete."

"You're surprisingly calm for someone imprisoned in an Eritrean prison."

"I can't say I'd stay there again," Hudson said. "But I know you guys are working to get the whole thing fixed and it will be over. I have to have that faith, you know? Or I'd go crazy."

Archer nodded. He started putting the papers back in his briefcase.

"I feel worse about the other man in my cell. He's been there for decades and there's no sign of release for him. He was telling me about the war of independence when he first met Mahmoud Mustafa. When the two of them, Mustafa and Hamid, were hiding from the Ethiopians under floorboards in a hut."

Archer leaned in closer and whispered, "Hamid Abraha?" He looked up at the guards but they hadn't heard or at least didn't react to it. "You're in a cell with Hamid Abraha?"

Hudson nodded. "You know him?"

"Know *of* him. Everyone knows of him."

Archer frowned again. "It seems really strange that they're keeping you in the same cell as him. I would have thought he'd be in solitary, considering the risk he poses to Mustafa. And you too, since your case is a current threat to his power."

"Five minutes," said the corporal at the back of the room, still unmoving.

"What else can you tell me?"

"Unfortunately, not much. There's something the president is playing close to his chest. There's a meeting tomorrow morning with the United Nations and the Secretary of State. With that international pressure, we are hoping the President will decide to save face and hand you both over to us at the embassy.

Ideally, it will be by tomorrow afternoon. But we're not holding our breath. We just hope that it's soon enough."

"Soon enough?"

Archer's eyes darted across Hudson's face. "Yes. Soon enough to get you out of the prison, before your health deteriorates."

Hudson studied Archer's face as the diplomat flicked through his notes. His brow was furrowed and his jaw clenched. "There's something you're not telling me."

"That's all that I know, that's everything," Archer replied.

"All that you know?"

Archer avoided his gaze. "That's all the official details."

"And the unofficial ones?"

Archer shrugged and shook his head.

"If there's something else, it's better that I know. And I know there's something else. I've dealt with official and unofficial reports for too long not to recognize it on your face, Archer."

"This is not a nation known for following international treaties or regulations."

"What are you saying, Archer?"

"There are rumors we've heard from people in the ministry that the president may rush through a trial on your case, and Mervyn's, and sentence you without any international presence. We would not be alerted until," Archer hesitated. "Until after the sentence."

"Surely you can still negotiate our release after that? You have enough political and diplomatic power."

Archer took a breath and leaned forward. "It's not that kind of sentence, Jones. There's no appeal process in Eritrea."

Hudson felt his heart rate rise. He was suddenly aware of just how dry his mouth was. "You mean that…" Hudson couldn't say it.

"Firing squad, usually."

"And you wouldn't know until…"

Archer lowered his voice further. "We have informants who keep us informed of it, but it's a process that's near impossible to stop. Especially if they keep denying it and refusing to tell us where you are both located. It's unofficial, Jones. It's a rumour. But we can't rule out the possibility of Mustafa pulling something like that even while the UN is in the country."

Hudson nodded feebly.

"We're doing our best."

"Sure." Those words didn't offer the consolation that they had just ten minutes earlier. The corporal's arms pulled Hudson to his feet. The two guards on either side held him up, and Hudson needed it. The small serves of kitcha didn't offer much nutrition and now the extra burden of Archer's revelations was weighing him down further.

"Tomorrow afternoon, Captain. We'll see you at the embassy then," Archer called out after him as he was pushed through the door and back into the idling truck. The hopeful tone didn't get through to Jones. He sat in the back of the truck, numb and lost in thought for the entire trip, barely feeling the jolts of the potholes in the road.

By the time the truck had returned to the prison Hudson had convinced himself he couldn't wait for Archer and the diplomatic solution. Tomorrow afternoon was no guarantee and if he returned to the cell and just had that thought running through his head then he'd go mad. No, that wouldn't do. He had to take actions into his own hands. The prison was nearly deserted when he was pulled out from the back of the truck. The sun was already beating down on the Eritrean desert and the soldiers doing their patrols around the prison had taken refuge in the buildings. Any time they needed to head out for their rounds, they did it quickly.

The guards weren't as strict in their head down rule as that first night Hudson had been dragged out of the truck with the other anonymous men and pushed into the prison. Hudson looked around and made a note of the lay out of the buildings. The fence around the prison was flimsy and structurally unsound. They could almost be jumped over instead of scaled. The security in the prison lay in the fact that most of the inmates were kept in the cells beneath the ground. Any attempt to escape required getting out of the shipping containers and past the guards on the stairs. For Hudson, that wouldn't be an issue unless they were moved to another cell. And considering what Abraha had said about the way they were being treated, they wouldn't be moved anytime soon.

Mervyn and Abraha were still in the same positions in the cell when Hudson was put back in. There were two empty plates of kitcha and one more next to them. Three cups of water sat near the door. Mervyn sat up.

"Where did they take you?"

"To see the Ambassador." Hudson sat down on the concrete next to him. "The Secretary of State is on his way to the country with a UN delegation to negotiate our release since the president is playing hardball."

"So once the UN and the Secretary of State put pressure on him, we'll be out?"

"One thing I can tell you about Mustafa," said Abraha from the blankets where he lay, speaking without opening his eyes, "is that he can't be expected to act in any normal or rational way. Though the pressure from the UN and the US would sway most leaders of smaller nations so they can save their reputations, Mustafa doesn't have that same instinct. He will push it as far as he can and try to show the US's grandstanding as a bluff."

"That's as much as the Ambassador said," Hudson agreed.

Mervyn looked blankly at the wall across the cell. "So we just have to wait here until he comes to his senses?"

"I don't suggest we do," Hudson said.

"What do you suggest?"

"We break out."

"With no weapons, and no idea where we are?" Mervyn asked.

Hudson shrugged. "We have to figure out what we do have."

Abraha sat up. "It's not unknown for people to escape from here. There have been some. They end up running across the desert, making a break at night, usually, when the moon is new."

"And exactly what do we have?" Mervyn asked. "I'm not skeptical. I'm a realist. We have one shot at this."

"If we can get outside, then to the right is the parking bay. If we get past there, hopefully out of view behind the fleet of trucks, it's not far to the fence."

"And then?" Mervyn asked. "We need some sort of plan, some direction to go. We don't even know where we are."

"You two are currently inmates at Adersesr," Abraha said. "Also known as Hadish Measker."

That changed things. Mervyn looked up. "Hadish Measker? Really?"

"Yes, unfortunately. Along with another ten thousand political prisoners."

"Is it a new moon tonight?"

Hudson looked at him incredulously. "It was pretty dark the night they brought me in."

"It is," Abraha confirmed. "There's not much else to do in here. I keep track of the moon cycles. Also, it's louder in here on a full moon with everyone else screaming to God and Allah and the devil. It's good to know when to expect it."

Hudson thought it was a bit strange but he knew not to judge the behaviors of someone who had been in a cell for the better part of the last two decades. "Why does the moon matter?" Hudson asked Mervyn.

"The patrol I was on when I was stationed here would travel down the highway not far from Hadish Measker on a new moon. The roads were darker and safer, for us."

"So we do have something," Hudson said. In the truck he was desperate and determined. Now there was hope to inspire that. "Do we know where to meet them? And when?"

Mervyn nodded. "We do tonight."

It was a gamble. It was the biggest gamble. If there were more than two guards in the hall, and they weren't both by the door when it opened, then it would be a short lived escape plan. If the guards didn't come that night the entire exercise was futile. The next night would not align with the moon and running into the desert was more of a suicide mission than Hudson intended taking on. If the trucks weren't there and there was no cover, then it would be over quickly. Or, if the guard patrol along the fence was in the wrong place at the wrong time. But, as Hudson reminded himself, desperate times call for desperate measures. Big pay offs, like escaping a prison, need a big risk. It requires a leap of faith. And they needed some luck. It hinged on these details aligning for them.

The wait until nightfall was unbearable. They tried to nap but their minds were racing too fast. Instead they sat in silence, each in his own thoughts. Several times the sound of boots came walking up the hall but they passed the cell door and disappeared into the distance. After an eternity, the sound of the metal plate sliding and the key sliding into the lock startled them. Time slowed. Mervyn and Hudson exchanged a glance – it was too early. The sun had set but it was still light outside. Faint shadows fell across the cell. Both knew the opportunity may not come again that night. The guard visits were too sporadic to be relied on.

Hudson nodded at Mervyn and he sprung to his feet, and leaned in the corner near the door. The door opened and the guard slid the first two plates into the room. He turned to the second guard behind him to pick up the third plate and a glass of water. Mervyn's hand shot out and grabbed the guard's wrist. He pulled him into the room, sending him sprawling on the concrete and throwing the water in the second guard's face. The shock of the water was enough. The quickness Mervyn showed caught him off guard and Mervyn grabbed the second guard's collar before he had a chance to react or call out or sound the alarm. Mervyn threw him on top of the other guard, checked the hall to make sure it was empty, then shut the door behind him.

Mervyn turned to face the two guards sprawled out on the concrete floor. Hudson was crouched behind the first guard, holding his arms behind him in a lock, making it impossible for him to move. Abraha held the first guard's pistol in both hands, pointed directly at the head of the second guard, who was frozen, his arms raised and leaning against the wall. Mervyn stepped over to the second guard and pulled his pistol from the holster, then checked him for any other weapons.

Abraha barked questions at the guard, interrogating him about the number of guards on duty and how many trucks were in the yard.

Hudson watched intently. The full rage of two decade's worth of time served in these walls was directly fired at the young guard. The guard gave the answers and Abraha translated them. The guard hesitated on one question, just paused for one moment and Abraha stood up above him and whipped his hand around, slamming the pistol butt into the guard's cheek. He hissed the question again and the guard answered quicker.

"It's possible to get past the hall if we move soon. He says there are few guards on duty now but the shift changeover is in twenty minutes. There'll be twice the number of guards then."

"I don't think it will fit," Mervyn said to Hudson.

"It's not going to." The original plan to escort Abraha out while Hudson and Mervyn wore the uniforms would have to be rethought.

"It probably wouldn't have passed any scrutiny anyway," Mervyn said with a wry smile.

"Your eyes are too blue."

"Tell them to strip anyway," Hudson told Abraha. "We can tie them up with the uniforms."

Hudson and Mervyn took a pistol each and flanked Abraha as they left the cell. Abraha locked the door behind them and smiled to himself. Hudson stepped quietly down the hall on the left and Mervyn kept to the right wall. Hudson slowed and looked behind to check on Abraha. The old man stood still in the middle of the hall, frozen in his step and looking down.

"Hamid?" Hudson hissed.

Abraha looked up, partially in a daze. He looked at Hudson, then Mervyn, then back down at his hands. He shook his head and turned around. Hudson looked at Mervyn – was the old man crazy? "I can't do it," Abraha said to himself more than the others. "I can't do it." He turned and stepped backwards to the door next to the cell he'd been in for countless waxing and waning moons. Without another word he slowly slid the key in the lock. Abraha pushed the door open slowly and looked inside.

"Quickly and quietly," he whispered to the prisoner then moved to the next cell. Hudson and Mervyn walked to the end of the hall. Hudson took a breath to steady himself then peered around the hall. A guard's boot flashed by at the end of the second hall, but the sound disappeared as the guard walked further away from them. Hudson touched his chest in relief, swapping a look with Mervyn.

Abraha had unlocked all five cells between theirs and the end of the hall and now a small group of prisoners, wearing dirty and torn clothes, their beards and hair unkempt and wild, kept step behind Mervyn. The second hall led straight to the door to the yard. It was a matter of getting past the intersecting hall and unlocking the heavy metal door. Then praying that the trucks provided enough cover to get to the fence.

Mervyn and Hudson leaned against the opposing walls and motioned for Abraha to cross the intersecting hall but the others to stay back. Abraha crossed quickly and flicked through the keys to find the right one to unlock the door. It was the third one he tried. As the prisoners held their breath the door clicked open and Abraha leaned hard against the heavy door, pushing it open carefully. It was the most fresh air he'd seen for years.

Then the shout came from behind the group of prisoners, from the hall with the open cell doors. A guard called out as he raced down the hall. Hudson ran to the door and held it open, waving the other prisoners to go through ahead of him. Mervyn fired a shot down the hall, hitting the wall near the guard's head and making him think twice about racing around the corner. The prisoners were all outside, and Hudson and Mervyn followed them. Mervyn pulled the door closed behind them, making sure it clicked shut. It would stall the guards just a moment.

There was a small amount of daylight left but already it was darker behind the trucks and Mervyn headed straight for them. Hudson grabbed Abraha by the collar and pulled him along, crouching behind the same truck. The other prisoners were in a daze. The light was dull but still took time for their eyes to adjust.

The light acted differently outside the walls and away from the buzzing light bulbs of the prison cell. They hadn't planned their escape. Even just two minutes earlier they had no idea their cell would be unlocked and they'd be led to the fresh air. The sun had disappeared over the horizon, leaving just a red stain in the eastern sky. The new moon hung in the eastern skies, bringing with it just a sliver of a chance for them to flee.

Hudson was measuring the distance to the fence while Mervyn kept his attention on the door. The closest part of the fence was almost one hundred yards away. The dirt road ran the other direction towards the security check at the gate. That wasn't an option. Guards from the gate were already running towards the disorientated prisoners with their weapons drawn. The first shot fired and hit another prisoner who crumbled immediately, grabbing his thigh. A guard stood over him, weapon trained directly at the man's body, as the other guards spread out to surround the other prisoners. A guard trailing the others looked towards the trucks and kept going, then doubled back. Mervyn cursed himself – he was trying to avoid any fire so they weren't seen behind the trucks. Mervyn fired once, hitting the guard in the upper stomach before he could let the other guards know. The sound of the gunshot was covered by another burst of fire from the guards.

Abraha was shaken, disorientated. Overwhelmed with the shouting and gunfire. For decades he was used to it, but years of solitary confinement take their toll too. The other prisoners were suffering in the same way. They ran for the nearest fence or for cover across the yard. It was a gamble that wouldn't pay off. Being captured again wasn't an option – they didn't want to go back into those cells, and suffer whatever torture the warden thought fit the crime. Abraha ducked behind the truck to avoid watching his fellow inmates being cut down with gunfire. The guards' machine guns rattled and the rounds tore through the dust caught in the red glow of sunset, then found their targets.

Abraha looked up at Hudson. It was Hudson who had started the escape and Abraha knew Hudson would find them a way out of it. Hudson nodded towards the back of the prison. Mervyn understood immediately. Going around the buildings would give them cover, and buy them time while the guards looked for them among the bodies wounded and bleeding in the yard.

Hudson scurried across and then covered Abraha's path. Mervyn followed at the rear. They collapsed against the wall and crept along the side. From that side of the building the sounds of the guards barking out orders and the prisoners pleading were muffled. For Hudson, it was a matter of figuring out how to get far away from that side of the building and getting to the fence on the other side. From where he stood, the fence was running further away. Doubling back and going for the closest exit was unthinkable. Hudson checked around the corner of the cell block then the three prisoners ducked behind the next building, staying out of the light.

The terrible pit that led beneath the building to the containers of prisoners below the ground opened up in front of them. Hudson stayed out of the light. The wall of the building was still radiating the day's heat back into the darkening night but a chill ran up his spine when he saw that ground giving way to the tunnels. One light glowed down the tunnel giving a supernatural glow warning of the horrors that lay beneath that dirt. Hudson just wanted to keep going.

He stepped out from behind the building. Then there was a click. Hudson knew he'd made a mistake. Just one error in thinking, one lapse in judgement – that was all it took. Hudson felt the gun barrel against his head. He put his arms out, letting his pistol fall to the dirt below. Mervyn turned and lined his pistol with the guard's head above Hudson's eye line. Hudson took a breath and let it out slowly. His heart was racing but everything was slowing down. Mervyn's face changed from panic to confusion, then a smile, and he dropped his weapon down to his side.

"Take that one. In there," the guard nodded towards the metal door. The guard's tone was hurried and hushed. Hudson looked around confused. Mervyn grabbed the metal handle and pulled it open for the others to enter.

Ali let Hudson go, releasing him to the floor in the small storage room. Hudson caught his breath and looked up at the guard and then at Mervyn.

"I thought you were dead," Mervyn said to Ali.

"Just shot," Ali said. He lifted his shirt where the side was bandaged. "The guy who shot me was another contact. He smuggled me back to shore then when I heard what they'd done to you, he helped get me in here undercover."

He looked at Mervyn's swollen eye. "I'm sorry I couldn't stop him from doing that."

"You're why we ended up in the same cell," Hudson said.

Ali nodded. "I knew you three would sort something out. Mister Abraha," Ali said, turning to the older man. "It's an honor to meet you, sir."

"Are we safe in here?"

"We are for now," Ali said. "If you guys hadn't done something tonight then I was going to have to figure something out and move you. The General has sent orders to prepare for an execution tomorrow evening or the next morning."

Mervyn and Hudson exchanged a look.

"When I heard the shots I knew you must have done something."

"If they find us, they'll move the execution forward a few hours."

"They won't." Ali moved across to the door and looked out to the yard under the dull yellow lights. "At the moment they probably think you bolted. A search party will be sent out. I'll go and run some interference and get a message through that you've been apprehended and being brought back to solitary. That will calm things down for the time being. The General will probably deploy some men to transfer you in the morning. The alarm will be raised when they don't find you. But by then you'll be somewhere else."

Hudson took this in. "You can arrange all of that?"

"It'll take time. But there's a guardhouse on the other side of the prison I can move you to." He handed Mervyn his AK-47 and Hudson the extra pistol. "Lay low here. Keep the light off," Ali said. "I'll be back with a truck in two or three hours."

"Two hours?" Mervyn asked. "Are we safe here for two hours?"

"It takes time for things to get calm after that mess you made out there." Ali opened the door then locked it from the outside.

"Are you sure he can be trusted?" Hudson asked Mervyn. They weren't in a position to strike out on their own or turn down Ali's plan, but it helped to know if you could trust the man who's smuggling you out of a heavily armed military prison.

Mervyn nodded. "His allegiance is not with the President. His interests are aligned with ours."

"I believe him," Abraha said. "He may pass for an Eritrean captain when he's ordering others around but he looks uncomfortable in that Eritrean uniform."

There was no way of knowing how long it was until Ali returned. The click of the lock of the storage room door snapped the three of them awake instantly from where they were crouching behind boxes at the back of the room. Mervyn steadied the barrel and pointed it towards the door, waiting for the blinding wash of the light. If it wasn't Ali, he'd have to shoot quick, without being able to see properly.

"Wait," Ali hissed, leaving the door open but keeping the light off. He turned and called towards the truck. A younger guard stepped into the storage room and handed Ali his weapon as he took a step towards a box and bent to pick it up. He saw Mervyn's barrel pointed at him and stood up. He reached for the gun that was usually slung over his shoulder but it was pointed at his head by his commanding officer. Ali closed the door and stepped towards the younger officer and hit the light.

"What are you doing, captain?"

"Hand me your pistol, private." He hesitated then handed it to Ali.

"Your uniform. The shirt will be enough."

The young officer hesitated again.

"I'd prefer to have it without blood, private."

Ali handed it to Mervyn who pulled it on over his shirt. After the private was bound and tied at the back of the room, Mervyn and Ali transferred Hudson and Abraha into the truck. They rolled slowly down the dirt road towards the guard shelter at the entry point. Ali slowed as they reached the checkpoint. Hudson and Ali sat crouched in the back of the smaller vehicle beneath a tarpaulin.

"I haven't been out of here since '96," Abraha said to Hudson.

"If we get our way, you won't ever be back."

Abraha nodded. He was hopeful, but found it difficult to believe.

The guard shack was on the south-eastern side of the prison, just beyond the boundary. It looked like it hadn't been used for years. A larger watchtower sat on the fence line further to the east, newer and with a higher vantage point. The light was on. Ali cut the engine and let the vehicle roll down the small hill to the shack. Rotted and aged boxes were in the front room behind the boarded up windows. Old weapons had been stored there without rounds for a while, but it was the only sign that the building had been used for anything in years.

"If you lay low here for the night, then we can move further tomorrow. There's a transport early we can get cover from."

"They won't look for us here?" Mervyn asked. "If we'd gotten out of the prison, then this seems like a good place to hide out."

"I ordered two patrols to already search through here for that very reason," Ali assured them. "In any case, your escape was four hours ago and on paper you're all in solitary confinement in the northern cell. No one will know you're not there until the General's men come for you in the morning."

Hudson became aware that Abraha wasn't there. He turned around and saw the older man standing by the window looking up at the new moon hanging in the sky.

"Is he ok?" Mervyn asked Hudson.

"He hasn't been out of that prison since ninety-six."

Abraha turned around and looked at Ali. "Where are you moving us to tomorrow?"

"Keren firstly."

Abraha looked at the sky, then back to the dull glow of the prison watchtower. The size of the prison didn't justify a watchtower. It was only when the unofficial size of the political prisoner population kept beneath the ground was considered that the watchtower and the security made sense.

"We can't leave all those other prisoners there," Abraha said, his voice cracking.

"What are you suggesting?" Ali replied.

Abraha looked at Hudson for support. He knew Hudson had seen the gaping mouth of the tunnel, the descent into the hell Mustafa had built.

"If you get us rounds for these weapons, then we might be able to do something. How many guards are there?"

"I can't believe you're thinking of this," Ali shook his head. "You just broke out of there."

"I know," Abraha smiled. "And now we're breaking back in."

8

President Mustafa sat in his usual chair on the balcony with a plate of fruit in front of him. He was a man of habit and ritual. He rarely varied his breakfast. He took it at the same time on the balcony. He would change his position on the balcony depending on the season and the sun's location. It was here, while he ate his boiled eggs, plate of fruit and a bowl of muesli that he would read the newspapers from the region and the other major papers from Europe and the U.S. When he took his second pot of coffee he would read the reports from the various ministries. His assistant would bring them to him with a rough outline of his schedule for the day. Mustafa would make any changes he saw were needed then head into the presidential office.

Mustafa read through the brief reports on the domestic affairs of Eritrea then put them aside. He sipped his coffee and opened the folder with the updated reports on the two American spies. The New York Times and Washington Post still claimed the prisoners were only a civilian tourist and a military lawyer sent to negotiate his release. Mustafa wasn't phased. The German and UK papers had reported that their roles were still undetermined and had made neither case more prominent in the last three days.

General Haile Sa'id climbed the stone steps to the balcony. His uniform was immaculate as always, stiff and pressed. He placed his hat on the extra chair and sat opposite the president.

"Another pot of coffee," Mustafa said to the waiter standing to his right. "I just read your report, General."

"Here's another one." Sa'id nodded, sliding another folder across the table. "The second one was moved to Adersesr prison last night. They're being taken care of, but they're in there under surveillance."

"And their embassy?"

"We're still unable to properly identify the first one. Our agent in Yemen identified him as the man he was following for some days before we captured him. That part is clear, but the rest isn't."

"Have you read these today?" Mustafa nodded towards the European papers.

"Briefly through La Republica."

"They're hedging their bets," Mustafa said, pouring coffee for himself and Sa'id.

"We'd anticipated them reporting the side of the Americans already but they're still refusing to speculate on whether the captives are spies."

"That's only going to help us," Sa'id nodded. "Your early statements have caught the Americans off guard. It's hard for them to refute the claims now."

"What time is the meeting?"

"Ten. I think it's a good move to go straight into a press statement after that before they've had time to react. Or release their own."

"That's a good idea," Mustafa agreed. He sipped his coffee. "Will you have that ready before the meeting?"

"I'll prepare it now. You can make it as soon as we leave the meeting."

The president put his cup back on the table and leaned forward. "I've never doubted you, Haile, but I didn't think this would come together as smoothly as it has."

"We were fortunate that they fell into place as well as they have, but there should not be any doubts."

"There were no doubts, Haile. But I had worries about it going as smoothly as this."

"You don't need to worry, Mahmoud. Everything has been thought of. Stick to the script and we will be victorious. Once we make some noise, the other leaders in the region will gather behind you. It's inevitable."

The president nodded, sipping the rest of his coffee as the general saluted and walked down the stone steps of the presidential residence. There was no doubt that things were falling into place. There had been some luck but if it hadn't been for this, the two Americans falling into his lap, then there would have been something else that would have come together. He looked again at the front page of the Eritrean newspaper, of the billowing smoke coming from the train tracks. The explosion on the railway had ignited the oil reserves nearby. The fire had been extinguished late last night after burning for three days. The efforts of sabotage on Eritrean infrastructure and as an attempt to hinder the Eritrean agricultural industry was an affront to the Eritrean people and would not be tolerated, Mustafa had said in his statement.

The same photo had been printed around the world along with the statements Mustafa had made about the US and the request that their covert spy operations in the region should cease. It wasn't without support from other leaders in the region, but at this point the other East African leaders were playing it conservatively and not issuing any other statements without more concrete evidence. The New York Times and Washington Post hadn't run the photo. They'd only run photos of the captive Americans. That was to be expected.

Mustafa looked at the report Sa'id had just delivered. The new photos of the damaged naval ship were only a few hours old. They'd be in the papers by the end of the day. There was a hole in the hull and cranes were holding it above the water level. Ambulances were on the dock pulling some seamen from the ship and giving them the treatment required. It was not one of the largest ships in the Eritrean navy but a medium sized warship. Size didn't really matter when it came down to it, just the fact that one of his ships had been torn apart by an explosion without cause. The explosion had been a small one, Sa'id's report stated, and probably designed to explode while the ship was further from shore. It was an unwarranted attack on a military vessel docked during a time of peace. An act of aggression without provocation or justification.

Mustafa decided he would take the report to the meeting. Sa'id would probably already have a copy with him, but it was best to be prepared. He wrote down some names of other leaders to call immediately after the conference and then called his assistant back from the lounge. Mustafa handed the day's schedule back to his assistant and told him to pull the other files from Thursday on the American captives and bring them to his office. Mustafa walked along the balcony overlooking Asmara and paused to look down the avenue at the city alive with traffic, the city he had rebuilt as his own nest of power over the last two decades. He smiled to himself. There are days when you must show the world what you're made of, when you must stand up and let your action define yourself. To let the world see the strength and power that lies within you. Today was going to be one of those days.

The office of the general was an uncluttered room overlooking the town. It was on the same side of the building as the president's office. It was, in fact, the only room on that side of the building, the one overlooking the town square, that wasn't an office or conference room or sitting room for the president and his business. Everything was in exactly the place it should be and in some ways resembled the general himself. His slender frame and uniform never had a single thing out of place. Never was a hair out of place, never a part of his uniform missing. He expected the same from his staff. He had been known to suspend an assistant if his tie was crooked. There had been times in the last few decades he would have been more severe, more drastic. A suspension was an easy let off in comparison.

The general's reputation preceded him in every room of Eritrea and many abroad. His partnership with Mahmoud Mustafa began in the early seventies, the second decade of the thirty years war, the Eritrean war of independence. It had been with General Sa'id's assistance that Mustafa had not only gained control of the party but also consolidated his grip over the country. While Mustafa's regime was feared, it was Sa'id that quietly inspired fear in the background to anyone who knew the real dynamic.

One of the more notable stories that floated through the halls was of the revenge for the university massacre. The story was at the forefront of almost every officer's mind the first time they met the general. He stood in front of them and they looked over the general's slim frame, decorated with medals of the land, his bony jaw jutting out from beneath his hat and the small dark beads of eyes. As the general's gaze looked over the younger officers, they felt a chill. It was inevitable.

In late 1974 the Eritrean People's Liberation Front had scored a few crucial wins against the Ethiopian army. The EPLF struck against the Ethiopian army in three key locations around Asmara, taking out some key bases and in the process destroying two barracks, a series of vehicles including three tanks, and stealing enough weaponry, arms and rounds to pose a sizeable problem to the Ethiopian army for at least the first half of 1975.

The success was short lived. The Ethiopian army was not going to lie down and take these without any resistance. In late December the revenge came. It was a quiet Tuesday night. The streets of the city were deserted after nightfall. The military presence made going outside a risk. Everyone had heard stories about people being picked up by the police or army and questioned, then disappearing. Any suspicion of involvement with the Liberation Front, however unfounded, was followed by severe punishment. It was easiest to avoid going anywhere that wasn't necessary.

On that Tuesday in late December 1974 the city was in the same quiet lock down that it had been for much of the last thirteen years. The Ethiopian army vehicles rolled through the streets looking for any sign of dissent and came to the university. Five officers walked through the campus, mostly deserted, and through the library to the neighboring auditorium. It was relatively empty too, with some students, forty seven, in different parts of the auditorium going through texts books and lecture notes.

The doors were locked on the university auditorium, and a handful of officers pulled the students together at the front of the auditorium. The sergeant addressed the students, demanding to know any links to the EPLF. A chill spread through the auditorium. The flutter of pigeons' wings could be heard as if it was some sort of omen. Though the students were sympathetic to the cause, and there was a strong pro-independence credo on campus, few students were involved with the EPLF. And certainly none were involved with the strikes against the Ethiopian army in the last few months.

The sergeant demanded answers. As he walked between the desks of students the other officers were breaking the piano at the front of the hall into pieces. The first student called forward was a mathematics undergraduate, Mahmoud Idris. He was told to kneel in front of the officers and put his hands by his side. They asked him about the EPLF. Idris didn't know. He had no political conviction though he leaned towards independence. He made no mention of it. A rifle butt slammed into his back and sent him sprawling across the floor and another student, a physics student named Pietro, came forward to help him up. The three rifles that were instantly trained on him convinced Pietro to go back behind the desk. The sergeant asked Idris again and still he said he didn't know. The sergeant walked towards the rest of the students and watched their reaction as his soldiers dealt with the student who had no answers.

The shock of the piano wire being strung around Idris' neck made him react instantly. The officer behind him wrapped it around his neck twice and pulled, a knee in Idris' back, leaning back with his weight. Idris kicked and pulled at the wire, desperately trying to breathe, unable to even make a sound. The silence and brutality of it stunned the other students, watching their classmate struggle and not even make the smallest scream. He felt the blood filling his eyes, looking up at his friends and classmates with desperation but knowing they couldn't do a thing. He kicked but the soldier was too strong. He pulled at the wire until his hands were cut and the blood had stained the skin around his neck and shirt. And then Idris went limp. His body was pushed to the side of the hallway and the physics student was called forward and told to kneel.

One by one they were pulled in front of their classmates and friends, a soldier already standing with wire in his hands as they stepped forward. Several tried to bargain their way out of it but the sergeant was having none of it. One student tried to give some information, any information, to buy time, but the sergeant knew immediately that it was false information and shot him in the leg, forcing him to watch the rest suffer while he bled, before he too was strangled with piano wire. The screams and cries were heard down the halls. There was only going to be one end of it. The bodies of the forty-seven students were dumped in doorways and hallways around the city.

The news of the massacre spread fast in hushed talk and tearful whispers and quickly reached the farmhouse in the hills where the top officers of the EPLF were hiding out. It was a base for a week, maybe two at the most. Then they'd move on and push south. Their plan was to strike again against the military, taking out a bridge into the area just before the monsoon season arrived. It would leave some of the military stranded and out of position. Then the EPLF would head south and attack from another angle. The news of the massacre made for a somber start to the new year. There had not been a strike like this against the civilians for a while. The Ethiopian army was growing desperate. A blatant massacre like this was chilling. It would only make the people feel like they were occupied even more, and spur more support for the independence movement. But it was at a cost.

"What good was all of this if the people we are trying to liberate are being killed?" Hamid Abraha asked the other leaders over a cup of coffee one morning.

"That's just what Mariam wants us to do."

"I am not suggesting we give in" Abraha said. "Don't misunderstand me. Just that we need to change our approach. Our people are being slaughtered."

"What do you suggest?"

Abraha looked around at the other ten leaders who were willing to die for the cause that he risked his life for. "I suggest we lay low for a few months and gain more support, more people, then lead another assault."

"Infiltrate the city and then fight out from there? From the first liberated city?" asked Mustafa.

"If we have that one strong hold then it gives Mariam one target. Our strength at the moment," Abraha continued, "is that he doesn't know where we are."

There was talk but no decisions that day other than no acts of revenge would be taken straight away. There would be a planned assault against the military strong holds, but nothing before then.

This plan didn't sit well with Sa'id. He'd joined the Liberation Front barely a year earlier and had earned some respect for his willingness to go straight into battle. He had a fearlessness that was widely admired. Sa'id had been at that same university eighteen months ago but dropped out in order to fight for his country's independence. One of the students in the slaughter was a cousin on his mother's side. When he'd heard about the massacre, the details of the piano wire and how his cousin's body, lifeless and bloodied with a gunshot wound in the leg, had been left in the doorway of an elementary school it made his blood boil. This was no longer just a political cause – if it had ever only been that – but now a personal war raged inside Sa'id. There would be no relenting until he'd been served the justice and liberty he sought.

That's how, three nights later, Sa'id led three newer recruits of the EPLF out of the camp in the hours after midnight. They rolled a car down the hill and drove the hundred miles to an army campsite. He waited for the sentry to walk around then grabbed him and broke his neck in one action. While the three other guerrillas crept around the darkened barracks looking for fuel cans, Sa'id slowly walked along the shadowed buildings and broke the necks of the sentries in his way. He boarded up the barracks and locked the doors. They were able to carry six fuel cans around to the front of the barracks where Sa'id was waiting. He poured the gasoline around each door and motioned for the recruits to pour more over the roof of the barracks. While they were on the roof Sa'id poured pools beneath each window. Anyone trying to escape would suffer, Sa'id made sure of it. If they survived they would wish they hadn't.

The flames danced high into the night sky and screams echoed through the barracks, waking the other soldiers. Sa'id and his consorts shot at those who ran into the base. Then Sa'id came to the general's quarters.

The general had been awoken by the gunshots. The dancing red light outside his window flung him out of bed and he pulled on his pants and opened the door. He was faced with the bony slim figure of Sa'id the guerrilla.

"Hello general. Are you going somewhere?" Sa'id fired the first shot into the general's leg. As the general collapsed and reached for his pistol Sa'id kicked his hand away and dragged him out to the middle of the base. "I want you to watch your men burn, general."

The younger recruits stood back, partly in terror of Sa'id. His eyes were small black beads of hate and vengeance. There would be no stopping him. After watching several burning bodies trying to escape from the windows and falling into the other flaming pool of gasoline before collapsing, the general reached for Sa'id. The guerrilla behind him shot him in the leg again and he collapsed in agony.

"I'm not without mercy, general," Sa'id told him in a low growling tone. "Though I'm in short supply." Sa'id reloaded the pistol and shot the general through the neck, then left him to bleed to death on the ground while watching the rest of his soldiers burn to death.

Sa'id drove the guerrillas away from the burning barracks without a word, away from the deathly red glow in the night sky, taking a long way back to the farm in the hills in case anyone tried to follow the tracks of the military vehicle the next day.

The news of what had happened spread quickly. When Sa'id woke in the early afternoon and walked into the kitchen to get a glass of water people were already looking at him differently. It was a look, a sneaked glance as their eyes darted for the shadows, that he would come to know, grow accustomed to and, eventually, expect.

The camp was split into two ways of thinking about the whole mess. The first was occupied by the elders of the liberation movement, Abraha and others who had been involved since the first shots had been fired at Mount Adal. They held the view that it was callous and irresponsible, a reckless act that – even though it may have been deserved – would be the downfall of the entire liberation movement. It was a small camp but an attack like that would not go without retribution. It was acts like that, with little planning and no proper organization, that would lead the Ethiopian army back to their base and would cost them all their lives.

The second line of thinking was held by the newer revolutionaries. They stood in awe of the kind of determination and violence that flickered behind the small dark beady eyes of Sa'id. Their instinctual need for vengeance, and the frustrations of having to obey orders handed down from a smaller group of leaders, were answered by the one violent act of defiance. The message sent to the Ethiopian army that the revolution would not be intimidated was loud and clear. Mahmoud Mustafa was one of the few leaders of the EPLF who shared the second line of thinking.

No immediate retribution against the Eritrean people came, and there was no clear strike against any of the guerrilla cells. No one could say if it was from lack of decisive power in the leadership struggle, or something to do with the charred remains of their soldiers. The Ethiopian leadership weren't the type to let things like this go without retaliation. The next mass slaughter of civilians was in February after the EPLF had taken out the bridges. The Ethiopian army raided the villages outside of Asmara. They forced the men to the riverside. The rivers in Eritrea don't flow all of the year, but now that the rains had come the riverbeds were full and flowing. There was nowhere for the villagers to run and no place to hide. The massacre was quicker this time, by gunfire, and the bodies left on the riverbanks.

*

General Sa'id met the president in his office, with walls covered in drapes and bookshelves filled with leather bound volumes of the political and philosophical texts Mustafa had first read as a young man in Syria. Leather couches divided the room between the desk and two reading areas. The mounted heads of African game animals hung on the wall, the most treasured being the lion's head in the center, in between other regal furnishings.

They walked to the car waiting outside, past the military guard. The presidential car was the fourth in the five car procession that snaked through the city blocks to the parliamentary building on the hill. More guards lined the sidewalk where the presidential car stopped. They stood at attention as the president, then the general, walked past. The officers kept their gaze straight ahead, looking above the heads of the general and president, partially from duty and partially, for those who knew better, out of fear of direct contact with the general's dark piercing and unforgiving gaze.

The Eritrean conference room looked out over the monument to the war of independence, a constant and not so subtle reminder for any foreign dignitary that Eritrea did have military capabilities. Ambassador Archer had stood at the window watching the parade beneath as the president's car eventually pulled to the curb. He had dealt with the president on multiple occasions but this time, considering the involvement of the United Nations, he was playing support to the Secretary of State, Tom Parkinson. Archer was often amused at the lavish parade that followed the president whenever he travelled. There was one time when the president had seemed amused that Archer took only one car from the palace to the embassy. Archer knew the president to be both warm and accepting at times and on other occasions he was harsh, stubborn and cold to the point of being impossible to deal with.

Archer turned back to the room and the large square desk in the center. Three United Nations representatives sat along one side. Empty chairs for the president, general and the Eritrean foreign ministry lined one side behind the small Eritrean flags. The delegation from the United States sat opposite them with the Secretary of State seated in the center, with assistant to his left and Archer on his right. The room was another elaborately decorated affair but paled in comparison to the regal essence of the palace. The gold leaf frames that hung around the oil paintings of war portraits were the most eye-catching pieces. Archer, Parkinson and his assistants stood when the President entered with his full guard and entourage. After the formalities were exchanged, they seated and Parkinson began.

"We will not accept anything except the full and unequivocal release of the two Unites States citizens you arrested last week," said Parkinson. "These are the tourist Donald Percy Mervyn and U.S. Army Captain Hudson Matthew Jones."

The General shifted his weight in his seat and shook his head dismissively. "This is not the first order of business," Mustafa said in a low and confident tone. He was accustomed to getting his way in life and conversation, and would not discuss anything out of order. "I am not prepared to begin discussion on releasing those two espionage agents until you accept responsibility for the attacks on our railway and harbor. They have been arrested in connection with these operations your government has been running on Eritrean soil."

These words hit Archer and the Secretary of State by surprise. They had heard of the attacks; it had been in the papers delivered in the morning, but at no point had it been linked with the U.S. military. The general's assistant slid the photos of the damaged naval ship and the burning railway across the table. The Secretary of State looked at the photos then dismissed them and turned to Archer.

"These tactics of intimidation will not be tolerated," Mustafa concluded. The room was silent. Sa'id's dark eyes surveyed the reaction of the U.S. delegation.

"These attacks upon Eritrean land are unfortunate," the secretary said, "but your suspicion of the United States government is unfounded and, to be frank, ridiculous."

The room was silent. Few Eritreans had heard anyone talk so directly to the president. Mustafa had expected a similar response. The claims were unfounded, but that was inconsequential to him. The senior United Nations official made a movement but the president began talking first, with the same calm tone as before, steady and deep. "The United States' influence in this area is sometimes baffling and, since it is founded entirely on diplomatic relations, not entirely stable."

"The United States has been supportive of the Eritrean government and your rule for many decades, President Mustafa," Parkinson said, making little attempt to mask the contempt in his voice. "I don't believe I need to remind you of the role President Bush and President Clinton had with you personally during your conflicts with your neighbors. The United States expresses condolences at the attacks and hopes that it does not ignite new tensions in the region. However, at this point we are only prepared to discuss the immediate release of the two US citizens you falsely arrested last week, Mervyn and Jones."

The president was unmoved. He sat back in his chair, leaning to his left and resting on the arm. His gaze rested above the U.S. delegations heads, briefly considering the painting on the wall opposite him, before he turned back to the table. It was clear he was not going to discuss any release today.

"This is a mediated meeting to discuss the release of these prisoners," said the head of the UN delegation. "This is the only issue on the current agenda for both parties. If there are other issues, then another meeting must be scheduled with both sides properly informed."

"Can I at least know under which charges you are holding them?" Parkinson asked.

"I am not prepared to discuss it at this point. When the reasons for your aggression on our soil are more clear, then we can discuss your two captured agents."

"They are not agents," Archer reminded the table, the tone in his voice leaving no doubt of his growing frustration. "They are U.S. citizens being held without reason and we believe with no due course."

Mustafa ignored the clarification. "I had planned to come to this meeting to discuss the activities of these, as you call them, citizens of the United States. But with the developments this morning…"

"What developments?" Archer demanded. The Secretary of State leaned forward between Archer and Mustafa.

"What right does your government have to sabotage us, a small nation, without provocation? What defense do you have for this espionage and these acts of destruction?"

"Those are not the issue of this conference." The United Nations delegate collected himself. "Those are not under discussion today, president. Secretary of State. If we could stay on topic, then we will achieve more."

"President," Parkinson said with a stern and steady voice. "We both know that those men are innocent of any charges that you have leveled at them. By not negotiating their release, you only draw more heat on yourself."

"That is not how I see it." Mustafa glanced at each of their faces, and at the United Nations delegation, then sipped the glass of water in front of him. He put it back gently and placed his hands on the table, the fingers entwined. And with that the president had all but declared the meeting over. Mustafa refused to budge. Any other questions just repeated the same circle he'd laid out.

"What the hell was that?" Archer demanded from the Secretary of State as soon as they were in the car. "How the hell did we walk out of that room knowing less than when we entered?"

"Calm, Archer."

"You want me to be calm after that? After that… atrocity in there?"

"I want to be able to get to the bottom of this, not have to watch out for the behavior and comments of my ambassador."

The rest of the drive across the city to the embassy was in silence. They both knew what would happen next. And time was of the essence. Together they worked the phones between the U.S. embassies in the region, speaking to the other ambassadors to gauge the political climate of recent days, with another line open to Washington. Another ran connected to London. Parkinson's assistant kept an eye on the media outlets. It wasn't too difficult; for almost a decade the only news outlets in Eritrea were the state sanctioned ones.

"Egypt says there hasn't been anything of note, but the railway attack was peculiar."

"Ethiopia says something similar."

"Have you spoken to Sudan?"

"Not yet. Yemen?"

"Yemen says it's not common for a ship of that size to be docked that far north."

"Where should it be?"

"In the archipelago."

"You call Sudan. I'll talk to Saudi Arabia."

"What about Israel?"

"These two first. We need to prepare the answering statement immediately. We can contact Israel after that, if needed."

"It's on," the assistant called out. Parkinson and Archer exchanged a glance then walked over to the couch facing the wall-mounted television. President Mustafa stood in front of the palace, the ever-present general behind him on his left, his other minister to his right.

"He knows how to make an event out of everything," Parkinson muttered.

"He's spent decades doing it."

"Earlier this morning our nation suffered its second attack within a week," Mustafa said on the television. He paused and looked around, letting the words from his deep baritone carry across the crowd of media gathered before him.

*

Mahmoud Mustafa moved from his small village outside Asmara to enroll in the university several years after the first shots were fired at Mount Adal. After one semester of his political science degree, he found himself getting more involved with the underground activity helping the revolutionaries. At the end of his first year of study, he backpacked up the horn of Africa, having no money for bus fares, and found himself in Cairo. He never returned for the rest of his classes. He spent his days working on a farm and learning political ideology from the retired professors who ran the farm.

Mustafa soaked up everything. He read textbooks on political theory, philosophy, history, Marx, Machiavelli, Napoleon, Caesar, and military tactics late into the night then woke early to tend to the herd of cattle. Just by engaging in conversation with the professors over several months, he managed to learn more than he would have if he'd stayed at the university. After five months work, and having read every book on the professor's shelves, they gave him enough for a bus ticket to Syria. One of the professor's old colleagues owned a place outside Palmyra. Mustafa spent the next eighteen months learning what he could from the guerrillas in the region and developing his own political ideologies. He would stay awake with the other young guerrillas, then once they'd fallen asleep, he would read into the night and write out his own notes. At three in the morning he would finally sleep for a few hours before the sun came up.

The land he'd left years earlier was changed. By the time he returned it was a country torn apart by the liberation movement and guerrilla warfare. The control of Haile Selassie and the grip of the Ethiopian army held firm but was increasingly under attack. They were striking against the civilians in the villages where they thought the rebels were hiding, and razing any building, farm or crop they suspected was aiding the guerrillas.

The rains came early in January '76 and stalled the movement of the EPLF through the towns and villages. In the months leading up to the end of the year the liberation movement had been slowly making small strategic strikes against the Ethiopian army. It was a slow burning plan. Each strike in itself wasn't a huge win but with a longer goal in mind it was all adding up. The early rains brought a halt to the plan.

After three weeks without much action and the now flowing rivers blocking the path they'd drawn out, there was nothing else to be done for now. Tensions within the camp were growing. The Ethiopian army had been busy during the year and the emotional toll of each of the massacres on the morale of the revolutionaries, the independence fighters, was felt after each one.

In mid-February, after another two strikes against Ethiopian military divisions, the retaliation came for those two strikes and, though it went mostly unspoken, Sa'id's crazed night of bloodlust where he torched the barracks. The branches of the EPLF were all making their way into the highlands when they heard about the Ethiopian army's attack in Asmara and the surrounding villages. The military rolled into the villages and opened fire on schools and homes when they knew people would be in class or at home. In Asmara, they waited for the holy day and fired upon the congregation in the churches throughout the city.

During a direct combat with EPLF and ELF in Woki Duba, the Ethiopian army turned their arms on the church where the townspeople had taken refuge from the gunfire in the streets. The screams were still ringing out as the dust and light pierced the walls of the church when the sounds of the Ethiopian army's retreat had faded. The next month the people of Agordat suffered through the same strategy from the Ethiopians.

In August, further to the west in Om Hajer, the townspeople were taken out to the riverside and interrogated about the presence of the liberation fronts. The men were lined up along the river so they wouldn't be able to run. When the general didn't get the answers he wanted he ordered his men to fire at the unarmed villagers, killing two hundred and fifty of the population.

They were acts of desperation. Fighting both the Eritrean People's Liberation Front and the Eritrean Liberation Front had left the Ethiopian military in a vulnerable position, and they weren't sure where to begin stopping their influence. At times it seemed that attacking the civilians, who mostly supported the liberation movement was their only clear plan. Despite the civilian support, the movement hadn't had any clear gains for sometime. The war of attrition was going nowhere and Abraha and his followers were growing weary. Each attack now needed to be more direct, more resolute and with a larger strategic purpose. The second half of the year had been spent designing these overall attacks and orchestrating the larger plans.

The hierarchy of the EPLF had never fully recovered since the death of Hamid Idris Awate. His charisma and unifying vision had drawn together so many of the liberation fighters under the same philosophy. It was for his vision that they still fought. It was for that philosophy and vision that the different parties had put their differences aside. The need to liberate their country and people was far more important than factional control over the movement. It was all silently agreed on, but after a decade of fighting, and with the influx of a new generation of revolutionaries whose ideals had been shaped by growing up in a country consumed with guerrilla warfare, there was rising tension.

Mustafa's place in the leadership circle of a dozen or so leaders was secured by his political intellect, but his ambition to lead the entire front was never taken seriously by Abraha and other members of the old guard of the EPLF. Mustafa had found a valuable ally in Sa'id. As the rains came down Sa'id and Mustafa would retreat to the far end of the farmhouse to discuss their own philosophies on Eritrean liberation. The plans they presented to the strategists in the guerrilla hierarchy were eventually dismissed.

The next step in Abraha's strategy involved sabotage. The mission was for Mustafa, Sa'id and three others to strike the roads near the rivers leading into Barentu. With those roads taken out, appearing to all onlookers as if it was due to the road conditions giving way with the recent rains, the advancing divisions of the Ethiopian army would be delayed and then forced to take another route into the city. That route would be patrolled by the EPLF who would organize an ambush.

It was simple, but not without risk. Mustafa was well known to the Ethiopians and there was little doubt that Sa'id was now on at least one of their files after the last year's activity. The intelligence collected by the EPLF showed that the Ethiopian army had only a few connections in Barentu.

This wasn't the way Mustafa wanted to approach it. He saw an opportunity to work with the other liberation front on the opposite side of the country, to the north on the coast, as being more important at this point. Several months ago the plan was still to capture these towns in the regions around Barentu. In principle, Mustafa agreed with that. But with more recent developments along the northern coast and armed altercations between the Ethiopian army and members of the ELF, Mustafa thought the EPLF should reassess and support their brothers in arms, splitting into divisions if needed. The ensuing battles in the north would certainly provide enough distraction to the Ethiopian army, no matter their size, to sabotage the bridges and roads like Abraha planned.

His arguments were shot down in a vote, nine to three. He wondered if that was why he was out leading the small group in the rain along the highways into Barentu, being sent on this mission more as an errand to put him in his place. At least Sa'id had volunteered to join him. The other two were recruits to the movement who had been with them for the last six months.

There were three roads into Barentu, meaning three that needed to be destroyed. The first highway to the south-west was easy enough to destroy. The dam further up river was on aging foundations. It didn't take much to set the waters racing down the hillside and across the already eroded road.

The four guerrillas walked into Barentu and spent the night in the apartment of a sympathizer in the south of the city before leaving at sunrise to take out the bridge on the south-east. It was dark and overcast when they came to the banks of the river. A faint red glow hung on the eastern horizon. Shadows stretched long. The rain came down lightly, getting in between everything and making the guerrillas' clothes stick to their skin. The four were walking separately, spread out over a hundred feet. Sa'id was the first to see the bridge and the lone military vehicle to the side of it. He signaled to the other three to stand back along the banks as he climbed the hill.

There was one soldier leaning against the front of the truck smoking a cigarette. Sa'id looked around from beneath the railing on the bridge. There had to be another soldier. He spotted him in the bushes, relieving himself against a tree twenty yards away. Sa'id fired at the smoker first, knowing the other soldier would take longer to react. The gunshot split the unearthly silence with a loud crack. He hit him with two shots to the chest while still hiding beneath the railing. The soldier hit the ground, the cigarette rolling from his lips, before he'd even had a chance to reach for his firearm. The other soldier called out, and turned while trying to pull up his trousers, moving just enough to take Sa'id's next shot in the shoulder instead of his chest. Sa'id fired again as the soldier reached for his weapon but it was too late.

Sa'id fired two more rounds into the soldier's chest and head for good measure. He reached down and picked the pack of cigarettes from the first soldier's chest pocket and lit one, then pulled the soldier's weapon from his holster. The first guerrilla had reached the bridge and scurried up the bank to the railing. His pistol was drawn, looking around for any other soldiers in the undergrowth. Sa'id weighed the soldier's pistol in his hand then fired at the guerrilla, sending him falling over the railing to the rocks below. The second guerrilla took a shot in the leg when he reached the bridge, then another to the head, flicking his head back before collapsing to the asphalt in a pool of blood. He was soaking in his own blood before he'd even realized Sa'id was the triggerman.

Mustafa approached the bridge carefully. He crept beneath it to the opposite side and peered over the railing with his pistol drawn. He could only see Sa'id standing, smoking calmly next to a slain soldier. Mustafa looked around, ears pricked to the deathly silence, waiting to decide if it was safe. He climbed up the bank, still hidden behind the Ethiopian truck. Sa'id looked over at Mustafa and tossed him the cigarette pack and lighter. Mustafa saw the Ethiopian firearm on the hood of the truck in front of him.

"You shot them?"

Sa'id nodded. "They had to die."

Mustafa leaned against the truck and lit a cigarette. They smoked in silence as the red in the sky dissolved to the grey and blue of the season. When they'd taken what they could from the bodies, Mustafa and Sa'id rolled the army truck back ten yards and repositioned the soldiers' bodies. Sa'id ripped open the fuel line and Mustafa cut a hole in the fuel can to make sure the rest of the gas followed down the sides of the bridge. They walked back along the river side as the bridge burned behind them.

Mustafa and Sa'id returned to camp after sundown, walking the entire way to stay off the highways and avoid any military on the way. Anyone else coming upon the scene would simply put the whole scenario down to an unfortunate meeting. It was just two guerrillas in the wrong place, both unprepared for the situation, and two soldiers that were able to stop them before they reached their destination.

When Mustafa and Sa'id stumbled into the mess hall their blood stained clothes caught attention immediately. Mustafa, a scowl on his face and a mighty storm of fury brewing above his head, walked straight up to the table where Abraha and the other ten leaders ate.

"What happened?" Abraha asked.

"You should know," Mustafa hissed at him.

"How could I know?"

"There was an ambush."

"And how was I meant to know?"

"You sent us into it based on your intelligence. You might have a problem with me or my ideas,"

Mustafa growled. "But sending us on a mission you knew would fail, and losing two other liberation soldiers, to prove a point, to try to get rid of me. That's just cowardly."

Abraha was taken back. The mere suggestion that he didn't care for the loss of life of his fellow freedom fighters, especially after he'd seen his friends and comrades killed over the last decade and a half took him aback.

"You're not fit for leadership," Mustafa said then turned out of the hall, the attention of everyone following him. The mess hall was silent. Abraha sat back down shocked. That there had been an attack, that men had lost their lives, was enough of a shock. But the personal attack had hit him just as hard. Abraha's mind whirled back through the details, the intelligence; the locations of the major military divisions; the way the pieces of the plan had fit together in the whole larger scheme. The plan had been simple. The margin for error was almost nil.

"Perhaps tomorrow we should reassess the overall strategy," Simeon suggested.

"That might be a good idea," someone else said as Abraha sat at the small table, numb, and trying to think of what he had overlooked. He'd lost his appetite completely. He excused himself from the table and went to his quarters. That was the moment he would think back to and label as the point his authority started to slip.

*

"Earlier this morning our nation suffered its second attack within a week." Mustafa looked across the audience packed together in front of the palace. The gathered crowd stretched across the small piazza and into the surrounding streets. Soldiers stood around as always. A small group of reporters were pooled closer to the podium. It was a larger media contingent than usual and that's what Mustafa had been counting on. The state controlled media didn't need such a large spectacle, though that never stopped Mustafa making these sorts of declarations when he wanted. But since the international media were already here for the meetings with the United Nations, Mustafa thought he'd take advantage of it.

"While the smoke still pours from the fires and our brave soldiers fight the flames back from the farms nearby," he continued with his fist clenched like a preacher with an enthralled congregation, "our peaceful navy came under attack. This morning an Eritrean vessel was docked near Alghiena. It was attacked without provocation. This is a direct and undeniable attack on the peaceful nation of Eritrean."

Mustafa looked around at the crowd, pausing for effect and waiting for just a moment. Flashes fired from the media pit. He continued. "These attacks will not go without retribution. The Eritrean people deserve their reply. We will not stand by as our peaceful region of this world is drawn into conflict once again by outside forces. Eritrea deserves better than that. The people of Africa deserve better. The member nations of the Arab League deserve better."

A roar went up around the piazza. General Sa'id pushed a smile away from his thin lips and remained at attention as the President leaned forward on the podium once again. "Eritrea will not tolerate these tactics of intimidation or espionage. It is time for the people of Africa to wrestle control of our own destiny back from outside influence."

Archer sat back on the couch and ran his hands through his hair. "Now he's claiming that not only civilians are spies but that it's an attack too?"

"It's one way to make an argument for a bigger role in the Arab League."

"You think that's all it is?"

"I'm not saying it's that simple," Parkinson said. "He's a dangerous man and we shouldn't assume that his argument will fail, or that others will see through it so quickly."

Archer chewed his lip. "He never…

"He said enough," Parkinson said. "He's gone on the offensive here, and now it's going to take more to stake our position. The words are out there and there are some who will take what he says seriously. He's put us in a position where we have to prove the claims are outrageously false, instead of him having to prove their validity."

Parkinson's assistant looked up from the laptop on the table. "Sudan has issued a statement in support of Eritrea."

Parkinson leaned over and quickly read the press release. "Call the ambassador in Khartoum," he said to Archer. "I'll call the White House."

9

Once the Soviets had withdrawn their support for the Ethiopians in late 1990, it was only a matter of time before their forces fell. The Ethiopian army lost morale without the larger force behind it and crumbled under fresh attacks from the liberation movement. Then the Ethiopian regime collapsed. In May 1991, the war of independence was officially over. The Bush administration oversaw talks that lead to the referendum and with less than one per cent voting against a separate Eritrean state, the liberation movement had succeeded after three decades of fighting.

Mahmoud Mustafa claimed office immediately. His position as the head of the EPLF was unquestioned. Any challenge would have been quickly defeated by the newly appointed General Sa'id. The General's power and ruthlessness had only grown since being appointed the most senior rank of a legitimate national military. No longer was he limited to the means available in

guerrilla warfare. Now he was able to command entire
divisions of the Eritrean army, direct fleets and order
strikes from the air force.

The forces were small, that was to be expected.
But the conscription laws that were passed to build the
military against any counterattack from the Ethiopians
in the west or Sudanese in the north were building the
size of the Eritrean military at an impressive rate.
Mustafa placed his valued comrades in high-ranking
ministry positions and assumed the position that was
rightfully his – the office of the President of Eritrea.
Officially, the position was temporary.

The arrival of the end of the war of
independence did not necessarily lead straight to the
arrival of peace. There were various factions of the
major liberation movements and even splinter groups of
the EPLF that all demanded a voice in the new republic.
Mustafa allowed them to speak but rarely listened to
what they had to say. As he saw it, the leadership he
had provided while fighting for liberation from
Ethiopia, and the way the other liberation movements
had been annexed or faded out on their own, was a
mandate for his rule.

It took three years until the dust of the liberation
movement began to settle. There were still some details
that were unclear, and disagreements over the exact
location of Eritrean borders. There was a sense of
paranoia that Mustafa carried with him, though he saw

it more as the precision of being careful. He'd been a wanted man since his early twenties but most of that time had been as a guerrilla fighter. Now he was the leader of a country and those who had once fought with him still dreamed foolishly of being part of some coalition.

The first whispers he heard of some sort of coup or uprising came through Sa'id's network of intelligence. All of the major members of the former liberation front were under some sort of surveillance, incarcerated in a state prison or otherwise accounted for. Several had taken roles in his administration and as hard as they worked, their roles were almost entirely in title only, particularly when it came to international issues. Others had fled across the borders to Sudan, Yemen or further north to Egypt.

Then there were the few who were too prominent or in too much of a volatile situation to be taken care of in the more traditional ways. Liberation leaders like Hamid Abraha. If any movement against their personal safety was to be made, particularly a fatal one, then their followers would more than likely incite massive unrest. Mustafa was forced to keep them in close quarters.

This information from Sudan wasn't Abraha's style. Abraha's approach was more direct. He insisted on negotiations and discussions that would bring about a democratic understanding. There was a lot of work to do until Eritrea was the democratic republic that Abraha and the other founders of the liberation movement had envisioned. Abraha was the only one still able to envision it. And he had taken it upon himself to ensure that the road to democracy was still being paved. Mustafa would have found these meetings and rallies much more endearing if they weren't so time consuming and persistent.

Mustafa still had concerns over the Ethiopian border but if a more direct threat was going to come from further north, then all attention would be turned towards Sudan. Mustafa released a decree claiming Sudan was housing a terrorist cell. He cut diplomatic ties and mobilized the military. The conscription rates kept the nation ready for any attack that may come, and ready to fire back if provoked. Sa'id kept the intelligence coming and Mustafa delivered impassioned pleas to the Eritrean people to ensure the Eritrean nation remained as solidified as it had been when they celebrated the victory of independence in the streets. The threats to his leadership weren't welcome, but he found that he could use these to his benefit if he played his cards right.

Mustafa kept the nation in a state of alarm for two years. Two years to lobby for entry into the Arab League as a full member status. Two years to entertain Abraha and his fellow revolutionaries and their plans for democracy. Two years to delay elections and the

implementation of the newly written Eritrean
constitution. Then two years later the terrorist cells
were flushed out. The threat was nullified and Mustafa
held more power over the nation than he had at the
beginning.

Hamid Abraha walked quickly down the street
sticking closely to the walls of the building and
crossing the street with his head down before slipping
into the mosque. Walking in the shadows had become a
habit now for over half his life and now he did it
without thinking. He walked along the right hand wall
inside the mosque sand through the small wooden door
into the back room. It was one of the few places the
leaders of the three major anti-Mustafa liberation fronts
could meet and discuss their strategies and philosophies
freely. Abraha thought he would be the last one to
arrive but there were only three other men in room
waiting for him. The chair for Yemane Tadese was still
empty.

The mood at these meetings was always stern
but some somber mood lingered like a layer of dust that
afternoon. Abraha didn't pick up on it immediately.

"Should we start, or wait for Yemane?"

"You didn't hear?"

"Hear what?" Abraha looked up, realizing for
the first time that the other men looked particularly
strained today. Between them they'd served in the war
of independence and now the war of democracy.

"Yemane was found last night strung up by the neck inside the warehouse that prints the Eritrean Sun in what the media are calling a cowardly suicide to avoid facing his crimes against the state and the president," said Hamid Isaak, his voice dry and tired.

"His suicide note called for an end to the protests and a full support behind Mustafa," added Dawit Himid.

Abraha sat down, taking it in for a minute. "Sa'id?"

"Unofficially," said Isaak. "And without a doubt. But they were never going to print that. And no journalist will make that connection, none based in this country, especially if they've seen the body."

Abraha didn't even want to ask about the body. "And they expect people to believe that he decried the protests and marches he was leading last month?"

"Either that," Isaak said, "or to realize the ruthlessness behind his killing and take it as a warning."

"It's a hell of a way to send a warning."

"Sa'id doesn't mess around."

Abraha reached for a glass and poured himself some water. Tadese had been one of his closest confidants even if their ideologies didn't line up perfectly. When facing a tyrant like the one Mustafa had grown into, these smaller differences didn't particularly matter.

Tadese had joined the liberation front barely half a year after Mustafa and had seen the same transformation from freedom fighter to self-serving tyrant. The news of his death came extra hard to Abraha since he'd spoken at length with Tadese that morning over coffee about the futility of the protests. Tadese had secured some political backing from Sudan who offered to help Tadese's rebel force with military backing.

For years the Sudanese had provided unofficial financial backing to Tadese's rebel group. Now Tadese had been promised official backing from their military, giving much needed strength against the firepower Sa'id wielded. Abraha had warned against it, saying it would retrocede Eritrea into another war for independence, this time from their own government. And, depending on who ruled Sudan when the fighting ended, leave them in debt to a regime whose involvement they didn't want. Tadese said it was something to consider, and shouldn't be dismissed so quickly; desperate times, he'd said, call for desperate actions.

"You think Sa'id did this in retaliation for just a week of protests?"

"I think it was a wider warning," Himid said. "Something to send a message to all of us."

"You're the only one of us that Mustafa respects enough to meet with regularly," Isaak said.

"This is a message to those he can't regularly attempt to intimidate in the palace."

"And how do you plan to react?"

"Personally, I'm watching my back and not doing anything for a few months," said Ibrahim Tadese, Yemane's younger brother. "I almost didn't come at all today and won't be here for the foreseeable future."

"We can't let these actions influence us."

"No?" Ibrahim asked. "We can't?

"We can't be intimidated by this kind of violence," Isaak said. "Or else we might as well resign ourselves living under this tyrannical rule."

"I'm not suggesting we surrender," Ibrahim said. "But we need a different tactic and I don't see any way forward with the same tactics we've been using. I can no longer condone these same protests. They're becoming pointless. We protested and rallied in Asmara and Keren for ten days and it raised no response from the palace."

"I can understand that you'd easily feel that way--"

"You can empathize, but you can't understand," Ibrahim said. "My brother was killed last night. You might say that it's a warning, that it's just a notice of caution, but it feels more like being sliced open with a blade for me."

The issue was not up for discussion. His mind would not be changed. The involvement of the Tadese name with the fight for Eritrean democracy died at the end of a rope, strung up above the warehouse of the last publication resembling anything of an independent press in Eritrea.

Three days passed without much noise from the regime or the rebel groups. The palace allowed a small and quiet funeral for Yemane Tadese two days after his body was found, but all reports of it were entirely blacked out in the media. Police and soldiers were located nearby to ensure the funeral didn't turn into another protest. Officially they were there to protect the mourners but the real message was clear. And there was little enthusiasm from the protestors.

Tadese's commitment to his country and the freedom of its people was renown. Never had the regime made such a strike against a prominent member of the rebels. There had been damage to property, arrests and other acts of intimidation. But Tadese's murder was something else completely. It was a direct strike against one of the popular leaders of the movement. It was more than a warning. It was a direct message of fear. General Sa'id was growing more and more brazen.

The monthly meeting between Abraha and Mustafa was scheduled for Wednesday afternoon. Mustafa had never succeeded in intimidating him. Once he'd begun to see through Mustafa's tactics and lies, he'd learned to avoid them. It became clear as the years

went by. It was clear once Abraha had realized the
control of the Liberation Front was slipping from his
grasp. Once he was removed from the leadership and
the blinding tasks of directing a plan of attack against
the occupying Ethiopian military, Mustafa's tactics
became immediately clear.

Despite that resilience, and insight into the way
Mustafa dealt with those he commanded, there had
been sleepless nights for Abraha since Tadese's funeral.
It was true that Mustafa respected, and perhaps still
feared, Abraha enough to meet with him, but it was
more of a strategy of keeping friends close and enemies
closer. Mustafa knew that fear was part of his
foundation for rule. Mustafa also knew that a strike
against Abraha in the same way he'd dealt with Tadese
would not pass so easily. There was a reason Tadese
was the one Mustafa had ordered to be executed and not
the more popular leader. Perhaps it was to do with a
link to Sudan. Perhaps it was testing the ground for
wider bloodshed. The truth remained that Abraha's
followers were more vocal, more loyal and even
numbered within his own support base.

Mustafa had to entertain Abraha almost as a
necessity to retain control and not let the peace he
controlled slip into an entire bloodshed. Would that
have happened if Abraha had been killed instead? It
was possible, but completely unknown. The extent of

Abraha's followers was never clear, but Mustafa himself would not test those waters.

Abraha waited in the usual foyer and waited for Mustafa's assistant to usher him in to the study, to be directed to one of the leather lounges. The wait was not as long as it had been for the last few months. Abraha had become accustomed to waiting for up to an hour for Mustafa's attention. It was the president's way of making sure Abraha knew his place. Of showing the president had business to attend to and that the protests in the street or any negotiation with those political parties not in his own cabinet were not of much interest to him. This week Abraha had to wait barely ten minutes.

"The president will see you now, Mr. Abraha." The assistant had once been a loyal soldier of the liberation front. Abraha recognized him. Now he was currying favors to the president for his own gains, however small they were.

"It saddened me to hear about the suicide of Tadese," Mustafa said. He reclined in the leather chair, motioning for Abraha to sit opposite him, and adjusted his suit jacket.

"I'm sure it did." Abraha looked around and noticed the new addition to the political theory books in the shelves behind him. A new volume of Marx sat on the table between the couches, next to a volume of Maistre.

"There's no need for unpleasantries, Hamid."

"The time has come for you to implement the constitution, Mahmoud. You have single-handedly stopped democracy in our country. You may call your party the People's Front for Democracy and Justice, but a democracy doesn't ignore their constitution, torture and arbitrarily detain citizens, and restrict freedoms of expression, association, and religion. Elections have not been held since Eritrea gained independence in 1993, the constitution has never been implemented, and political parties are not allowed. This is not what we envisioned for our people."

Abraha sat back in the couch. He faced Mustafa squarely and spoke gently, softly enough to make the president sit forward to hear what he was saying. "If you really want to act on your heartfelt sorrow for the... suicide... of Yemane then you should honor it by implementing the constitution that you, and he, and other notable leaders of the war of independence fought for."

Mustafa smiled. Abraha certainly knew how to phrase an argument. "I don't believe this is the right time," Mustafa said with the confidence and aloof air he had been honing. "The nation of Eritrea is not as stable as it may seem. Diplomatic ties with Sudan are still not entirely settled. Ethiopia is still a threat, poised and waiting for any moment of weak leadership to latch on to and exploit. And there is the looming conflict with Yemen. Eritrea requires a strong steady hand."

"A conflict with Yemen?"

Mustafa nodded, shrugging. "It's inevitable."

"The people of Eritrea, President, do not want another conflict. They want their democracy. They want the republic that they were promised to be implemented. The people of Eritrea have suffered for over three decades through an ongoing war of independence, civil wars, and the disputes over the borders. Have they not suffered enough? Do they not deserve the republic they were promised by the People's Liberation Front?"

"Suffering does not lead to freedom in itself, my friend. If the government of Eritrea falters even a little now in this hostile climate in the horn of Africa, then the war of independence may have been fought for naught."

"Every country gets the government it deserves. Are you living up to the kind of leader the Eritrean people deserve?"

For a second Mustafa's expression changed, ready to engage. It was the kind of look that passed over his eyes in the seventies late at night as the guerrilla leaders began the late night philosophical discussion. It was a younger Mustafa, a mind willing to engage in argument and find the best solution. But the look was fleeting and was replaced again with the cool and aloof expression of the leader of the only legal political party in the nation. "I will take your comments into consideration, Hamid. And give it some thought before we meet again."

Out of habit, Abraha didn't go directly home. His home address was known to the regime – that was to be expected. But going directly home, or using the same path as usual, left him open for ambushes. He'd always been careful about that. Abraha left the palace feeling confident about the meeting. But he wasn't sure how far he'd gotten through to Mustafa. That fleeting look, the glance that he was ready to engage with an actual discussion, it gave Abraha some hope.

Abraha turned left outside the palace and walked back towards the docks. He turned right and wandered along the empty business street into the industrial area of the city, close to the port. He wasn't particularly sure where he was going, just knowing that he'd gone right last month, and he had to go a different route. Then when he saw it he realized which way he'd come.

The warehouse was dark. Barely a week earlier it was a whirring force of information, printing pages upon pages each day before being distributed through the city, and trucked across the country to Keren. Other newspapers started going bankrupt or coming under scrutiny the year before. There were few bastions of actual balanced reporting. Now with the Sun closed down and the police tape still on the doors, the media was entirely under the state's control.

Still, Abraha had hope. There were underground meetings, and very small presses. And there was that fleeting look. Maybe he was holding onto that too much. He could be forgiven – there was little to hold onto for hope lately. Abraha played that scene over in his mind as he walked. Was there something he could have done differently? Was there something he could have said that would bring the President around to see the right course of action was to allow democracy?

These questions ran through his mind over and over and before he had realized it, Abraha was standing on the street outside his flat. He'd walked the entire way without being conscious of it. That was a mistake that could have been fatal if he'd wandered into an ambush. It was a moment of distraction that he rarely allowed himself. And while his thoughts were elsewhere, he'd made it all the way home, somehow oblivious to the quiet foreboding stillness of the night. He stood on the pavement, looking up at his apartment and knowing something was wrong – his kitchen light was on.

"Good evening, Hamid." The voice was unmistakable. It spoke before Abraha was even in the room. Then he turned and saw, sitting in the kitchen and calmly sipping a glass of scotch, the small dark eyes of General Sa'id. Something about seeing the

General out of his usual context was disturbing. Having him sitting in the full military regalia that he insisted on wearing at every possibility, even at the small wooden table with the one rotten leg in Abraha's kitchen, was chilling.

"General." Abraha entered cautiously, keeping an eye on the General and looking around for any of his soldiers.

"You can relax, Hamid. It's only us here. But with one signal my men can enter quickly from the car they've parked outside."

"You should have told me you were coming. I could have prepared you something."

"That's not necessary."

Abraha shrugged and reached for a glass from the cabinet above his head. He turned to the sideboard where he kept the scotch. He unscrewed the top and poured it to be half full. He slowly screwed the lid back on and placed it on the sideboard, reached further than needed, his fingers around the metal handle of the revolver. Then he felt the general's left forearm on his back. A blow between the shoulder blades shocked him. Sa'id drew his pistol and had it against Abraha's skull before Abraha had a chance to pull his weapon from the drawer, or even stand up.

"I could fire now and end it." Sa'id forced the words out through his tightly clenched jaw.

"End it right now. Don't think I wouldn't. Don't think I don't want to, that I haven't wanted to have this opportunity for the last two decades. And don't think for one second I haven't already looked for where you keep your weapons, Hamid." Sa'id stepped back, his pistol still trained on the older man. "I could say it was self-defense. I could say anything I want, who's going to stop me? No one could say anything different, and no one would. But I won't."

"Because you're a coward? Because lowly invertebrates don't have spines?"

"Don't test me." Sa'id's words came out slow and firm. There was no mistaking the meaning. "It's only because Mustafa wants you alive. For now." He drained the rest of the glass of scotch before he continued. "But that's the curious thing, you see. What happens to you tonight is not up to me, or the president. He wants you alive, but I couldn't care less either way. So you get to choose.

"Either you get to die a hero of the resistance and commit suicide like your friend. A hero of the resistance," Sa'id repeated it to himself, marveling at the stupidity of the title and the futile death it would represent. "Or you accompany me and you'll be charged with treason."

"Treason?"

Sa'id pulled a document from his coat and read it. "'For the intentional attempt to weaken and

compromise the government and security of the
Eritrean nation.' That's what he's written here." Sa'id
slid the arrest warrant across the table, signed by
Mahmoud Mustafa and dated that same day. "So what
will it be, Hamid? You can finish your drink while you
decide."

10

Hudson woke from a light sleep. He was sore, especially his right shoulder. He and Mervyn had spent two hours in the back of a truck moving weapons and ammunition out from the guards' storage rooms and into the abandoned shack outside the prison walls. Ali had driven, provided cover, and kept the other guards from suspecting anything. Now the shack was stocked with firearms and ammunition and ready for the early morning strike that Hudson had come up with to free the other political prisoners. Abraha had laid low in the shack and organized the crates by weapon type and gauge.

Hudson moved through the small shack towards the front room. A figure seated in the dark at the window gave a start when he entered the room.

"Can't sleep?" Hudson asked Abraha.

"Barely a minute." Abraha was sitting near the window of the darkened guard post. "It's been years since I've been out of that place. You'd think I'd be able to enjoy it. Instead, I just keep sitting here, looking up at the stars and making sure that there aren't any guards coming this way."

"It will take time, I'm sure."

"I think I might have given up hope of getting out of there."

"You don't have to hope any more," Hudson said. "Now you can think about what to do next. Where do you think you'll go?"

Abraha let out a deep sigh. "I hadn't even thought about it. I suppose Mustafa and his general will still be chasing me when he finds out I've escaped. My family, or what was left of it, is probably dead or in another part of the world. Maybe I need to leave the country too."

"Maybe you should get some rest. We'll start moving in an hour."

"It might be too late to get any sleep tonight." Abraha nodded towards the eastern sky. The first strains of the sun were seeping over the horizon. The stars had gone and now the sky was a dull grey. Red streaks had begun to stain the sky.

"What's that old shepherd's saying," Hudson asked. "Red sky at morning, shepherds take warning?"

"I hope it's a warning for them, not for us. But I hope we get our flock out of there."

"I hope you're right." Hudson let out a wry smile.

The plan was to start an hour before the guards' change of shift at dawn. At that point, Ali explained, there would be the fewest number of guards on the grounds for the entire day. If they wait any longer, then they'll be against twice the number. The dawn surprise attack was the best strategy. The entire thing was a crazy idea, Ali had said. They should be halfway across the country in the night so when the General's men came in the morning, they were already gone. But once Abraha had made his case, Hudson had agreed and that was that. There was more to do before they could head across the countryside to the border, or the shelter of the U.S. embassy. And there was still something else Hudson had to do.

The three men split the thermos of coffee and loaf of bread Ali had left them. There was little talking among the three as they drank the coffee and ate the bread. Their appetites were small but they knew it could be quite sometime before they got to eat again. There was a lot at risk, but the payoff was bigger. Freedom for the entire political prisoner population, over ten thousand men, and though they wouldn't all be armed, there'd be enough to overpower the guards.

The sound of Ali's truck rolling down the dirt road rumbled into the heavy silence. There was not much left to say. It was time for action. The truck was loaded with the weapons and ammunition they'd smuggled out hours earlier. Mervyn finished off the coffee then stood up and pulled a rifle over his shoulder. He checked that it was loaded and that he had enough rounds with him, then picked up the other bag Ali had brought him.

"Good luck."

"You too."

Hudson watched him walk out into the morning then disappear into the darkness of the landscape. After little more than thirty feet he was gone, engulfed in that pre-dawn pit of gloom. The red streaks in the sky looked like cuts and abrasions now, from one horizon to the other. Hudson and Abraha climbed into the back and lay flat against the bed of the truck, empty bags covering them. Ali climbed into the front of the truck. He peered against the fog of the morning. He couldn't see Mervyn at all.

He started the truck and rolled back up the dirt road to the checkpoint. Ali had moved one of his other most trusted guards to the checkpoint early in the night. The movement and the frequency with his comings and goings would have drawn attention from anyone else who wasn't also sympathetic with the prisoners. Addis had caught Ali's attention when he was smuggling extra water to the prisoners in the hole the week before. Ali marched Addis into his office for the required disciplining. Addis was a young soldier, barely twenty years old. It was clear he was too liberal for the General's army.

He was one decision away from being in the prison himself, locked up for refusing to serve the required conscription. Ali didn't discipline Addis and because of that he knew he could trust him when he needed a friendly and sympathetic accomplice on the checkpoint.

Addis stood to salute his superior officer. Again he didn't note the comings and going in the log.

"Addis," Ali leaned out of the truck cab and called the younger soldier over.

"Yes, sir?"

Ali lowered his voice. "Something is about to happen," he paused to make sure the message was clear. Addis nodded. "When things happen, you need to not wear your uniform. This is important."

Addis realized just what Ali meant. "Yes, sir. Tell me what you need me to do, sir."

Ali threw him a civilian jacket so he wouldn't freeze in the early morning desert temperature.

"You'll know when it starts. Clear the exits, then come to the southern block."

"Yes, sir."

Donald Mervyn crept up to the fence under the cover of the darkness. When he'd left the hut, he could barely see a few yards in front of him. By the time he'd reached the prison fence he could see the grey outline of the buildings across the fence and the rocks rising further ahead. The complete lack of light only helped him, and so he knew he had to work fast. He was beneath the guard tower by the fence. From the windows, they couldn't see him but in fifteen minutes it would be light enough that any guard patrolling on the ground would be able to see him. Mervyn pulled the wire cutters out from the bag and pushed it up against the wire. The cutters were dull. He had to press hard to get them to even dent the wire let alone cut through the fence. He was unable to wrestle the fence loose in case it made too much noise. Mervyn had to just use blunt force to get through the wire.

The sky had turned a dull grey by the time he'd made the first two incisions. The plan relied completely on his ability to break through this first part of the fence. The hole had to be big enough for him to fit through without rattling the wire too much and attracting the attention of the guards. Mervyn pushed through the fence as the first shadows became clear. It had taken far longer than they'd anticipated and he cursed under his breath, thinking of Hudson and Abraha in the truck, waiting for the signal, wondering what had happened to him. Mervyn climbed through the small hole in the fence as quietly as he could, then pulled the rifle and bags through. He had to work quickly.

He doused the rags from the second bag in the engine oil Ali had given him, then threw them under the stairs to the watchtower. There were a pile of cigarette buts and discarded matches lying in the dirt. He threw the oil around the posts beneath the tower. He lit the next ball of rags and threw it towards the stairs. He was struggling to light the match on the old box when from the corner of his eye he saw a match fall. A guard had stepped out to smoke and had dropped his match on the oily rag. It went up in flames immediately. The blue flame leaped towards the pool of oil and the guard cried out. His cigarette dropped three feet to the right and lit the next rag.

Mervyn had the next match lit instantly and threw it towards the other rags near the tower supports. He pulled the rifle over his shoulder and the bag of ammunition then crept out from the tower along the fence while the guards cried out.

If it was still dark, like they'd anticipated, then Mervyn would still be covered by the shadows. As it was, he had to race for cover before any of the guards saw him. Their attention was drawn to the flames beneath them and covering the only exit from the guard tower. Mervyn waited in the shelter provided for him by the block of cells to the south and watched another patrol of guards come running to help their comrades trapped in the burning tower. The flames had engulfed the steps completely now, and the oil burned at such a high temperature the metal was already bending out of shape.

Ali had sat in the truck for a while watching the sky grow lighter. There was only so long he could stay there before he drew attention. He slammed the door closed and dropped the keys into the truck bed where Hudson lay still.

"I'm going to do a quick round," he mumbled just loud enough for Hudson to hear. Ali walked past a guard patrol who saluted him as they passed. He walked into the guard's kitchen where three patrols of officers were resting around one of the tables.

"We're just taking a break before we do our rounds, sir," one of them informed him.

"No rush, officer."

Ali picked up a mug from the kitchen area and filled it with black coffee. He kept one ear on the conversation between the guards but no one mentioned anything about capturing a prisoner. Ali walked past the table again and closed the door behind him, turning and locking it. He put the coffee down in the hall and left it. He wasn't in the mood for coffee. Ten less guards to deal with could only be a good thing.

When he'd walked back out of the hall and into the yard he heard a shout. A cry. A patrol was running quickly to the eastern tower. They called out to him, pointing and yelling,

"Fire."

Hudson and Abraha were already out of the truck when he got back. Hudson turned quickly when he heard footsteps and aimed the rifle directly at Ali, then dropped it when he realized who it was. He threw the rifle to Ali and picked up another from the back of the truck. "Eight guards ran out of the pit."

"That's half of the ones down there."

"Did you see Mervyn?"

"Not yet, but none of the guards mentioned him."

The sound of footsteps racing along the dirt startled Hudson. He raised the rifle and lined Addis up in his sights, then dropped it again when Addis stopped and raised his arms.

"Sir."

Hudson and Abraha exchanged glances.

"Take these," Hudson handed him half a dozen rifles. "We're arming the prisoners and breaking out of here."

"Yes, sir." Addis let a smile break across his face. Hudson and Abraha picked up as many rifles as they could. "Let's go."

Ali led the way, down into the pit. It got dark quick. There was one dull and flickering light every ten yards. Hudson and Abraha followed Ali as if they were still prisoners with Addis bringing up the rear. Ali took the attention of the first guard and Addis took him out with one shot. The next guard came running from the small station at the sound of the shot, his rifle drawn, but Ali landed the first blow to the stomach before Addis fired again. Hudson was impressed – the kid was a good shot.

They wound down the stairs, unlocking the first shipping container that had been converted to a cell. Ali stepped inside and declared them free men. "We are overthrowing the guards," he cried out. The men were still mostly asleep.

"Take your weapons and climb up the stairs."

Addis led Hudson and Mervyn deeper underground. The air was thick and Hudson found it became harder to breathe the further underground the band descended. Hudson remembered the reports he'd read about there being ten thousand men in this prison. That was the number the regime had not refuted. The real number of men buried in this living coffin, this hellish African gulag was anyone's guess.

Addis greeted each guard and said something Hudson and Mervyn didn't understand. Then, with the guard's attention drawn away, they were dealt with quickly. The next level of prisoners unlocked. The guard's bodies were left in the cells they'd been guarding. By the fifth level under ground, the air was dusty and dank, and each breath was a chore. The light was nearly impossible. Hudson could only make out two steps in front of him.

"Last one," Addis whispered.

"What's all that noise?" a guard called out.

"There's some disturbance," Addis called back into the dull light. "It started in the eastern tower. The prisoners got wind of it."

"There's been nothing down here."

"I've been sent by the major to check."

There was no response. Addis glanced back at Hudson then took a step forward. A shot fired out, leaving a ringing in Hudson's ears.

"You just stay there, officer."

"No need to fire, officer." Addis took an aggressive tone. "How would you explain that to the major?"

"I'm not sure I'd need to." The beam of a flashlight searched the stairs for the group descending. As the beam made its way up and over the wall Mervyn lay down on the stairs, his head at the bottom. He struggled to see anything, even his own hands. He lined his pistol up with the source of the light then fired just above it. A direct hit. The torch fell as the guard's body dropped. The light shone directly into Mervyn's eyes and lit his face up. He had no way to line up his next shot or move away as he lay on the stairs.

Hudson stepped forward and fired into the dull outline of a figure behind the light. The figure dropped his automatic weapon. The guard reached for his pistol but Hudson was quicker, firing again twice and hitting the shoulder, then head. Addis took out the third guard. Mervyn picked himself up from the stairs, brushing the dirt off. He was lucky, he knew it. There was safer ways to break that stand-off but none of them had come to mind.

"Good shot," Mervyn said to Hudson. "Really good shot."

Hudson helped him up, and handed him the flashlight. "Let's unlock these souls and get back to the surface."

*

President Mustafa sat in his usual chair on the balcony with a plate of fruit in front of him. He was a man of habit and ritual. He read through the files his ministers had submitted to him over night. The reports coming from the embassies in Washington and London were encouraging. Mustafa had the international attention he'd been wanting. He had the focus of the international media and other leaders in the region had been speaking out to back his position or, at the very least, contacting him to give their unofficial endorsement. They were watching the developments very closely said the leaders of Sudan and Ethiopia.

Libya had publicly spoken out to support Mustafa and his cries of too much foreign influence.

"Good morning, President," the General said as he climbed the stairs.

"Good morning, General."

The second pot of coffee arrived as the General sat down and looked through the newspapers laid out on the table.

"I heard there were some protests last night." Mustafa said it in a casual manner as if asking the General about his evening meal.
"Small ones, president. A group of hoodlums were looting the city center. There was some property damaged but they have been apprehended and dealt with."

"Very good," Mustafa said, not even looking up from the report from the Parisian embassy.

Small protests were a rare occurrence but they never bothered Mustafa. The military squashed any unrest before they got to a point of posing any real threat to his hold on power. Even the protests during the Arab Spring that had raged on for five days in Asmara and three days in Keren had barely caught Mustafa's attention. They'd burned cars and buildings two blocks from the palace.

The noise and smoke from the explosions were bothersome but as far as being an actual threat to his power or his day-to-day habits, the protestors never posed a threat. The general had taken care of it. The last member of the foreign press had left Eritrea the year before and since the only media that remained was state controlled, the protests and deaths were easy enough to wash away. The only reason the protests the night before had caught Mustafa's attention was because of the presence of the UN dignitaries and the foreign media in Asmara.

A junior officer called up to the balcony from the courtyard. "General Sa'id?"

"Yes?" Sa'id leaned over the railing and looked down.

"There's an urgent message for you, sir."

"Excuse me, president." Sa'id descended the stairs to the courtyard.

"General," the officer said, holding out a piece of paper. "There's been a fire reported at a prison."

"Thank you, officer." Sa'id took the faxed memo from the officer. "That will be all." He started reading over the message as he climbed the stairs to the president's balcony. Mustafa put down the Washington Post and picked up the Corriere Della Sera. "Are we meeting with the UN delegates today?"

Sa'id was reading over the memo.

"General?"

"Yes, president?"

Mustafa looked up and saw Sa'id's furrowed brow reading over the memo. "What is it?"

"There's a fire at Adersesr."

"Just a fire?"

"Three guards were killed in the flames."

"That's unfortunate." Mustafa turned back to his paper.

"It's not that, president. That's where the Americans are being held."

"They weren't hurt, were they?"

"No." "So, we'll just keep it from the international media. They don't need to know."

"Of course." Sa'id sighed. "That's not what I'm worried about, president."

Mustafa put the newspaper back on the table. "Is there something else I need to be informed about?"

"Nothing else, president. I'm just concerned about the security of the prison. Two suspected spies, the largest collection of political prisoners in the country. It could be problematic if this fire wasn't accidental."

"Suspected spies, general?"

Sa'id shrugged. "Spies."

"Does the memo say anything about the cause of fire being suspicious?"

"It doesn't say anything about the cause."

"In my experience," Mustafa said, "that means there is nothing else to worry about."

Sa'id nodded and sipped his coffee. The president turned back to his paper. There were so many times before that the president had proven right. His intuition and leadership had gone hand in hand many times before and Sa'id always stood by Mustafa. There was something bothering him about this. Second guessing the president never led to anything beneficial. Any time that the president had dismissed something and Sa'id still felt troubled about it, the situation dissolved into nothing. The president had been right. But still, even after reminding himself of this, Sa'id couldn't shake the ominous feeling hanging around.

"What time are the meetings this morning?"

"At eleven. Do you want me to move them back?"

Mustafa chewed his lip and flicked through the Washington Post. "No. There's no need to change any schedules."

Sa'id nodded. He answered the president's questions, then excused himself and went back to his office. He closed the door and picked up the phone to dial the extension to Adersesr. It rang five times before it was answered.

"This is General Sa'id," he said immediately, cutting off the officer answering. "Update me on the situation with the fire, officer."

"Yes, sir." The guard reacted immediately to Sa'id's tone. "The fire is under control and has been extinguished."

"What damage?"

"Just the one watch tower, sir. There were no casualties."

"The other memo mentioned there were guards trapped in the tower."

"Yes, sir. They were rescued. Two have been treated for smoke inhalation. They're being taken care of, sir."

"No other damage?"

"None, sir."

"Why did it take you so long to answer the phone, officer?"

"I apologize, sir. There has been a lot of movement this morning and all guards have been mobilized to secure that wing."

"I understand, officer."

Sa'id hung the phone on the hook and leaned back in his chair. The president was right. There was nothing to worry about. Sa'id looked to the clock above the bookcase. There were still two hours until the next meeting with the ambassador and the UN dignitaries and a lot of work to do before then.

*

The remaining guards were put in the prison block that Abraha and Hudson had been locked in only the day before. Hudson and Abraha handed out cups of water and what food they could find to all the prisoners.

Suddenly they had over ten thousand men to feed. Their lips were dry and beards unkempt. The men blinked hard against the light of the new morning as they sat around the prison blocks.

"Where's Addis?" Mervyn asked.

"In the office," Ali said. "We had to keep the communications manned. Some news got out about the fire before we stormed the under ground cells."

"Should we expect company?"

Ali shook his head. "Addis has been broadcasting news of the fire but a stable recovery."

"Hudson? A word?"

Hudson nodded and followed Mervyn around the corner. "What they do doesn't necessarily affect us," Mervyn said. His hand was around Hudson's forearm, gripping tightly. "We have our own objectives. We can't forget that."

"There's time," Hudson urged. "Abraha helped us. I think it's only fair we help him."

"We liberated him an army," Mervyn said. "I don't know how much more we can do."
Hudson looked around at the thousands of political prisoners now sitting in the sun for the first time in God knows how long.

"And we don't know how much time the kids have." This last point hit Hudson hard. He knew Mervyn was right. But leaving Abraha here didn't seem right either.

"What if they can help us?"

"How?"

"Numbers would help us."

"Some would. Not this many. It would only make it more difficult."

"Of course not this many. There are thousands here."

Addis came running from the building. He was out of breath when he reached Ali and Hudson but couldn't keep the sparkle from his eye.

"What is it?" Ali demanded.

"The general called, but I told him everything was under control."

"Good. Wait – which general?"

"Sa'id," Addis nodded.

"And he didn't suspect anything?"

"It didn't sound like it. He sounded concerned, but I assured him it was under control."

Ali sighed. "I'm glad you were on the radio."

"That's not the good news." Addis looked around. "I was talking to other officers stationed near Asmara. There were riots last night. The military squashed most of the uprising but it's still going in parts."

Ali's eyes were wide. He looked at Abraha. "So…"

"So," Addis continued before anyone could stop him. "A movement is underway that are not expecting another ten thousand to join them. And most of the army are mobilized from the bases outside Asmara. Their security is low."

The question of what next had lingered in the mind of all of them before they'd smuggled themselves back into Adersesr but not one had for a moment considered that a rebellion would already be underway in the capital city.

"Most of these men are not fit for raiding the presidential palace," Mervyn said. "Most of them need medical treatment. They could barely walk around the yard, let alone over throw the government. And then there's the question of how to get ten thousand men there."

"I know how we can," Addis said. "If we can convince everyone to join them in Asmara."

"I don't think that should be a problem," Abraha smiled. "That's what we've been living for all this time. Let me talk to them."

Ali nodded, and led the older man to the closest tower, looking over the sea of prisoners. He handed Abraha a megaphone. "They're all yours."

"Gentleman," Abraha said. With all these eyes on him, his voice found a strength that his frail frame had obscured. "My name is Hamid Abraha and I am glad to say we are all free men."

A hushed reverence spread through the crowd before a cheer went up at the mention of freedom. A small chant of "A-bra-ha, A-bra-ha," passed around the crowd. "Is that really him?" Hudson heard someone say, followed by someone else saying, "I thought he'd died." "It is him," several voices exclaimed. Mervyn exchanged glances with Hudson. Perhaps there was something more worthwhile than cutting and running. Perhaps Jones had been right.

With all of the surviving guards locked in the cells, the prison was quiet and deserted. Addis worked the front gate. His plan was simple – since the other prisons had heard about the fire and the damage to the prison, Addis simply radioed the surrounding prisons and requested several trucks from each. With unrest in the capital growing, there wasn't time to check orders. The vehicles were transported without guards since, as Addis had instructed, the guards at Adersesr would be sufficient.

The small fleet of trucks at Adersesr, the ones Hudson Jones knew only too well, were quickly filled by those eager to storm the presidential palace, to join with those who had already begun the uprising to gain control of their city. Over a thousand men had fit together in those over packed tin vehicles as they'd headed out into the desert.

"I don't know whether to be happy or sad," Abraha said to Hudson as they watched the last of the trucks disappear into the horizon. "It seems we've been fighting for independence for so long. Then when we got it, we had to fight for it again against ourselves. I'd hoped that by the time I got to this age the fighting would be over."

The first trucks from the other bases arrived in little over an hour. Addis checked the paperwork then gave them directions to the other wing of the prison. That's where the men were waiting. Those willing and able to storm the capital were waiting for extra trucks. Those who were too frail, weak or old were staying at the prison in the guard towers and keeping the prison secure.

Once the first two trucks had wound their way around the prison it was easy to disarm them. Extra guard outfits were used by the prisoners to keep up appearances but once the visiting guards were out of the vehicle, there was no mercy shown. Their bodies were dragged into the shipping containers beneath the ground. The trucks were filled up as soon as they were parked and then headed back into the desert, taking the southern road. Slowly, waves of men, political prisoners locked up by Mustafa's regime, were heading towards the rioting and smoke filled streets of Asmara.

"Sir," Addis called out after the third wave of men had left Adersesr. "There's reports the president is on the move."

"Where to?"

"They only say the convoy headed west."

"West?" Ali looked at Addis. "What's out west for them to head to?" Ali and Hudson looked over the map pinned to the wall. There were no bases or major cities for a long way. Ali pointed to the next town west across the map. "There's no chance a man like Mustafa will risk being open for that long a time."

"West of Asmara?" Abraha asked, looking up from the desk as he slowly made the connection. "I think I know."

*

Haile Sa'id straightened his uniform then knocked briskly three times on the president's door. He gripped the brass handle and pushed it open. The president sat in his usual place on the couch with one leg up on the leather cushion. The newspapers that he'd been reading at breakfast were in a pile on the coffee table beneath the folder in which Sa'id had placed the UN brief. Mustafa put down the book he was reading when Sa'id entered the room.

"Is it time?" Mustafa looked down at his gold watch.

"It is. But I don't think we can." While he spoke that last part, Sa'id's voice trailed off.

Mustafa looked at Sa'id blankly.

"That is to say, sir, that we're unable."

"Why not?"

"I'm sorry?"

"Why not, general?"

Sa'id strode across the room to the full-length windows and pulled the curtains back. "The city is in flames, president. They are calling for blood in City Square."

Mustafa looked out the windows with his hands on his hips. He rocked lightly backwards on his heels and took in the clouds of smoke rising from the city.

"I see you haven't had the ability to take control of this."

"It's escalated, President." Sa'id's tone was firm.

"Clearly they are protesting about the foreign influence in the area." Mustafa leaned forward and looked to the far left out the window. "The people are angry about the attacks in the north of their country. This is understandable. And I will get them their answers, the justice that the Eritrean people deserve."

Sa'id turned away from the window. As he looked at his president he came to realize the gap, the huge amount of distance between the president and what was happening. The distance between the president's fight for this country and his position now in the palace. He wasn't even able to tell if Mustafa was serious about the protests – had he forgotten how those attacks had happened? Had he lost track of the unofficial story and the line they'd been feeding the press? It all appeared to Sa'id as though it was a vision from above. And not necessarily one he wanted.

"The protests had died down after last night, Mahmoud. But the few who were still causing unrest this morning were joined by more than we were prepared for." Sa'id looked up. "They appear to have come from Adersesr."

Mustafa turned quickly on his heel. The expression said it all. Sa'id nodded. "It was more than a fire."

"And you did nothing?"

"I looked into it even after you said not to worry," Sa'id answered, his voice rising and his tone unrelenting. "It was covered up and by the time I did find out it was too late."

Mustafa rested on the desk. He had heard Sa'id raise his voice plenty of times when talking to lower ranking members of the party, of the revolution, of the military, but never to him. It took him back. Mustafa looked up.

"We must leave. Now." Sa'id was stern.

Mustafa nodded, still shaken and uncertain. If Sa'id decided that leaving is the right move then he will trust his second in command. "Prepare the motorcade," Mustafa said weakly, then reached for a glass of water on the desk. His throat was dry. His head felt light. He stayed like that perched on the edge of the desk as Sa'id left the room and closed the door.

Mustafa walked over to the windows again and looked at the smoke rising above the city skyline. This was a day Mustafa had sworn would never come. He had witnessed the rise and fall of his contemporaries around Africa and the Middle East. There was a modesty he had kept during his reign. His rule was not one full of pageantry and regal procession. He wore a tailored suit to his presidential office and not a decorated uniform or gold plated jewelry. He had learned lessons from history, all those hours burned while reading the strengths and failings of the great rulers of history. He had given his best years to fighting for the liberation of this nation, then the rest of what he had to ruling it. There was a sinking feeling in his stomach and he knew he had been blind. Even at this late hour he could not pinpoint what went wrong and though he would keep turning the question over in his mind, he knew there was nothing he could do about it.

Mustafa walked across to the desk and sat for, what he could only assume, was the last time at his presidential position. His movements and breath were deliberate and steady as he reached for the third drawer. He pulled out the papers and placed them on the mahogany and leather desktop. The false bottom of the drawer came loose with a dull click and he placed that on top of the papers. The gold plated pistol lay there,

lonesome and cold. Mustafa wrapped his thick fingers around the butt and pulled it out. He checked the round in the chamber and felt the weight of the weapon. It was a fine piece of craftsmanship. That was unquestioned. The pistol had sat in that drawer, loaded but unused, for the best part of three decades since it had been given to him by the Russian president after taking office. The lines of the weapon were straight and precise.
For the briefest of moments Mustafa considered firing it straight into his mouth. But the thought passed quickly. This was not his way. He was the president and had nothing to be ashamed of. He stood by his rule and his legacy. There were few who could rule a nation as he had for a quarter century and have as proud a record as he had. He had given all he could to the country, even losing two wives in the process.

For decades his only job was suffering with the nation and making the difficult decisions on behalf of the people. Their lives were better because of his service. No, suicide was not an option for a man of his caliber. He slid the leather holster under his suit jacket and clipped the pistol into place. His city and nation might be in flames but he would guide the people through this mess, through this darkness, as he had before. A stronger Eritrea would emerge from the ashes.

Mustafa picked up the phone and dialed his son's house but there was no answer. He tried again but

it rang out without answer. Mustafa gathered some
other personal belongings and put them in his leather
briefcase. There were the three books he never travelled
without – dog-eared volumes of the writings of Maistre
and Marx, and a slim volume of Macchiavelli – though
perhaps now more out of habit or superstition than a
desire to reread them. For some reason he put his late
wife's necklace in the bag before he clicked it shut.

Mustafa marched confidently down the hall past
the general's empty office and to the garage. He pulled
the suit jacket down and tight to hide the gold plated
firearm in its holster – there was no need to alarm
anyone any further. The staff was already busy running
around, preparing for the convoy's exit. Drivers stood
at the ready but had not been given the orders yet.
Mustafa slipped into the third vehicle in the procession.
Sa'id was barking orders to the drivers and some other
ministers as they prepared to pull out. His face was red
and enraged.

Mustafa closed his eyes and leaned his head
back on the leather headrest. There were times when it
was not possible to know everything that was going on
around the nation. There were times when a president's
focus had to be concentrated on one particular issue, or
a handful of them. These were the times when you
came to know the quality of staff and ministers you'd
surrounded yourself with. For Mustafa, Sa'id was the
most reliable and efficient right hand man he could

have asked for. And it was times like these, as the nation's capital was rioting, that he had to trust Sa'id's judgement and direction. Sa'id better knew the situation beyond the walls at the moment.

"President," Sa'id slid into the seat opposite Mustafa. "Preparations are coming along. It seems rioters have spilled into the surrounding blocks and we're waiting for a clear exit past them before we leave. Then we'll be heading west."

"As you think best, general." Mustafa's mouth was still dry. "Do you have any water?"

"I'll have some brought over for you." Sa'id nodded, his eyes flicking down to the president's side as the suit jacket fell open. "I'll be travelling with you. The other vehicles are carrying the rest of the cabinet and essential staff. I haven't been able to locate Davide." Sa'id spoke this last part quieter and with reservation, his dark eyes focused on the president and looking for any sign of his reaction.

Mustafa chewed his lip and looked at the staff lining up for the other cars. "I know. I tried calling him."

"He was meant to be in Keren this week. So we can just hope he's there and we will meet with him later. My staff has orders to locate him and have him rendezvous with us."

"Fine work, general."

"Thank you, sir. We will move out as soon as possible," Sa'id climbed out of the car. "I'll have that water brought over for you."

It was almost an hour and a half before Sa'id gave the order to pull out of the presidential palace. Even then it was less to do with a clear stretch of road to the highway and more to do with the amount of ground made up by the rioters to the north-east. One of the Soviet built T-55A tanks that Mustafa had purchased from the Bulgarians led the procession of thirty armored vehicles. It ran the lights and cleared the traffic then peeled off to return to City Park as the procession reached the city border and accelerated onto the highway.

Sa'id stared straight ahead as they passed the city streets while Mustafa looked out the window to survey the destruction of his city. His heart sank a little further but he resolved he would unify these people again. The president chewed his lip as he considered the strategy he would need. He thought of Napoleon in exile, kept on the island of Elba, as the procession accelerated to a hundred miles an hour. He thought of Lenin in the armored train.

The first explosion shocked everyone. It was a loud and deafening crack and boom.

Just as the sound dispersed and the shock passed, the crunch of the first car landing and skidding along the asphalt on its side screeched through the desert air. Then the second roadside bomb detonated and the explosion tore through the second car, flipping it forward and landing on its roof. The road was blocked. The procession screeched to a halt. Gunfire came from the desert dunes but it wasn't clear from where. Shots thumped the cars. A door opened from the second car and the driver crawled out, firing wildly towards the sounds of the gunfire. His one-man stand was cut short as bullets tore through his chest and he collapsed onto the boiling asphalt. A scream came from the car as the minister for finance crawled towards the driver. His body took three bullets to the chest before collapsing.

Mustafa turned to look behind them. Smoke was pouring out of a car he guessed to be ten or eleven. Drivers took up the arms Sa'id had handed out and started firing into the glaringly bright hills. Without being able to see their assailants, their shots just landed in the dirt or flew far overhead. Then Mustafa saw it. In the dirt and the brush. A rebel moved forward and hurled a grenade towards the cars.

He threw three in an arc before scurrying back to shelter. The grenades flew through the air and exploded near the cars behind Mustafa and Sa'id. One hit the dirt and skidded beneath the fifth vehicle, sending it spinning onto its side in a flurry of screaming metal and smashing glass. Mustafa picked up one of the weapons at his and Sa'id's feet and rolled the window down an inch. He kept his head down behind the bulletproof glass and let the AKM rifle fire into the direction of the movement. He took them out in one hit.

"Go," Sa'id ordered the driver. "Take out those in the foxholes." The driver hesitated and Sa'id turned his weapon towards him. "Now, officer."

"Yes, general." The driver opened the door and ran behind the overturned vehicle for cover. He fired into the foxholes then darted behind the vehicle. He'd hit three on the ground before he took a shot to the head. The thump of rounds flying into the doors came again and Mustafa dropped below the window.

Sa'id climbed out of the car as Mustafa fired through the small gap in the window. Sa'id jumped into the driver's seat and clicked it into gear. The tires squealed and he floored the accelerator. Bullets hit the back of the car but made no serious damage. Another grenade exploded somewhere far behind them. Sa'id didn't even turn to see where it had landed. Once he was clear of the second demolished car, he yelled directions into the radio, "Cars four and five follow me and the rest continue to Keren." He turned the wheel hard, heading off the road to a dirt track that coiled through the heat of the Eritrean landscape, as the ten remaining vehicles wound their way along the highways through to Keren.

*

The small utility vehicle barreled through the Eritrean countryside with the canvas top pulled back. The air conditioning was busted and the sun beat down on the car unrelentingly. Somewhere across the horizon in the nation's capital, there were thousands of men pouring in to an already volatile city, preparing to storm the presidential palace. Ali and Addis had led the last group of prisoners to a small base to the east of Asmara and were arming the uprising. For Hudson and Mervyn, there were other things to do. And Abraha knew where they had to be.

Abraha was yelling across the sound of the engine as Hudson drove. "There was a farmhouse," he said, turning around so Mervyn could hear him in the back seat. "It wasn't big and had hardly any more than running water. Even that was unreliable. But there was a basement that connected with a barn on the other side of the property. There were times during the seventies when it saved us in a big way. The Ethiopian army would be closing in and we would go under ground. They razed the house in a fire in eighty three but the tunnels remained."

"And you think they're going there?"

"If the palace is under siege in Asmara, the other cities won't lay restless for long. The other presidential properties won't be safe for him to hide out."

Abraha looked around taking in the whole sight. The horizon amazed him. The sky was so blue. He hoped that he'd be able to remember the way to the farmhouse after all these years.

"What is your plan once we get there?" Mervyn asked. "If there's any sign that they've already arrived then we should be cautious."

Hudson agreed. "We don't even know how many of them there'll be."

Abraha scanned the landscape for the dirt road into the hillside. Just after he started to think he'd missed it or it had been covered up, the two hills lined up and the tell tale tree loomed. Hudson swung the steering wheel hard right and the small vehicle accelerated up the rocky incline.

Hudson pulled the car in behind some overgrowth and the three men armed themselves then climbed the small embankment the rest of the way. The farmhouse was deserted. The effects of the fire three decades earlier could still be seen around the southern walls and guttering. Parts of the wall were missing. There was no glass in the windows. The tin roofing had been left to fall off and the entire building had suffered under the weather. Mervyn moved to the right of the small main house, staying as close as he could to cover.

He'd swung the AKM rifle over his right shoulder and held it steady as he slowly stepped around to the side.

Hudson stayed back further, heading to the left. He could see the barn further along the dead, dry, abandoned fields behind the farmhouse. He looked up and saw Mervyn moving towards the front door, motioning for Abraha to follow him. The older man's grip on the rifle was tight and he held it steady as he moved in behind Mervyn. Abraha's attention wavered and he looked around too much.

Hudson stood next to the northern wall and motioned to Mervyn that it was clear. Then the first shot rang out. The bullet flew past Hudson and hit a tree behind him. He dropped to the floor immediately. Mervyn and Abraha were crouched low against the wall. Hudson peeked over the window ledge then dropped again when another shot was fired from inside the house. He pressed his back hard against the wall. A sound from the other side caught his attention. He turned and fired, seeing a head disappear behind the wall as the bullets took out another chunk of wall.

The silence hung like a storm cloud over the farmhouse. Any moment the sky would crack and the rain would tear down. The gunman around the corner had been dealt with for now but there was no telling how long that would last. Hudson peered around to where Mervyn was crouching, looking through the wire door, shaky on its rusted hinges. Mervyn held up two fingers and leaned back on the wall. That was the only two figures he could make out in the dark den of the farmhouse. There could be more but he couldn't be sure.

From where he sat, Mervyn could see them looking out the other windows. He weighed the options. Taking them out from where he sat was one, but it would probably bring other guards running. He looked at Abraha crouching behind him and motioned for him to stay put, keeping an eye on the other two. Mervyn turned and ran to the southern side, checking the corner and moving around, coming up behind the guard who had just fired at Hudson. The guard was out of uniform, in worn and tattered clothes. Mervyn scanned the flat ground around the farmhouse but couldn't see any other assailants or any cover. The guard stepped forward and fired at Hudson again, then scurried behind the corner for cover as Hudson fired back. That was all the time Mervyn needed to cover the ground along that side of the house. He kept low so the other guards inside the house couldn't see him and then stuck the barrel of the gun into the guard's back.

"Drop your weapon."

The guard froze, hands slightly raised. Mervyn grabbed the AKM rifle and threw it away from the house, out where Hudson could see it. "I've got him," Mervyn called out to Hudson. There was a tense silence. Hudson peered around the corner, still keeping low.

"I guess we're even now."

"I guess so," Mervyn grinned, then stuck the rifle barrel further in the guard's back. "You tell your comrades to come out. Throw their weapons out and come out with their arms up slowly."

Hudson could see the terror in the young guard's face. It was not an expression he'd seen in the faces of the guard's that morning. It was youthful terror. If Mustafa had brought this man along as a guard then he must have been low on men. Hudson's thoughts were distracted when two other guards came out.

"Tell them to come out," Hudson repeated. The guard called out in a tongue Hudson didn't recognize.

"Slowly," Mervyn reminded him.

Hudson kept his rifle trained on the two guards slowly walking around the farmhouse.

"Throw the weapons over there."

The other two guards obeyed and threw their AKM rifles to the dirt path around the building. Hudson patted them down and pulled a pistol from one of the men and threw that away too.

"How many other guards are there?" Mervyn asked. "And where is Mustafa?"

The guards shook their head. They were confused. "We know nothing about Mustafa."

"Where are the other guards?" Mervyn said it slowly, digging the rifle in slowly.

"There are no other guards."

"There are no guards."

Mervyn took a breath then hit his hostage over the head and pushed him to the ground. He pushed the rifle in his face. "Don't lie to me. Where is Mustafa?" Mervyn grabbed the guard's shirt and threw him backwards into the farmhouse wall. His patience was growing thin. Abraha walked around the corner slowly and kept his rifle trained on the guards with their back to him. Hudson pulled a knife from the pocket of the second guard and threw that away. Hudson looked down at Mervyn. The young guard's eyes opened wide. "Hamid Abraha," he muttered.

"Where is Mustafa?" Mervyn fired a shot into the air.

The other two guards looked at the guard with puzzled expressions then looked up as Abraha walked around behind Hudson.

"I don't know where Mustafa is. Why would I?"

Mervyn stepped back and looked at Hudson.

"Maybe he's telling the truth," Hudson said quietly to Mervyn. "He's not in any uniform."

They looked at the other two guards on their knees. All three were looking at Abraha with a stunned reverence. "Mister Abraha, sir," the second guard said.

"We're not guards, sir. We don't know where the president is."

"Then why are you here?"

The guards exchanged glances. Mervyn stepped forward, his rifle pointed at the first guard.

"Answer him. Why are you here?"

"We were hiding here," the third one said, finally speaking up. "We have been trying to raise money to buy Abraha from prison."

"We were hiding in another small town but we had to leave."

"Raising money?" Abraha asked.

"Yes, sir. We are your supporters."

"It's an honor to meet you, sir."

"If they're not with Mustafa…" Mervyn started.

"Then he's still on his way." Hudson looked down the rocky ridge to the distant highway.

"Who is?"

Hudson exchanged looks with Mervyn. "There have been protests and riots in Asmara all morning. We lead a break out of the prison and now we have information that Mustafa and his close supporters have left the palace."

"We believe he is on his way here."

"Here? Why?"

"We used this to hide from the Ethiopians in the '70s," Abraha said. The three guards sat in awe as their leader spoke.

"There's a dust cloud coming off the highway," Hudson said. "It looks like just one car, but we don't have much time."

"Listen," Mervyn said. "If you're really his close supporters, you're going to help us now, aren't you?"

"Yes, yes of course."

"Are there any other people in the farmhouse?"

The three men exchanged glances, "Well," the third guard said eventually. "There are the children."

"You have children here?" Abraha asked. "This is no place for children."

"Not our children," the second said meekly.

It all clicked for Hudson. He saw it clearly. It all added up. The reasons for demanding the ransom were redundant. Where the money was going wasn't important, just that the way they were going about it was torturous and violent and not without its victims. After all he'd been put through it the last week, he almost had trouble accepting that he was standing in front of the very men he'd been chasing. He felt the blood rush to his head. Hudson's mouth went dry. Before Mervyn could stop him, Hudson launched himself towards the guards, dropping his weapon and aiming for their throat. "You're barbarians. You kidnap children to raise money for freedom? You're sick."

Mervyn pulled Hudson off the guards, pushing him back into the dirt. "Easy, Hudson. We've found them. As long as they're safe, it's fine."

"It's them, alright," Hudson knew it was. He turned back to the three men kneeling with their arms held in front of them. "You will make this up to them and you will make this up to me."

The guards led the way through the dark house. A thick layer of dust and dirt covered everything. A few well-trodden paths wound through the small house. The only thing that looked like it had been made in the last half century was the lock fitted on the small bedroom at the end of the hall. Sayid opened the door and pushed it open. Hudson walked into the dark room, stepping over the barely visible objects on the floor and opened the rusted shutters with a violent push. The children squinted up and looked at him. Their ankles were shackled to the floor with thick chains that were fixed to the floor with heavy grey bolts. He sat on the bed next to the eldest one.

"You must be Sarah," he said.

She looked up, staring and not answering. She looked over the strange man sitting next to her and slowly nodded.

"My name is Hudson. I'm a friend of your father." Hudson looked at the other children. "He asked me to come here and take you to see him."

"You know papa?" Sarah's voice was quiet and hoarse. She licked the corners of her mouth nervously.

"Yes. He's waiting to see you."

"Where is he?" Robel spoke up.

"He's in a country across the sea where I live. We're going to go and see him."

Helen reached across to Hudson and wrapped her hands around his neck, sobbing into his shoulder. "He told me all about you. Sarah, Helen and Robel."

"I miss papa," Helen whispered.

"Hudson," Mervyn said, motioning to his watch.

"Right," Hudson said, then turned to Sayid. "What are you waiting for? Unlock them." He placed Helen on the bed. "Before we go to papa," Hudson said. "We have to stay here and hide and be very quiet. Then we'll fly across the sea to papa. Do you think you can do that?"

"We can do that," Sarah said.

The tunnel entrance was through a small hatch in the kitchen floor. A floorboard lifted up and a false cupboard that was otherwise unable to be moved, swung open to the dull and dusty cavern of the tunnel to the barn. Abraha led the way with a dull torch. Mervyn and Hudson exchanged a glance; for the second time that day they were going into stale and nearly unbreathable air.

"We didn't even know this was here," Omar said.

"It seems like it might not have been used since we were last here," Abraha said half to himself. Mervyn wiped some dusty footprints from the kitchen floor then pulled the door closed behind them just as he heard the sound of an engine come to the summit of the hill then shut off.

President Mustafa and General Sa'id looked around the kitchen of the farmhouse. "I can't believe this is still here," Mustafa said. The time hiding out in the house, underground in the stale air and under fear of being found and executed without trial by the branches of the Ethiopian army, was far from idyllic. But now, over three decades later and far removed from that danger, it was hard to not reflect on the whole experience with some nostalgia.

"Part of me wondered if we'd ever come back here," Sa'id revealed. "So I never had the place destroyed."

"I don't suppose any supplies we left here are still good," Mustafa smirked.

The general shook his head. "I think the best thing to do is to hide out underground for some days and let the initial turmoil pass over us," Sa'id suggested, handing the president a flashlight. "After that we can get some information from the cities and reassess our situation."

"That's the best course of action to take at this point," Mustafa agreed. He walked into the kitchen and pulled at the floorboard. It came up easily. Then the cupboard. The stale smell of the cold, dank air hit him and he recoiled. "A few days?"

"At most."

Mustafa led the way down the tunnel. It was still large enough to walk through as long as he was hunched over. Some parts of the dirt walls had given way and he crawled over them. The general replaced the floorboard and pulled the door closed and was not far behind. For extra security, the EPLF had built separate escape tunnels. They were designed primarily for emergency use and were crudely constructed. The first one had given way years earlier. The second was still useable Mustafa noted as he continued towards the room at the end of the tunnel beneath the barn. The flashlight flickered as Mustafa continued down the dark corridor. He smiled to himself as he remembered carving out some of the walls. The stone walls were slightly wet to touch.

"There's a puddle here, Sa'id," Mustafa warned his accomplice. "Watch out for it."

There was a reinforced door at the end of the tunnel and above that a doorway into the barn. He prayed that it wasn't rusted over, that he could open it as soon as they got to the end of the tunnel. The flashlight flickered again and Mustafa kept going, feeling his way until he reached the welcome cold sensation of the reinforced steel door.

"I found the door," he said. "It's stuck."

"Right behind you," Sa'id called out. They pushed hard on the door, heaving their shoulders into it. On the fourth effort it gave way and they stumbled into the dark and cold room.

"Where's that door in the roof?" Mustafa asked himself.

"Point your flashlight up here, Sa'id."

Before either of them could make out the latch to find their way into the barn, the door slammed shut. Sa'id turned and dropped his flashlight leaving the whole room in deathly darkness. Sa'id looked up at the sound of a match being lit. It sparked and glowed, igniting a kerosene lamp on the small table in the corner.

"Leave it on the floor and keep your hands in the air."

Both the president and the general jumped. Until now they'd not even considered they wouldn't be alone down there. A hand reached towards the lantern and turned the flame up, illuminating the weary and unshaven face of Hamid Abraha and chasing the shadows to the wall. The figures of five armed men with their rifles trained on the president and Sa'id became clear.

"Have a seat," Abraha said. "But keep your hands on the table. No one will hesitate to shoot you if you don't."

Mustafa swapped a glance with his general then moved slowly and sat down, keeping his hands on the table. Sa'id hesitated.

"Please, general." Abraha's offer was accompanied by a jab in the ribs from Mervyn's rifle. It convinced him. He sat reluctantly at the table in the chair to Mustafa's left, with his fingers spread out on the surface. His small dark eyes darted around the room, searching for a way out of the room and a way to turn the tables and hold these ruffians at gunpoint.

"Last time we spoke, Mahmoud," Abraha said, "you told me you would think something over before we next met."

Mustafa took a deep breath and let it out slowly. He repressed his frustration. He was the president – he would not be talked down to. He would get what he wanted. "What do you want, Abraha?"

Sa'id could see the gold plated pistol out of the corner of his eye. It hung behind Mustafa's jacket. He could assume the other men hadn't spotted it yet.

"The same thing I've wanted for the last half century, Mahmoud. Freedom for myself and my people."

"Your people?" Mustafa laughed. "What makes you think these are your people? Or that you're anything like them?" He leaned forward on the table and lifted his hands. Hudson stepped forward and kept the rifle pointed at directly at Mustafa.

"Hands on the table, president."

Mustafa let out a hard sigh and glanced quickly towards Sa'id. He put his palms flat on the table. "I've given everything to these people, Hamid. Everything. And do you see what they're doing? Did you see my palace in flames? These people are ungrateful for all that we've done for them. We watched our friends die for decades. We killed for these people's freedom. We gave them independence but that wasn't enough. They always want more. These people don't even know what is best for them. They're imbeciles, peasants - rodents that stand in the way of greatness. It takes a certain kind of man to do what we did, Hamid. Most men want freedom but they're unwilling to make the sacrifice. We are stronger. We are a better caliber of men. We are able to stand and give what others are unwilling. We give things that these others are even unaware of. Then they have the nerve to question us when we tell them what is good for them? Ha! They don't even know what is good for them. It takes great men like Napoleon and Alexander and Zedong and Stalin – men like you and me, Hamid – to stand by their visions and form great nations. These commoners couldn't make those choices if they had them in front of them. Don't you understand that, Hamid?"

Abraha leaned back in his chair, his face now half engulfed in the shadows. "Have you read any Maistre lately?" A knowing look flashed across

Mustafa's face. It was fleeting, but Abraha knew the president understood his point. "Have you?"

Sa'id leaned forward on his chair, keeping his weight to the front but careful not to attract the attention of Abraha's men while he bided his time.

"Maybe the point for you is not that the people get the government they deserve, but that the leader gets the nation he deserves. What type of leader have you been, Mahmoud? One that thinks the people owe him? That's not a leader, Mahmoud. Leaders make the sacrifices that others cannot, – about this you are correct. But that sacrifice doesn't become reward. The sacrifice keeps going, Mahmoud. And a leader understands this and does it willingly, don't you agree?"

There would be no answer. Mahmoud leaned forward and dropped his left shoulder, dragging his hand across the table. That was enough for Sa'id. The general moved like a flash and slipped his hand across the president's chest, grabbing the gold pistol and firing it through the jacket to where Hudson stood before he'd even pulled it from the holster. Hudson dropped to the ground, instinctively firing the automatic weapon as he fell.

Abraha fell to the side, pulling the table over him for cover. The lantern fell but didn't break. Sa'id drew the pistol and turned, firing at the wall where Mervyn stood, but he'd already moved, firing at the general in the dull light. The table flipped over as the deafening sound of gunshots exploded in the room. Sa'id dropped to his knees, turned and fired to where the other men were. The prickly scent of sulfur over came the musty damp smell. And then there was silence and stillness.

Abraha lifted the lantern and saw Sa'id standing in the center of the room with the pistol trained directly at him. Sa'id's small dark eyes were enflamed, enraged, like a trapped animal. His lips stretched into a wry and sinister smile.

"As I recall, Hamid, this is how we last met."

Abraha shrugged. "But now your control on the nation is slipping, general. The people will not be intimidated into forcing the new revolution underground."

"Since you like your philosophical discussions," the general said, spitting the words out.

"Maybe you can wax lyrical on this one. Those who do not learn from history are doomed to repeat it."

"Who do you think is doing the repeating, general? It seems to me that you are now the occupying force in a country that wants democracy." Abraha lifted the lantern, turning the flame up to send all the shadows to the far corners of the small room. "Just as you're the outnumbered occupying force in this room."

Sa'id looked around. The president was on the floor, looking up at Sa'id and Abraha through tired eyes. His hand was pressed to his side but it didn't stop the blood from flowing. It barely slowed the flow. Hudson pressed against the wall and helped himself to his feet, his rifle trained on the general. He'd been hit in the right calf but still had the strength in his left leg to stand. Mervyn lay on the ground, with his rifle pointed up at the general. The gun fire had claimed two of the kidnappers and only Omar remained, against the door, unharmed but in shock at seeing his brothers bloodied bodies in the light.

"Hand me the pistol, Sa'id."

The general stood firm. Sa'id's jaw muscle clenched and unclenched beneath a layer of sweat. The lack of ventilation was getting to him. He could feel the blood pulse through his head.

"How many rounds do you think that pistol holds, general?"

"There's one left." Sa'id kept his eyes on Abraha.

"Then you should use it wisely."

Time moved slowly through the thick air. No one dared move, fearful of starting another gunfight. Sa'id finally dropped his gaze from Abraha and looked at the president. "It's been an honor, sir." That was all he said. Then turned the pistol on himself and fired through his skull.

Mervyn righted the overturned chair, climbed onto the it, and opened the hatch into the barn. The sunlight came through, catching the dust and gunpowder smoke in the light. Abraha bent down over the body of the president and pushed a shirt into the wound. It was futile. Mustafa had been hit in the stomach by several shots. His body shook and twitched as he looked up into the eyes of his one-time ally, his eventual adversary, and the only man he'd ever considered his philosophical equal. He swallowed hard. His mouth was dry and his breathing was labored.

"We buried so many in this field," Mustafa said to Abraha. "I never thought I'd be another. Not at this point."

"Don't try to speak, Mahmoud," Abraha said. "You don't need to say anything else."

"I did my best to serve the country, Abraha." It came out from Mustafa's lips almost as a plea for redemption. Abraha wanted to reassure him that he'd lived up to the promise they'd taken, but they both knew under this light of death that hindsight brings so much perspective and truth.

"You were a fine and determined fighter for independence."

Mustafa nodded, knowing that after all these years, it should be that chapter he should be most proud of. If his legacy was to be measured only by that fight for independence then he would be glad. Mustafa nodded, smiled and with his last breath muttered a simple, "thank you." Abraha took off his coat and draped it over the president's body.

Mervyn and Omar helped push Hudson through the hatch into the barn. He walked over to the empty ammunition case in the corner.

"It's me, Hudson," he called out then opened to see the three children curled up together. The pistol he'd given them as a precaution was in Sarah's right hand, her left was around her siblings. She handed it to him.

"That was loud and lots of gunfire."

"There was a lot of noise," Hudson said, making sure the pistol was unloaded before he slipped it in his pocket.

"Did you get hurt?" Robel asked.

"Just a little, but it will be ok."

"We got scared," Helen said.

"It's over now," Hudson smiled at them.

"Now we can see papa?"

Hudson nodded. "Now we can go and see papa."

11

It was a solemn car ride back to the capital. The desert highway was empty and grey. The sun was lingering on the horizon as they drove with the shadows long in front of them. Mervyn drove while Abraha sat in the passenger seat. Hudson sat in the middle of the back seat with the children. Helen and Robel were exhausted and slept with their arms around each other, their heads propped up on the torn vinyl seats. Sarah looked out the window into the sparse desert extending as far as they could see. The cool air blew her knotted hair off her face. She turned and smiled at Hudson then put her head on his shoulder and let her eyes fall closed for a moment.

No one really felt like talking. There wasn't much to say. In some ways there'd been a victory won today but the mood in the car was far from celebratory. It had been a victory, Hudson was sure of that, and more than completing an assignment and fulfilling his word to Daniel.

Abraha looked exhausted and Mervyn didn't look well. Hudson didn't feel much better. They'd had less than eight hours of sleep between the three of them over the last day and a half. Mervyn's shoulder had been taped together and a bandage had stopped the bleeding. The bullet had passed through the flesh and he was fortunate that it was just a flesh wound. Hudson's calf was tender and he had trouble putting almost any weight on it.

They'd put the bodies of the slain in ammunition crates. Abraha suggested burying them in the field with the other dead from the war of independence but Hudson was sure that the international community would need to witness the body of such a large leader. Omar had stayed at the farmhouse to keep watch until tomorrow when they could return for the bodies. Mustafa's duties were not over, even in death.

."Death is a such a messy affair," Abraha had said. "It's such a personal and intimate experience but we have this need to broadcast it as far as we can for some."

"Some people are larger than life when they're living," Hudson replied. "Their death is no exception."

Much of the center of the city was in smoke and ruins when the small vehicle reached the city border. There were streets that were in ruins and needed to be driven around. Some explosions had ripped up the streets in what Hudson could only imagine were from the tanks. There were smashed shop windows and overturned cars still on fire. Glass was shattered across the streets, partly from shop windows, the broken cars, and the remains of Molotov cocktails being hurled at the military.

Trees along the boulevard had been toppled, blocking large parts of the road. Mervyn drove past the courthouse, half of which had been burned. One of the tanks from the monument to the war of independence had been toppled and set alight. The flames were now all out but the black husk remained. The crowds were getting thicker the further they drove towards the palace.

"I think we're going to have to walk," Mervyn said still a mile away from the palace. The chanting crowd could be heard through the buildings.

"What are they saying?" Hudson asked Abraha.

"Freedom will rise," Abraha said, smiling. "It was a slogan from the early days, back in the sixties."

The military had been disarmed. Hudson couldn't tell if it was from the rioters gaining control through numbers or if it was due to Ali and Addis and the extra military power they'd brought with them.

There was no doubt that the sight of incoming armored vehicles and tanks would have lifted the spirits of the rebels. With Sa'id and Mustafa both leaving the city, there would have been a hole of experience at the top of the army leadership.

Daniel's information on the communications base had led to a strategic take over of certain parts of the Eritrean military. It was another part of the U.S. forces, the division Mervyn had been assigned to months earlier, that had acted on that information. Whether that stunned the co-ordination of the Eritrean forces, and perhaps led to aid the escape from Adersesr, Hudson had yet to find out. He leaned on a makeshift walking cane and held Sarah's hand in the other. Mervyn carried Robel, though Hudson could see him grimacing each time he had to twist around another protestor in the crowd. Helen walked alongside her sister.

All the state buildings had suffered under the onslaught of protests all day. Sarah and Helen walked wide-eyed, staring at the damage. A young boy hurled another brick through a window in front of them, then he turned and ran before the crash of glass on the second story. Abraha had stopped to ask one of the chanting men what had happened. Abraha turned back to Hudson and shrugged. "All he knows is that Mustafa is gone. The palace is empty. They've overrun it. And there are protests all through the streets up to the presidential palace."

"The embassy is down this street," Hudson said. "I think it's best if we get some treatment then come down."

"I agree," Abraha said. The expression on his face was relief.

"You go ahead," Hudson said. "We'll come after you soon."

The emotion swelled in Abraha's face. The battle he had been fighting for most of half a century was at an end. It was criminal to keep him from the palace that had been overtaken by the citizens.

"Go," Hudson said. "It's your victory you have to celebrate."

"I couldn't have done it…" Abraha started, searching for the words.

"Go," Hudson said again. "We'll come down after you."

Hudson and Mervyn carried the children as best they could and came to the gates of the embassy. It was heavily armed as expected but largely untouched. It was a whole other thing that the rioters had their sights on. Hudson leaned heavily on his cane as he approached the guard.

"Captain Hudson Jones and Sergeant Donald Mervyn to see Ambassador Archer."

"Identification, Captain?"

"It's in the embassy," Hudson said. "The ambassador will be able to identify me."

Hudson started to laugh. He'd just realized how the five of them would have appeared standing there, dirty and worn clothes, gunshot wounds, unshaven, and barefoot children dressed in little more than rags. Mervyn allowed himself to laugh too.

"Is papa in there?" Helen asked.

"No," Sarah said. "Papa is across the sea. We will have to fly there."

Archer walked down the path to the front gate with two armed guards

"Thank heavens, Jones. We thought you'd been killed."

"They tried, sir. But we wouldn't let them. I'd like to introduce Sergeant Mervyn."

The children were taken to be bathed and fed, while the freshly bandaged Hudson and Mervyn sat with Archer and the other high-ranking officials at the embassy. Hudson and Mervyn recounted a rough version of their escape, partnership with Abraha and how they came to find the children. They'd left out the part about Mustafa, though neither of them knew why exactly, and it hadn't been something they'd discussed. It seemed respectful somehow. Their story was that Abraha had taken them to hide out in the farmhouse.

Archer nodded his head as he sipped a cup of black decaf coffee. "I'd say you two have had a rather punishing few weeks."

"I can't speak for Captain Jones here, but I'm beyond exhausted at this point, sir."

"I can imagine," Archer said. "President Mustafa left the city at some point this morning and missed the meeting with the United Nations delegation. The people have over run the palace but there's been no sign of the president. Word is he was heading for Keren when his procession was attacked by rebels on the highway."

"Keren?" Mervyn said. "I thought he was heading west."

"Why would you think that?"

"We heard it on the street," Hudson said. "Abraha was talking to some of the protestors."

"It seems strange you were put in the same cell as the leader of the opposition," said Parkinson.

"Yes, sir," Mervyn said. "We thought that too, but it was designed by the contact I had in Yemen."

"Stranger things have happened," Parkinson declared. "And now we just have to file the paper work. You're dismissed, gentlemen, until tomorrow morning. The flight will be at 0500 hours."

"Yes, sir."

Mervyn helped Hudson down the stairs. "Do you feel like going out to witness a revolution, Captain?"

"I wouldn't miss it, Sergeant."

The streets were full of shadows though the sky still glowed with a full light. There was no more destruction. There were no bricks or Molotov cocktails being hurled through the streets. Tanks that had moved through the city before, either for the army or the stolen ones hi-jacked by Ali, now sat idle and still in the streets while children played around them. The unofficial and unconfirmed news of Mustafa's death had lightened the mood. His death had unified the people of Asmara and now they rejoiced. It was unofficial, but that was good enough for them.

Hudson and Mervyn walked slowly through the streets. The city would not get much sleep tonight. Strangers were singing and dancing in the squares and intersections. Anywhere it was large enough to gather, they were singing and dancing. The crowd was thicker as they pressed towards the palace. It seemed like every one in Asmara and all the surrounding villages had come out in force tonight.

Above the palace, the Eritrean flag flew high above the rooftops and was still shining in the light from the setting sun. There was movement on a balcony. Beneath that were the steps from which Mustafa gave his addresses to the media. The microphone and speakers were being set up. Attention from the square turned to the steps as the speakers crackled to life. Normally the speakers served those immediately congregated at the steps of the palace. This evening there were a lot more people demanding to hear what was said. The crowd pushed forward and swept Hudson and Mervyn along. They moved out to the side since Hudson was having trouble keeping up with the pushing crowd.

A small figure moved to the microphone and started speaking. The volume was far too low and the crowd started chanting again, then singing the national anthem. The volume peaked and the voice boomed over the people.

"Ladies and gentleman, I give you Hamid Abraha."

The crowd cheered. Chants of "Ab-ra-ha,"

Hudson and Mervyn exchanged glances as Abraha made his way to the small podium. Even from this distance they could tell his beard had been trimmed and his hair cut to a respectable length. He wore a suit and had his hair pushed back. He waved to the crowd and leaned heavily on the podium.

"Thank you," he said. "Twenty years ago we won a victory of independence from our neighbors. Today we have won freedom from ourselves." A cheer went up around the crowd, a roar that would not be stifled. "You, the Eritrean people have stood up and declared that no more will we live under the rule of someone else. We, the Eritrean people, demand that we govern ourselves." The crowd was chanting his name again.

Abraha stopped and waited for something resembling silence. He was as tough as nails – that had certainly been proven – but he was not a young man any more. And, as Hudson and Mervyn only knew too well, he hadn't had any rest for nearly thirty-six hours.

"This is a time of transition, and a time of growth. This is the time that the strength of our nation will be forged. The future will be cast now and Eritrea will grow from the mold we design now." The crowd answered back as one.

"We cannot do this alone. We have each other but we must also call on our friends. Our allies. I did not survive or escape from Adersesr alone. We cannot build a country on our own. We have seen the worst of this country, my friends. But now I ask for you to join with us all to make Eritrea into the nation we all know it can be."

A deafening roar rose from the crowd. "Ab-ra-ha! Ab! Ra! Ha!" Hudson couldn't help himself. He lifted his fist in the air and started chanting along with the Eritreans. He turned to look at Mervyn who was doing the same. They shrugged and laughed and kept chanting.

Abraha stood at the podium waving to his supporters, the thousands in the street who believed in the same Eritrea he did. Abraha waved to all of them, shaking their hands and talking and dancing with them for as long as he could as the sun cast a red sky again over Eritrea.

*

It was almost a month later when Hudson and Lauren pulled into the car park of the Prince Of Eritrea and walked into the restaurant. Hudson put the car in park and leaned over to kiss his wife. They lingered for a moment, looking into each other's eyes, then climbed out of the car.

"Hudson," Daniel called out from the back. He rose from the table and started walking toward the door with his arms outstretched. Sarah and Helen turned and jumped off their chairs, weaving around the chairs and their father's legs to reach Hudson first. They wrapped their arms around Hudson's legs. Daniel looked up, alarmed. "How's your leg?"

"It's great. A much quicker recovery than the prognosis."

"That's good."

Hudson shrugged, then broke into a grin. "Except it means I have to go back to work sooner."

"Come on, girls. Let Hudson sit down." Daniel took the Jones' jackets and put them behind the bar. "It's good to see you both," Daniel said. "Let me get you a drink."

"I'll have a Jack on the rocks," Hudson looked to his wife. "Tonic water?"
Lauren nodded. "Tonic water, thank you."

"Just a tonic water?" Daniel asked her.

"You do know that we're celebrating tonight, right?"

"We are too, actually." Hudson smiled and winked at Daniel.

Lauren placed a hand over her stomach. "The doctor gave us the news this afternoon."

"Congratulations. That's even better news."

"It's really great," Hudson said, beaming as he followed Daniel to the table. He pulled out the chair for his wife.

"Here," Lauren said, handing Daniel a small box. "It's just a little something."

"You didn't have to get me anything," Daniel said. "Your husband already gave me the best thing I could ask for."

"Happy birthday, Daniel," Hudson said, placing a hand on his shoulder. "It's been a good one?"

Daniel sat back and looked at the kids playing.

"I didn't know they made ties that small," Hudson said as he watched Robel at the end of the table.

"He asked for one, actually. My brother's wife sewed it this afternoon."

"How are they settling into Mississippi life?"

"Robel in particular has been having trouble sleeping. He wakes up screaming. But in the day he's fine. Sarah's adjusted the best. I haven't started them at school yet. Maybe next semester, I don't know yet."

"That's understandable."

"Is Donald coming?"

"I spoke to him this afternoon. His flight was supposed to land about an hour ago and he was coming straight here. I thought he'd be here already."

As if on cue, Mervyn walked through the door. "You give horrible directions, Jones."

"We found the place alright," Hudson laughed back.

"Everyone, this is Melissa," Mervyn motioned to the short brunette standing next to him.

"Melissa, this is Hudson, the kids, everyone else."

"How long are you in town for?" Daniel asked.

"Just three days."

"Where are you staying?"

"With Jones actually," Mervyn said. "I hope he gives better directions back to his house."

Once the party had settled into the restaurant and ordered their meals, Daniel called Mervyn and Hudson over to the bar.

"Now that you're both here," Daniel said. "I wanted to show you this." He pulled out a newspaper from behind the bar. "It slipped out of the American news cycle but I thought you'd like to see it."

Though neither of them could see it, Mervyn and Donald both grabbed it. The front page showed Abraha opening the refurbished government building. His beard was gone completely and his hair was cut short. The bags under his eyes were taken back and unsurprisingly, he looked healthier than he had after a decade and a half in prison.

"What does the article say?" Mervyn asked.

"The election is in ten months," Daniel said. "Until then he's been appointed interim president."

"Is he running?" Mervyn asked. "He'd be a shoe-in, wouldn't he? The way they were chanting his name in that square was amazing."

"I actually spoke to him last week," Hudson said. "He thinks he's too old for statesmanship. That he wouldn't be able to run a country at his age."

"How old is he?"

"That's one thing he wouldn't tell me," Hudson laughed and sipped his Jack. "But he did sound like he could be talked into standing for election."

"Is there anything else in the article?" Mervyn asked.

"Not much. It's a conservative Egyptian paper," Daniel looked up. "Eritrea now has five newspapers but I haven't seen any of them yet."

"That's an improvement."

"Certainly is."

"It just says that the nation has been redesigning the government for democracy," Daniel said as he quickly scanned the article. "That Eritrea has been going through administrative change and upheaval since the riots last month that lead to President Mustafa and his top general committing suicide."

"Suicide?" Mervyn asked, swapping a glance with Hudson who looked down quickly at his Jack.

"Yes," Daniel said. "They found him and General Sa'id in a farmhouse in the Eritrean highlands, west of Asmara."

"Who would have thought?" Mervyn asked.

Hudson nodded. "I guess every leader gets the death he deserves."

"I guess so," Mervyn said.

ABOUT THE AUTHOR

Practicing in the areas of bankruptcy, tax, business planning and formation, and estate planning, including wills and probate, Randall R. Saxton is the founding attorney of Saxton Law, PLLC, which serves as general counsel for Randall Saxton Real Estate, Inc. and R&S Development, Inc. Randall also serves as the JAG officer for the Mississippi State Guard, Vice President of the Mississippi State Guard Association, on the Board of Directors of the Madison Chamber of Commerce, and on the Executive Committee for the Madison County Republican Party. He does volunteer work with the Mission First Legal Aid Clinic and as a Mediator for the Jackson Municipal Court.

Randall is a graduate of Mississippi College, where he majored in History and English, receiving his Bachelor of Science degree in 2006. He also holds a Master of Social Sciences in Administration of Justice, before attending law school at the Mississippi College School of Law, and graduating from there in 2010 as a Doctor of Jurisprudence.

He is married to Madeline W. Saxton, Regional Business Development and Marketing Coordinator for Jones Walker, LLP, and is a member of First Baptist Church in Jackson. His family enjoys photography, traveling, and their corgi, Hudson.